The Highwayman

The Highwayman

H.C. Bailey

MINT EDITIONS

The Highwayman was first published in 1915.

This edition published by Mint Editions 2021.

ISBN 9781513281322 | E-ISBN 9781513286341

Published by Mint Editions®

MINT
EDITIONS
minteditionbooks.com

Publishing Director: Jennifer Newens
Design & Production: Rachel Lopez Metzger
Project Manager: Micaela Clark
Typesetting: Westchester Publishing Services

Contents

I

THE COMPLETE HERO

Harry Boyce addressed Queen Anne in glittering verse. She was not present. She had, however, no cause to regret that, for he was tramping the Great North Road at four miles by the hour—a pace far beyond the capacity of Her Majesty's legs; and his verses were Latin—a language not within the capacity of Her Majesty's mind. Her absence gave him no grief. In all his twenty-four years he could not remember being grieved by anyone's absence. His general content was never diminished at finding himself alone. He chose the Queen as the subject of his verses merely because he did not admire her. She appeared to him then, as to later generations, a woman ineffectual and without interest; a dull woman physically, mentally, and perhaps morally; just the woman upon whom it would be hardest to make an encomium of any splendour. So he was heartily ingenious over his alcaics, and relished them.

From this you may divine much that you have to know about the soul of Harry Boyce. It was more given to mockery than enthusiasms, apter to criticisms than devotion, not very gentle nor very kind, and so quite satisfied with itself and by itself. To be sure, it was yet only twenty-four.

You discover also other things less fundamental. He was something of a scholar, as scholarship was reckoned in those placid days. He had even some Greek—more than Mr. Pope and quite as much as Mr. Addison. His Latin verses would have brought him a fellowship at Merton if he had been willing to take Holy Orders, "I may take them indeed; but how believe they have been given me?" quoth he to the Warden with a tilt of one eyebrow. Whereat the Warden, aghast, wrote him off as a youth unreasonable, impracticable, and impish. Many others had the same opinion of Harry Boyce before the world was done with him. Few of them saw in his antics the uncertain spasms of too tender a conscience. But you must judge.

Of course he was poor. He could only boast a bob wig, a base thing, which, for all the show it made, might have been a man's own hair. He wore no sword. His hat lacked feather and lace. His coat and breeches were but black drugget, shiny at each corner of him and rusty everywhere. His stockings were worsted, and darned even on his excellent calves. His shoes had strings where buckles should have been, and mere black heels—and low heels at that. As you know, he could walk at a round pace with them—a preposterous, vulgar thing. There was nothing in him to give this poverty a romantical air. To be sure, he had admirable legs, but the rest was neither good nor bad. He was of the middle size and a wholesome complexion. You would look at him long and see nothing rare enough to be worth looking at. If you looked longer yet you might begin to be surprised: his so ordinary face was extraordinary in its lack of expression.

The man who owned it must be either very dull of heart and mind, or self-contained and of self-control beyond the common. But whatever the heart might be, no one ever took the eyes for the eyes of a fool. They were keen, alert, perpetually on guard. There is a letter extant—it was indeed a dear friend who wrote it—which mocks at Harry for his "curst stand-and-deliver stare." But it is a queer thing that most men had to know Harry Boyce a long time before they remarked that his eyes were not quite of the same colour. The common English grey-green-blue was in both of them, but one had a bluer glint than the other. The oddity, when it was discovered, seemed to make the challenge of the eyes more defiant and more baffling, as though they gleamed from the shadow of a mask.

Not that anyone cared yet whether he wore a mask or his soul in that placid, ordinary face. Who should care a pinch of snuff for "a scholar just from his college broke loose" with a penny farthing in his pocket, who had to pioneer young gentlemen through their Horace and their Tully for his bed and board? When you meet him, Harry Boyce was happy in having caught for his pupil a young fellow who had not merely money but brains, and so sublime a condescension that Harry was not sent away from table with the parson when the puddings came. Mr. Geoffrey Waverton was pleased to have a value for him, and defended him from his natural duty of being gentleman usher to Lady Waverton. So, Mr. Waverton having taken horse, Harry was free to go walking.

It was late in a wet autumn, and all the clay of Middlesex slippery as butter and, withal, affectionate as warm glue. Harry kept to the highway. Though its miles of mud and water were, on the surface, even worse than the too green meadows or the gleaming brown furrows of plough land, a careful man could count upon its letting him go no further than knee deep. When he came to Whetstone, Harry's feet were brown, shapeless, weighty masses, but he had not lost either shoe, and he was still in hopes of reaching Barnet and a pint of small beer before it was time to struggle back. At the worst a dry throat and wet legs were a cheap price for escaping the voice of Lady Waverton, who, in the afternoons, read the romances of Mlle. de Scudéry aloud.

He could see the tufts of smoke above Barnet and its church on the hill-top. He was winding down to the bottom of the valley from which that hill rises, when eloquence arrested him. He may at other times have heard profanity as copious, but never profanity so vehement or at such speed. The orator was a woman.

Harry stood to listen with critical admiration. Madame mixed the ugly and the pleasant rarely; she made a charming grotesque. Her mind was very far from nice and provided her with amazing images; but she had a pretty, womanly voice, and hard though she drove it, it would not break to one ugly note. Disgusting epithets, mean threats, poured out in mellow music. Harry splashed on round the corner. He was eager to see her.

In the morass at the cross-lanes by the green, a coach was stuck—a coach of splendour. It was a huge thing as big as a room, half glass, half gold and garter blue, and it swayed luxuriously on its great springs. Six horses heaved at it in vain with great splashing and squelching, and a whole company of servants, some mounted, some afoot, struggled with them.

The profane woman had half her body and two gesticulating arms out of the coach window. She was plainly neither a drab nor in liquor. Harry halted out of range of the splashes to examine and enjoy her. She had been comely, and still could hold a man's eye with her curves of neck and bosom. The piquant features must have been adorable before they sharpened and her cheeks faded and the lines came. Her abundant hair must once have been gold, and was not yet altogether grey.

"You filthy slug," said she. "Samuel! Stand to it, I say. Damme, I'll have a whip about that loose belly of yours! Now pull, you swine, pull. Odso, flog the black horse. You, devil broil your bones, lay on to him. What now? Od rot you, Antony, you'll see no money this month, you—" She became unprintable. As she took breath again, she saw Harry Boyce calmly contemplative. "You dog, who bade you stand and gape? Go, give a hand there, I say."

Harry touched his hat. "By your leave, ma'am, I am too busy admiring you."

"William, put that rogue into the ditch," said she.

All this while a man in the coach had been writing, calmly intent upon his tablets as though there was not a sound or a rage within a mile. He now stood up, and, while his lady was still execrating through one door of the coach, he opened the other and came out. Two of the servants, obedient to the lady's oaths, were approaching Harry, who waited them with calm and a swinging stick. The man waved his hand at them and they turned tail. But he had no further interest in Harry. He stood to watch the struggles of his horses and his men. He was of some height, and, though past middle age, bore himself with singular grace and vigour. He had still a rarely handsome face—too handsome, by far, for Harry's taste. The features were of an impossible, absurd perfection. There was something superhuman or fatuous, at least something vastly irritating, in his assured calm, his air of blandly confident supremacy.

He walked on to the leaders and, with a gesture and a word, set the whole team pulling at an angle. Meanwhile the lady had earnestly continued her abusive orders, but none of the servants now professed to heed her. Dragging the horses on, or labouring hand and shoulder at the wheels, they were now effective, and they watched the man's eye as though it were an inspiration. Wondering why he did, Harry, too, put his weight on a wheel. The horses found a footing in the mire, the coach was dragged on to the higher, firmer ground beyond.

My lady subsided. The man came back to the coach and touched his hat to Harry. "I'm obliged for your help, sir," he said, and climbed in. They drove away towards London.

As the servants swung to their saddles, "Who's your obscene lady?" said Harry.

"What, don't you know him, bumpkin?"

"She will never be him. Her shape is all provocative she."

This humble wit was not remarked. His ignorance occupied them, "Oh Lud, not to know the Old Corporal!"

One of Harry's eyebrows went up. "That the Old Corporal? Faith, I am sorry for him."

He received a handful of mud in his face. With a cry of "Rot your impudence," they splashed off.

While he wiped the mud out of his eyes, Harry felt a very comfortable self-satisfaction. It was agreeable to pity His Grace of Marlborough. For the Duke of Marlborough was still the greatest man in Europe, the greatest man in the world—credibly the greatest man that ever lived. A pleasant fool, to marry such a wife and to keep her.

Harry Boyce at no time in his life had much admiration for human eminence. In this, his hungry youth, he was set upon despising rank and power, great fame and pure virtue, as no more than the luck of fools. He would always atone by finding sympathy and excuses for any rogue's roguery. Highly fortified in this faith by the exhibition of Marlborough's matrimonial happiness, he trudged back.

The delay over the coach had left him no time for small ale at Barnet. Mr. Waverton, though amiably pleased to deliver Harry from attendance on his mother, required constant attendance on himself. He would be, in his superb way, disagreeable if Harry were not in waiting when he was wanted to take a hand at ombre. Harry liked Mr. Waverton well enough, as well as he liked anybody, but found him in the part of offended majesty intolerable. So there was some hard walking back to Whetstone. On the way his temper was not sweetened by two horsemen at the gallop who gave him a shower-bath of mud.

As he came through the village, behold another coach labouring up to the high road from Totteridge lane. This had but four horses, no array of outriders, no gilt splendours. It was a sober, old-fashioned thing, and it rumbled on at a sober gait. "Some city ma'am," Harry sneered at it, "much the same shape as her horses."

But half an hour after he saw it again. Where the road was dark through a thicket it had come to a stand. "Oh Lud," said Harry, "here's more fair madames in the mud. They may sit on it till they hatch it for me." But he wondered a little. It was indeed nothing very strange in such an autumn to find a coach stuck upon the highway. But two for one afternoon, two so near was a generous provision. And hereabouts, where the road ran level and high, was a strange place for a coach to choose to stick. "Madame seems to be a gross girl," quoth Harry.

And then he saw what made him step out. There were two men on horseback by the halted coach—two men with black upon their faces which must be masks, and that in their hands which must be pistols.

"Egad, the road's joyful to-night," said Harry. "And two and one make three," and he began to run, and arrived.

Of the two highwaymen one was dismounted. The other, holding his friend's horse, held also a pistol at the coachman's head, muttering lurid threats of what he would do if the coachman drove on. The dismounted man was half inside the coach where two women shrank from him, and thence his blusterous voice proceeded, "Now, my blowens, hand over, or I'll rummage you. A skinny purse? Come, now, you've more than that. What's under your legs, fatty? Stand up, I say. Ay, hand out the jewel-box. Now, my tackle, what ha' you got aboard? What's under that pretty tucker?" He threw the jewel-case out into the mud and, leaning across one woman, reached with a fat, foul hand to the younger bosom beyond.

He was prevented by a whistle and a cry, "Behind you, Ben." His companion announced the arrival of Harry.

Ben came out of the coach with an oath and thrust his pistol into Harry's face. "Good e'en to you, bully. Now cut and run or I'll drill you. Via, my poppet."

Harry looked along the pistol and stood fast. The highwayman was no bigger than he, and bloated. "I am studying arithmetic, Benjamin," said he.

"Burn your eyes, be off with you; run while you may."

Harry laughed and swung his stick at the mud. "But, I wonder, is it addition or subtraction? Is it two and one makes three, or—"

"Kick the bumpkin into the ditch, Ben," the man on horseback advised.

"Off with you," Benjamin thrust him back, and in the act the pistol wavered. Harry slashed with his stick at the pistol hand. A yell, an oath, and the shot came together—a shot which went into the mud and sent it spattering about them. Harry sprang away from Benjamin's rush and brought his stick down on the hindquarters of the horses. They plunged forward, and the man in the saddle, wrestling with them, let off another aimless shot. Harry dodged round them and lashed them again, and they bolted down the road. He returned to fling himself upon Benjamin, who was ramming another charge into his pistol. "It seems to be subtraction, Benjamin," said he, embracing the man fervently. "One from two leaves one," and they swayed together, and he found Benjamin's body soft.

Benjamin, panting, cursed him. "Od rot you, why must you meddle, bully? What's your will, burn you? Ha' done now, and—" Benjamin went down on his back in the mud with Harry on top of him. "Ugh! What's the game, bully?"

"I think you call it the high toby," said Harry delicately and began to sing to the tune of a catch:

"Oh, three merry men, three merry men, three highwaymen were we. You in a quag and he on a nag and I on top of the three."

"Lord love you, are you on the road?" Benjamin cried. "Why, rot you, did you want a share then? You should ha' said so, bully. Come on now, my dear, let's up. We do be gentlemen and share fair enough."

"I warrant you I am having my share," Harry laughed; "and I like it very well. But oh, Benjamin, there would have been nought to share if I had not come up. No fun at all, Benjamin." He wrenched the pistol away. "'Tis I have made the business joyous. You are a dull fellow by yourself."

"Rot you," said Benjamin frankly. "When Ned comes back he'll shoot you like vermin."

On which they both heard horses, and both, according to their abilities—Benjamin in the mud, and Harry keeping a sure hold of him—wriggled to look for them.

Harry laughed. It was certainly not a returning Ned. These horses came from the other way, and there were four of them and each had a rider. "I fear your Ned will come too late, Benjamin—if, by the grace of God, he comes at all." So said Harry, chuckling, and to his amazement Benjamin also laughed. Why should Benjamin find consolation in the coming of this *posse*? It was not credible that they could be allies of his. Highwaymen did not work in gangs of half a dozen.

The four horsemen, urged by the shots or by what they saw, came at a gallop and reined up almost on top of Harry and Benjamin. One of them, a little man with a lean, brown face, called out, "By your leave, sir! What's this?"

"It's a rude fellow, sir," Harry said. "I fear a lewd fellow. By trade a highwayman. The highway, indeed, is his life's love, his adored mistress. Observe how he cleaves to it." He compressed Benjamin, who squelched, into the mud, and rose, standing on Benjamin's chest and stomach.

Benjamin groaned, and the eyes behind his mask rolled towards the little man.

"Filthy dog," that little man said with sincere disgust. "Can I serve you, sir?" he touched his hat to the women in the coach.

"Why, Benjamin has a friend, one Ned. Ned hath a pistol or so and two horses which have bolted with him. But he may yet persuade them to bring back his pistols and him. Now, if you would be so good, it would be convenient in you to ride on and destroy Ned."

"It's a pleasure, sir," the little man showed his teeth. "And the fat rogue there, can I help you with him? Shall we take him on to the constables?"

"Oh, I thank you, but my Benjamin is docile. I'll e'en tie him up with his garters, and all will be well."

The little man scowled at Benjamin. "I shall hope to be at his hanging," he said incisively. "Sir, your most obedient! Ladies!" he bobbed at them and rode off, his three companions close about him in eager talk.

As they went, Benjamin let out a cry of anguish: "Captain!"

The little man and his company used their spurs.

Harry looked at their hurry and then down at Benjamin.

"Now why did you call him that, my Benjamin?" said he. "Indeed, why did you call on him at all?"

From behind the mask Benjamin's prominent eyes stared sullenly. He said nothing.

Harry shook his head. "I feel that I do not know you, Benjamin. I must see more of you," With which he fell upon the man again and twitched off the mask. The wig came with it. Benjamin was revealed the owner of a big, bald, shiny head with a face which was puffed and purple. "You were right, Benjamin," said Harry sadly, "You were kind. To wear a mask was charity, nay, decency—what breeches are to other men. That obese and flaccid nose—pah, let us talk of something else." He lay upon Benjamin and tugged at his sword-belt. Benjamin writhed and groaned. His sword was caught underneath him, the hilt deep in the small of his back. Harry hauled the sword-belt off at last and gripped at Benjamin's wrists. He began to struggle again. "Do not be troublesome or I'll tap the beer on your brain. So." He hauled the belt taut about the fighting arms and made all fast. Then he sat himself on Benjamin's legs, which thus ceased to be turbulent, and, taking off the garters, therewith tied the ankles together.

Sighing satisfaction, Harry picked up the pistol and sword, spoils of victory, and rose at his leisure. He contemplated the hapless highwayman with benign interest for a moment, and turned to the coach. "You are still there, ladies? Benjamin is flattered and so am I. But the play is over. He will not be amusing for some time, and at any moment he may be profane. I see him bursting with it. Pray drive on and remove your chaste ears." He restored to them the jewel-case.

"Put him up on the box, sir," the younger woman cried.

"I beg your pardon, madame?"

"We will take him to the constables at Finchley."

"But why? He is beautiful there, my Benjamin, and I doubt he was never beautiful before. And I have planted him so firmly. I think if we leave him there he may grow and blossom. Do not dig him up again yet. Imagine Benjamin in flower! A thing to dream of."

"You are pleased to be witty, sir. Come, we have lost time enough. Put the rogue up, and do you mount with us."

Harry became aware that this young woman had a brow of pride. It was ample and broad and, after the Greek manner, it rose almost in a line with her admirable nose. A noble head, to be sure, but alarming to a mere human man. So Harry thought, and he touched his hat and said: "Madame, your most humble. Pray what do you want with my Benjamin? Your gentle heart would never have him hanged."

Her eyes made Harry feel that he was impudent, which, unhappily, amused him. "I desire the fellow should be given up to the law, sir," she said coldly. "Have you anything against it?"

"Oh, ma'am, a thousand things, with which I'll not weary you. For I see that you would not understand. You are very young (as I hope). Perhaps you may soon grow older (which I pray for you). Let this suffice then. My Benjamin may deserve a hanging. Who knows? We are not God, ma'am, neither you nor I. Therefore I have no mind to be a hangman. And you—why, you are young enough to wait another occasion. And so I give you good-night. Home, coachman, home."

The young woman stared at him as though he were grovelling stupidity, and then lay back on her cushions with a "You will drive on, Samuel."

Harry made his bow, and then, as the coach began to move, there was a cry: "Alison! Alison! It is not right!" The older woman leaned forward, and for the first time he remarked a gentle, motherly face, much lined and worn. "Sure, sir, you will ride with us," she said, and he liked the voice. "We may carry you home."

Harry smiled at her. "Nay, ma'am. I am too dirty for such fine company."

"Drive on," said Mistress Alison. And the coach rolled away.

Harry looked down at the wretched Benjamin, whose eyes answered with apprehension and anxiety. "What's the game?" said Benjamin hoarsely. "I say, master—what d'ye want with me?"

Harry did not answer. He was finding that motherly face, that pleasant voice, curiously vivid still. This annoyed him, and he forced himself back with a jerk to the oddity of events. "A queer business, my Benjamin," he said. "Who was your captain, I wonder?"

Benjamin scowled. "I know nought o' no captain."

"Ah, I thought you did. But I fear you have annoyed the captain, Benjamin. Now what had you done—or what had you not done?"

"It's not fair, master," Benjamin whined. "You do be making game of me, and me beat."

"I am rebuked, Benjamin. Good-night."

"Oons, ye won't leave me so?" Benjamin howled. "I ha' done you no harm, master. Come now, play fair. What d'ye want of me?"

"Nothing, Benjamin, nothing. I like you very well. You are a beautiful mystery. Pleasant dreams."

The hapless Benjamin howled after him long and loud. Thereby Harry, who had a musical ear, was spurred to his best pace. "It's a vile voice," he reflected; "like Lady Waverton's. The marmoreal Alison was right. He would be better hanged. But so also would Lady Waverton. She will acridly want to know why I am late. Well! It will be a melancholy satisfaction not to tell her. That will also annoy Geoffrey, who'll magnificently indicate that I owe him an apology. The poor Geoffrey! He is so fond of himself!"

His evening was as pleasant as he had anticipated. He won two shillings from Lady Waverton at ombre, which made her angry; and lost them to Geoffrey, which made him melancholy. For Mr. Waverton loved (in small things) to be a martyr.

II

The House of Waverton

M r. Waverton had an idea in his head. That was not the least unusual. It was, unhappily, a wrong one. That was not unusual either. We must have a trifle of Latin. Mr. Waverton, studying Horace, desired to translate, *Civium ardor prava jubentium* "the wicked ardour of the overbearing citizens." In vain Harry urged that he was outraging grammar. Mr. Waverton did not believe him, did not want to believe him—the same thing. Mr. Waverton was convinced that he had an insight into the soul of Horace which Harry's pedantic eyes could not share. He explained, as one explains to a dull child, the rare poetic beauty of the sentiment which he had produced. The hero whom Horace was celebrating, you know, was the man superior to the common herd. Now common men (as even Harry might be aware) are all overbearing. It is this quality in the vulgar which most distresses fine souls (like Mr. Waverton) who desire nothing but their just rights.

"I dare say it is," Harry yawned. "If Horace had wanted to mean that, he would have said so."

"I often think, Harry, you dry scholars have no sense for the thought of a poet," said Mr. Waverton elegantly, and lay back in his chair and surveyed Harry.

He was a handsome lad and knew how to set it off. He had height and bulk—almost too much of that indeed, and so made light of it by a careless, lounging ease. At this time he was only twenty-two, but of a precocious maturity. He had the self-possession—as well as the full-bottomed wig—of experience and worldly wisdom, and would have liked to hear you say so. In its dark aquiline style his face was finely moulded and imposing, and already it had a massive gravity. "A mighty grand fellow indeed," said Lady Dorchester once, "if only his mouth had grown since he was a baby." It has to be admitted that Mr. Waverton's mouth, a small, pretty feature, was oddly assorted with the haughty manner in which the rest of him was constructed. The ladies who lamented that were, for the most part, consoled by his eyes—large, dark eyes of a liquid melancholy. But my Lord Wharton complained that they looked at him like a hound's.

Mr. Waverton was an only son, and fatherless. He had also great possessions. From his house of Tetherdown all the fields that he could see stretching away to the Essex border were of his inheritance. His mother was no wiser than she should have been. She consisted spiritually of admiration for herself, for the family into which she had married, and the son whom she had borne. "After all," said Harry Boyce in moments of geniality, "it's wonderful the boy has come out of it so well."

Mr. Waverton, thanks to vacillation of himself and his mother, doubt as to what career, what manner of education, what university, could be worthy his talents, went up to Oxford at last and (for those days) very late. After doing nothing for another year or two, he decided (which was also unusual for a gentleman of means in those days) that he had a genius in pure literature. Therefore Harry was hired to decorate him with all the elegances of Greek and Latin.

The appointment was considered a great prize for a lad so awkward as Harry Boyce. It might well end in a luxurious competence—a stewardship, for example, and marriage with my lady's maid. "That is, if you play your cards well, sirrah," the Sub-Warden felt it his duty to warn Harry's difficult temper.

"Oh, sir, I could never play cards," said Harry, for the Sub-Warden was a master at picquet. "I am too honest."

Yet he had not fallen out with Mr. Waverton. It is probable that he was careful to keep on good terms with his bread and butter. But he had always, I believe, a kindness for Geoffrey Waverton, and bore no ill will for his parade of supremacy. Tyranny in small things, indeed, Mr. Waverton did not affect. He had a desire to be magnificent. Those who did not cross him, those who were content to be his inferiors, found him amiable enough and, on occasion, generous. . .

"Shall we try another line, Mr. Waverton?" said Harry wearily.

"I have a mind to make an epigram," Mr. Waverton announced. "The arrogance of the vulgar, the—the uninstructed—perhaps I lack the *mot juste*, but *quand même*—the mansuetude of the loftier mind. A fine antithesis that, I think." He stood up, walked to the window, and looked out. Away down the hill the fields lay in a mellow mist, the kindly autumn sun made the copses glow golden; it was a benign scene, apt to encourage wit. Mr. Waverton lisped in numbers, but the numbers did not come. He turned to seek stimulus from Harry. "You relish the thought?"

"It is a perfect subject for your style," said Harry.

Mr. Waverton smiled, and turned again to the window for productive meditation.

A third man came lounging in, unheard by Mr. Waverton's rapt mind. He opened his eyes at the back which Mr. Waverton turned upon Harry and the space between them. "Why, Geoffrey, have you been very stupid this morning? And has schoolmaster stood you in the corner? Well done, Mr. Boyce. I always told you, spare the rod and spoil the child. Shall I go cut a birch for you?"

"I wonder you are not tired of that old jest, Charles," said Waverton with a dignity which did not permit him to turn round.

"Never while it annoys you, child."

"Mr. Waverton is in labour with a poem," Harry explained.

"And it's indecent in me to be present at the ceremony? Well, Geoffrey, postpone the birth." He sat himself down at his ease in Geoffrey's chair. He was a compact man with only one arm. He looked ten years older than Geoffrey and was, in fact, five. The campaign in Flanders which had destroyed his right arm had set and hardened a frame and face by nature solid enough. That face was long and angular, with a heavy chin and an expression of sardonic complacency oddly increased by the jauntiness of its shabby brown wig.

Waverton turned round wearily upon the unwelcome guest. "Well, Charles, what is it?"

"It is nothing. My dear Geoffrey, if I had anything to do or anything to say why should I come to you?"

"*Merci*, monsieur," Waverton smiled gracious indulgence.

Mr. Hadley chuckled, and in French replied: "Yes, let's talk French; it embellishes our simple wit and elevates our souls above the vulgar."

There is reason to believe that Waverton liked his French better in fragments than continuously. He still smiled condescension, but risked no other answer.

"Come, Geoffrey, what's the news?" Mr. Hadley reverted to English. "Could you say your lessons this morning? And did you wear a new coat last night?"

"You may go if you will, Harry. Mr. Hadley will be talking for some time," Waverton said. "Indeed, he may, perhaps, have something to say."

Harry was used to being turned out for any reason or none. He well understood that Waverton was not fond of an audience when he was being laughed at. "If you please," he said, and made his bow to Mr. Hadley.

"Why, what's the matter? I don't bite. You are too meek for this life, Mr. Boyce." He looked at Harry with some contempt in his grey eyes. "Oons, you're a man and a brother, ain't you? Sit down and be hearty. Lud, Geoffrey, why do you never have a pipe in the room?"

"It's death to a clean taste, your tobacco smoking, and I value my wine."

"Value it, quotha! Ay, by the spoonful. You ha' never known how to drink since they weaned you. And you, Mr. Boyce, d'ye never smoke a pipe over your Latin?"

"I hope I know my place, Mr. Hadley," Harry said solemnly.

Charles Hadley stared at him. "Hear the Scripture, Mr. Boyce: 'What shall it profit a man though he gain a pretty patron and lose his own soul?'"

"You are very polite, sir," said Harry.

"Upon my honour, Charles, this is too much," Mr. Waverton cried in noble indignation. "Mr. Boyce is my friend, and you'll be good enough to take him as yours if you come to my house."

Charles Hadley was not out of countenance. He eyed them both, and his sardonic expression was more marked. "You make a pretty pair," said he. "When two men ride a horse, one must ride behind. Eh, Mr. Boyce? I wonder. Well, Geoffrey, it's a wicked world. Had you heard of that?"

"The world is what you make it, I think," said Mr. Waverton with dignity.

"Oons, I could sometimes believe you did make it. A simple, pompous place, Geoffrey, that is kind to you if you'll not laugh at it. And full of petty, pompous mysteries. Maybe you make the mysteries too, Geoffrey. Damme, it is so. It's perfectly in your manner," he chuckled abundantly. "Come, child, what were you doing on the highway yesterday?"

Harry stared at him. "When you have finished laughing at your joke, perhaps you will make it," said Waverton. "Pray let us have it over before dinner."

"My dear child, why be so touchy? Were you bitten? Well, you know, this morning one of my fellows brings in a miserable wretch he had found on the road by Black Horse Spinney. The thing was half-dead with wet and cold. He had been lying there all night—so he said, and it's the one thing I believe of him. He was found trussed as tight as a chicken in his own sword-belt and his own garters. Damme, it was a fellow of some humour had the handling of him. He had not been robbed, for there was a bag of money at his middle. He professed that he could tell nothing of who had trussed him or why he was set upon. He would have nought of law or hue and cry. Egad, empty and shivering as he was, he wanted nothing but to be let go. A perfect Christian, as you remark, Geoffrey. Now, you or I, if we had been tied up in the mud through one of these damned raw nights, would take some pains to catch the fellow who did the trussing. But my wretch was as meek as the Gospels. So here is a silly, teasing mystery. Who is the footpad that is at the pains of tying up a fellow and never looks for his purse? Odds fish, I did not know we had a gentleman of such humour in these parts. I suspect you, Geoffrey, I protest. There's a misty fatuousness about it which—"

"By your leave, sir," a servant appeared, "my lady waits dinner."

"Then I fear we shall pay for it," said Hadley, and stood up.

"You dine with us, Charles?" Mr. Waverton was not hearty about it.

"I'll give you that pleasure, child. Well, Mr. Boyce, what do you make of my mystery?"

Harry had to say something. "Perhaps your friend was carrying more than guineas," he said.

"What then? Papers and plots and the high political? I don't think it. If you saw him—a mere tub of beer—and a leaky tub this morning, for he had a vile cold in the head and dribbled damnably."

"I give it up then. Have you let him go?" They were moving out in the corridor and Hadley did not answer. "Is he gone?" Harry said again.

Hadley turned round upon him. "Why, yes. Does it signify?"

"I wonder who he was," said Harry.

Upon that they entered the drawing-room of Lady Waverton. It was congested and dim. The two oriel windows were so draped with curtains of pink and yellow that only a faint light as of the last of a sunset filtered through. The wide spaces were beset with screens in lacquer, odd chairs, Dutch tables, and very many cabinets,—cabinets inlaid with flowers and birds of many colours; cabinets full of shells, agates, corals, and any gaudy stone; cabinets and yet again more cabinets full of Eastern china. In the midst Lady Waverton reclined.

She had been handsome in a large, bold style, and might still have been but for excessive decoration. Her dress was voluminous white satin embroidered in a big pattern of gold and set off with black. It was low at her opulent bosom, to the curves of which the eye was directed by black patches craftily fixed. There were many more patches on her face which, still only a little too full and too loose, had its colours laid on in sharp and vivid contrasts. Her black hair was erected in symmetrical waves high above her brow, and one ringlet was brought by glossy, frozen curls to caress her bosom. She held out the whitest of hands drooping from a large but still fine arm for Mr. Hadley to kiss.

"You are a bad fellow, Charles Hadley," she pouted. "You make me feel old."

"There's a common childish fancy, ma'am."

"You never come to see me now. And when you do come, 'tis not to see me."

"A thousand pardons. Mr. Boyce delayed me awhile with the beauties of his conversation."

"Mr. Boyce?" she looked at Harry as if wondering that he dared exist. "Go and see why they do not bring in dinner."

Having thus diminished Harry, she proceeded, without waiting for him to be gone, to criticize him. "You know, I would never have a chaplain in the house. This tutor fellow is of the same breed, Charles. They tease me, these men which are neither gentlemen nor servants. Faith, life's hard for the poor wretches. They are torn 'twixt their conceit and their poverty. They know not from minute to minute whether they will fawn or be insolent. So they do both indifferent ill."

Harry, who chose not to hear, was opening the door. There came in upon him a woman—the young woman of the coach. Even as he recoiled, bowing, even as he collected his startled wits, he was aware of the singular beauty of her complexion. Its delicacy, its life, were nonpareil. The first clear process of his mind was to wonder how he had contrived not to remark that complexion when first he saw her.

Lady Waverton lifted up her voice. "Alison! Dear child! And are you home at last? It's delicious in you. You seek us out first, do you not? My sweet girl!" Alison was engulfed. Conceive apple blossom in the embraces of a peony.

The apple blossom emerged with a calm, "Dear Lady Waverton."

"You are a sad bad thing. I writ you five letters, I think, and not one from you."

"You are so much cleverer than I am. I had nothing to say." Alison's voice was sweet and low, but too sublimely calm for perfect comfort in her hearers. "So here I am to say it and make my excuses," she dropped a small curtsey, "my lady. Why, Geoffrey, I thought you had been back at Oxford!"

Mr. Waverton came forward, smiling magnificence. "I am delighted to disappoint you, Alison."

"Nay, never believe her, Geoffrey," Lady Waverton lifted up her voice and was arch. "I vow she counted on finding you here. Why else had she come? I know when I was a toast I wasted none of my time going to see old women," she languished affectionately at the girl.

"Dear Lady Waverton,"—if it was possible, Alison's voice became calmer than ever—"how well you know me. And how cruel to expose me. If Geoffrey had his mother's wit, faith, I should never dare come here at all."

"It is not my wit which you need ever fear, Alison," Geoffrey's eyes were ardent upon her.

"Why, you are merciful. Or is it modest?"

"I can be neither, Alison. I am a man."

"My dear Geoffrey, I am sorry for all your misfortunes." She turned from him to Mr. Hadley, who was content in a corner. "Have we quarrelled?"

"We never loved each other well enough."

"Is that why I am always very glad to see Mr. Hadley?"

"It is why he can tell Miss Lambourne that she looks divinely beautiful."

"That means inhuman, sir."

"Which is not my fault, ma'am."

Geoffrey was visibly restive at his exclusion, "Charles never could pay a compliment without a sting in it."

"That is why they are agreeable, sir," said she.

"That is why they are true," said Hadley in the same breath, and they laughed together.

Lady Waverton interfered imperiously. "Alison, dear, come sit by me and tell me all about yourself."

"Faith, not with the gentlemen to listen," said she, and was saved by Harry and the butler, who came in together announcing dinner.

Lady Waverton rose elaborately. "Give me your arm, Charles. My dear Alison—"

"But who is this?" Alison said, and she stared with placid, candid interest at Harry. With equal composure Harry stared back. But there was no candour in his expressionless face. For he had become keenly aware of her beauty. It was waking in him desire and already something deeper and stronger, and he vehemently resented the disturbance. He had no wish to be troubled by any woman, and for this woman, judging her on her behaviour, he felt even a little more contempt than the store which he had for all her sex. It was cursedly impertinent in her to be such a joy to the blood. She stood there, her eyes level with his eyes, and dared to look as strong as he— slighter to be sure, but not too slight for a woman, and delectably deep bosomed. There was life and laughter in that calm Greek face, and the vivid, delicate colour of it maddened him. The great crown of black hair was just what her brow needed for its royalty. He could find no fault in the irksome wench. Even her dress, dark grey as her eyes, perfectly became her, perfectly pleased in its generous modesty. And she knew of her power too. There was a mocking confidence in every line of her.

"But who is this, Lady Waverton?" she was saying again.

Lady Waverton tried to draw her on. "'Tis but Geoffrey's new factotum."

"My good friend, Harry Boyce, Alison," said Geoffrey with a patronly hand on Harry's shoulder.

Harry made his bow.

"Faith, sir, we have met before," she smiled.

"No, ma'am," Harry bowed again. "I have never had an honour, which, sure, I could not forget."

Her brow wrinkled. Lady Waverton swept her on, and Harry in the rear had the pleasure of hearing Lady Waverton say: "A poor, vulgar wretch, my dear. An out-at-elbows scholar which Geoffrey met at Oxford and keeps out of charity. He is too soft of heart, dear boy, and such creatures stick to him like burrs."

The dinner-table was a blaze of silver, but otherwise not bountifully provided. Lady Waverton looked down it with pride. "I am of Mr. Addison's mind, my dear," she announced. "Do you remember? 'Two plain dishes with two good-natured, cheerful, ingenious friends make me more pleased and vain than all your luxury.'"

"Why, then, you must now be sore out of countenance," Alison protested. "For I am not good-natured and I vow Mr. Hadley is not cheerful." Mr. Hadley's face, set in contemplation of the food, shed gloom and apprehension. "But perhaps Mr. Boyce is ingenious."

"I hope so," said Hadley.

It was Harry's task to carve, which dispensed him from answering the girl or even looking at her. One not abundant fowl and a calf's head smoked before him. Under a heavy fire of directions from Lady Waverton he did his duty.

Miss Lambourne may have suddenly grown weary of Lady Waverton's eloquence upon the daintiest bits of these unexciting foods. She may have been waiting for the moment when Harry would have no occupation to prevent him listening to her. While my lady was still explaining the superiority of her calf, as bred and born in the house of Waverton, to all other calves, just when Harry had finished his work, Miss Lambourne broke out: "Faith, I was almost forgetting my splendid story. I wonder, now, have any of you met any ventures on the North Road?"

Harry began to eat. Charles Hadley ceased an anxious examination of his plate and looked at her. Lady Waverton cried out: "Dear Alison! Don't tell me you have been stopped. Too terrible! I vow I could never bear it. I should die of shame. They tell me these rogues are vilely impudent to a fine woman."

Geoffrey exhibited a tender agitation. "Why, Alison, what is it? Zounds, I cannot have you go travelling alone! You must give me news when you make a journey, and I'll ride with you."

"Thank you for your agonies. But the virgin in distress found her knight-errant duly provided. He rose out of the mud romantically apropos. To be sure, I think he was mad. But that is all in the part. The complete hero. Geoffrey, could you be a little mad?"

"More than a little," said he with proper ardour. "Pray don't torture us, Alison. Let us hear."

"It's on my mind that I am going to hear news of my funny friend," said Hadley solemnly. "Don't you think so, Mr. Boyce?"

Harry, who had been eating with the humble zeal appropriate to a poor scholar, looked up for a moment: "Why, sir, I can't tell at all. If you say so, indeed—" and he went on eating.

"Come, are you in it too, Mr. Hadley?" Alison cried.

"In it, odds life, I am bewilderingly out of it," quoth Hadley, and again told his tale of the mysterious man found tied up in the mud who knew nothing of his assailants and wanted no vengeance on them.

"That's our Benjamin," Alison laughed. "Oh, but you did not let him go?"

"Not let him go, quotha! For what I know, he was a poor, suffering martyr, though to look at his nose, I doubt it. And yet he was fool enough. Nay, how could I stay him?"

"Why, send him to gaol for a rogue and a vagabond. Should he not?" she invited the suffrages of the table.

"Dear Alison, to be sure, yes," Lady Waverton murmured. "These fellows must be put down."

"You owed it to yourself to look deeper into the matter, Charles," said Geoffrey gravely.

"Come, Mr. Boyce, your sentence too," Alison cried, wicked eyes intent upon him.

He met them with bland meekness. "Indeed, ma'am, I can't tell. It's Mr. Hadley's affair."

"From a virtuous woman, good Lord deliver us," Hadley groaned. "You would make a rare hanging judge, Alison. Now, i' God's name, let's have your tale. What's the rogue to you?"

"Oh, sir, a great joy. Why, he gave me the only knight-errant ever I had. A vile muddy one, to be sure, but poor maids must not be choosers. We were driving home, Mrs. Weston and I, and by Black Horse Spinney we were stopped by two highwaymen. They had just begun to be rude, when out of the mud comes my knight-errant, bold as Don Quixote and as shabby withal, and with a pretty wit too—which is not much in the way of knight-errants, I think. He scared the highwaymen's horses and set them bolting with the one fellow which held them, then he knocked the other down, took his pistol, and tied the rogue up in his own garters. Oh, the neatest knight-errant ever you saw. Then we bade him put the fellow on the box and drive on with us. But monsieur was haughty, if you please. He wanted none of our company. Off he packed us, for me to cry my eyes out for love of him. Which I do heartily, I warrant you."

"Alison!" Geoffrey cried, and laid his hand on hers.

"Faith, yes, give me sympathy. I have loved and lost—in the mud. To be sure, I can ne'er be my own woman again till I find him and give him—a brush, I think, and maybe a pair of breeches too, for his own can never recover their youth. Dear Geoffrey, help me to find him."

Geoffrey had taken his hand away in a hurry. He contemplated her with cold reproof. It did not trouble her. She was giving all her attention to Harry; gay, malicious eyes challenged him to declare himself, mocked him for his modesty, vaunted what she had to give.

"Damme, this is madder and madder yet," Hadley broke in. "Who is your Orlando Furioso that's a champion of dames and too haughty to ride in their carriage; that ties up highwaymen and forgets to tell the constable where he left 'em? Odso, I thought I knew most of the fools in these parts, but there's one bigger than I know."

"Dear Alison—I could never have survived it—but you are so strong—and what a person! My dear, I could not bear to think of him. A rude, low fellow, to be sure," Thus Lady Waverton coherently.

Alison laughed. "I doubt I'm not so delicate," Then she leaned towards Harry. "Well, and you? Come, Mr. Boyce, why leave yourself out?"

"I beg pardon, ma'am?"

She made an impatient sound. "And what do you think of my hero?"

"I wonder who the gentleman was, ma'am," Harry said.

Her eyes fought a moment more with his bland, meaningless face. "Faith, I think he's a fool for his pains," said she.

"Grateful woman," Hadley grunted. "Humph. *Spretae injuria formae*, ain't it, Mr. Boyce? Give miss a construe."

Harry gave a deprecating cough instead.

"Oh, be brave, sir," she jeered.

"I am afraid it means 'the insult of slighting your beauty,' ma'am," said Harry meekly.

Lady Waverton straightened her back and looked ice at him. But the butler was at her elbow, whispering. "Colonel Boyce?" she repeated. "What Colonel Boyce? Who is Colonel Boyce?

"It might be my father," Harry suggested.

"Why, Harry, I never knew you had a father," Waverton sneered amiably.

"Is your father a colonel?" Lady Waverton was torn between incredulity of such presumption and rage at it.

"Not that I know of, my lady. But he has always surprised me."

"Shall we have him in, Geoffrey?" said Lady Waverton.

"My dear mother!" Geoffrey waved his hand to the butler. "Ask the gentleman to be so good as to join us."

Mr. Hadley turned in his chair, and over the remnants of the fowl and the calf's head directed a grim smile at Harry. "Thank you for a very pleasant dinner," said he.

III

A Man of Many Worlds

There came in a man of many colours. Dazzled eyes, recovering from their first dismay, might admit that his splendours were harmonious. A red coat with gold buttons, a waistcoat of gold satin embroidered in blue, breeches of blue velvet with golden garters were topped by a face burnt brown and a great jet-black periwig. He carried off all this with airy ease. "My lady, your most humble and devoted," he bowed to Lady Waverton. "Harry, dear lad," he held out his hands, and Harry, rising, found himself embraced and kissed on both cheeks.

"Colonel Boyce is it?" said Lady Waverton with some emphasis on the title.

"In the service of your ladyship," he laughed, and bowed to her again, and turned upon the company. "Pray present me, dear lady." She made some stumbling about it, but Colonel Boyce appeared to enjoy himself with an "I account myself fortunate, ma'am," for Miss Lambourne; with a "My boy's friends are mine, sir—and his debts too," for Geoffrey; and to Mr. Hadley, "You have served, sir?" with a look of respect at the empty sleeve.

Hadley nodded. "Ay, ay. The red field of honour. Well, there's no life like it."

"That's why I left it," Hadley grunted.

"Come, sir, draw up a chair and join us," Geoffrey said. "Be sure you are very welcome."

"Ten thousand thanks." Without enthusiasm Colonel Boyce looked at the calf's head. "But—egad, I am sorry for it now—but I have dined."

"At least you'll drink a glass of wine with us?"

"Oh, I can't deny myself the pleasure, sir." He drew up a chair, Geoffrey reached at a decanter, and so Lady Waverton rose and Alison after her.

Colonel Boyce started up. "But no—not at that price. Damme, that would poison the Prince's own Tokay. Nay, you are too cruel, my lady. I come, and you desolate the table to receive me. Gad's life, ma'am, our friends here will be calling me out for my daring to exist."

Lady Waverton was very well pleased. "Sir, you will let me give you a dish of tea. I warrant the men were already sighing to be rid of us."

"Then I vow they be blind," quoth Colonel Boyce, and opened the door, from which he came back with a laugh to his glass of port. Over drinking it he went through all the tricks of the connoisseur and ended with a cultured ecstasy.

"I see you are a man of the world, Colonel," Hadley sneered.

"A man of many worlds, sir," the Colonel laughed easily.

"I wonder which this is?"

"Why, this is the world of good company and good fellowship—" he smiled and bowed to Geoffrey—"of sound wine and sound learning."

"Sir, you are very good. But I hope my wine is better than my scholarship. This is our man of learning," he slapped Harry on the shoulder. "And Harry counts me a mere trifler, a literary exquisite, an amateur of elegances."

"If your scholarship has the elegance of your wine, Mr. Waverton, you do very well. I doubt my Harry is no judge of the graces. He has always been something of a plodder."

"Have I?" Harry found his tongue. "How did you know?"

The Colonel laughed. "He has me there, the rogue. The truth is, gentlemen, I have not seen him in these six years. Damme, Harry, you are grown no fatter."

"Servitors don't make flesh," said Harry.

"And soldiers don't make money. Still; there's enough for two now, boy."

"I am glad you have been fortunate," the tone suggested that though the father had quite enough for two; there would be none to spare for the son.

"Why, sir," Waverton was grandly genial, "I hope you don't mean to rob me of Harry. He's the most useful fellow, and, I promise you; I value him."

"Thank you very much," said Harry.

"I'll take you into my confidence, Mr. Waverton," the Colonel leaned across the table.

"Then I'll take my leave," said Hadley.

"No need, sir. At this time, we all know, there are higher claims on a man than a friend's or a father's."

"I feel like a pawn," Harry complained.

"Egad, sir, a pawn may save a queen or check a king."

"But do you suppose it enjoys it?"

"Are you away to the war, sir?" Geoffrey smiled. "I doubt our Harry has no turn for soldiering."

"You are always right, Mr. Waverton," Harry nodded at him.

"It is not only soldiers who fight our battles, Mr. Waverton," said the Colonel with dignity. "There's danger enough for a quick wit and a cool judgment far behind the lines. And you need not go to Flanders to find the war. It's flaming all over England, all over—France," he dropped the last word in a lower tone, as if his heat had carried him away and it was a blunder. He flung himself back and emptied his glass, and looked gloomily at the empty decanter. "Why, Mr. Waverton, you have made me into a babbler. It's time you delivered me to the ladies."

"Aye, aye," Hadley yawned. "Let's try another of the worlds."

They marched out, but the Colonel and Waverton, waiting on each other, were some distance behind the other pair.

"You must know I have often had some desire for the life of action," said Mr. Waverton.

To which the Colonel earnestly, "I have never known a man more fit for it," and upon that they entered my lady's drawing-room.

Miss Lambourne was singing Carey's song of the nightingale:

> *"While in a Bow'r with beauty blest*
> *The lov'd Amintor lies,*
> *While sinking on Lucinda's breast*
> *He fondly kiss'd her Eyes.*
> *A wakeful nightingale who long*
> *Had mourn'd within, the Shade*
> *Sweetly renewed her plaintive song*
> *And warbled through the Glade."*

On the coming of the men the wakeful nightingale broke off her plaintive song abruptly.

Lady Waverton, who was again at full length on her couch, then opened her eyes. "Delicious, delicately delicious," she sighed. "Why did you stop, dear?" she controlled a yawn. "Oh, the men! Odious creatures!" she rose on her elbow and looked at them, and looked down at her dress and patted it.

Colonel Boyce accepted the challenge briskly, and marched upon her. "Egad, my lady, your name is cruelty."

"Who—I, sir? I vow I never had the heart to see any creature suffer."

"Nay, your very nature is cruelty. You exist but to torture us."

"Good lack, sir," says my lady, well pleased, "and must I die to serve your pleasure?"

"Why, there it is. We can neither bear to be with you nor to be without you. I protest, ma'am, your sex was made for our torture. 'Tis why you parade it and delight in it."

"Lud, sir, you are mighty rude," my lady simpered. "I parade my sex? Alack, my modesty!"

"Modesty—that's but another weapon to madden us. Fie, ma'am, why do you clothe yourself in such beauty but to flaunt upon our senses that sex of yours?" My lady was duly shocked and hid behind her fan. "Aye, there it is! We catch a whiff of paradise and straightway it is denied us. Our nightingale there is silent when we draw near. Our Venus here hides herself when our eyes would enjoy her. As His Grace said to me, you women are like heaven to a damned soul."

"You are a wicked fellow," said Lady Waverton with relish.

Geoffrey at his elbow put in, "'His Grace,' Colonel?"

"The Old Corporal, Mr. Waverton. The Duke of Marlborough."

"You have served with him, sir?"

Colonel Boyce gave a laugh of genial condescension. "Why, yes, Mr. Waverton, I stand as close to His Grace as most men."

After a moment of impressive silence, the Wavertons vigorously directed the conversation to the Duke of Marlborough. Colonel Boyce made no objection. In the most obliging manner he admitted them to a piquant intimacy with His Grace's manners and customs. He mingled things personal and high politics with a fascinating air of letting out secrets at every word; and, throughout, he maintained a tantalizing discretion about his own position. My lady and Mr. Waverton were more and more fascinated.

So that Miss Lambourne had good opportunity to try her maiden steel upon Harry. As soon as he came in, he withdrew himself to a cabinet of medals in a remote corner. Mr. Hadley approached the harpsichord and reached it just before it fell silent. Miss Lambourne looked up into his face.

"Yes, shall we lay our heads together?" said he.

"But I doubt mine would turn yours."

"If you'll risk it, ma'am, I will."

"La, sir, is this an offer? I protest I am all one blush."

"Then your imagination is bolder than mine, ma'am. I mean—"

"Oh, fie for shame! To disgrace a poor maid so! To betray her weakness! It is unmanly, Mr. Hadley. Sure, my father (in the general resurrection) will have your blood. I leave you to your conscience, sir," which she did, making for Harry.

Mr. Hadley, remaining by the harpsichord, contemplated them, and with his one hand caressed his chin. "It's a fascinating family, the family of Boyce," said he to himself.

Miss Lambourne sat herself down beside Harry before he chose to be aware of her coming. He started up and obsequiously drew away.

"You are very coy, Mr. Boyce," said the lady.

Harry replied, with the servile laughter of a dependent, "Oh, ma'am, you are mocking me."

"Tit for tat"—Alison's eyes had some fire in them.

"Tat, ma'am?"

"Lud, now, don't be tedious. Sir, the house of Waverton is entranced by your splendid father: and Charles Hadley (as usual) is entranced by himself. You have no audience Mr. Boyce. Stop acting, and tell me— what is wrong with me?"

Harry considered her with calm criticism. "It's not for me to tell Miss Lambourne that she is too beautiful."

"Indeed, I thought you had more sense."

"Too beautiful," Harry persisted deliberately; "too beautiful to be good company."

"That will not serve, sir. You are not so inflammable. Being more in the nature of a tortoise."

"If you had a flaw or so: if your nose had a twist; if your cheeks had felt the weather; if—I fear, ma'am, I grow intimate. In fine, if you were less fine, you would be a comfort to a man. But as it is—permit the tortoise to keep in his shell."

"I advise you, Mr. Boyce—I resent this."

Harry bowed. "I dare to remind you, ma'am—I did not demand the conversation."

"The conversation!" Her eyes flashed. "What do I care if a lad's impudent? Perhaps I like it well enough, Mr. Boyce. There is more than that between you and me. You have done me something of a service, and you'll not let me avow it nor pay you. Well?"

"Well, ma'am, you're telling the truth," said Harry placidly.

The lady made an exclamation. "I shall bear you a grudge for this, sir."

"I am vastly obliged, ma'am."

The lady drew back a little and looked at him full, which he bore calmly. "I suppose I am beneath Mr. Boyce's concernment."

"Not beneath, ma'am. Above. Above. Do you admire the Italian medals? They are of a delicate restraint." He turned to the cabinet and began to lecture.

Miss Lambourne was not repulsed. He maintained a steady flow of instruction. She waited, watching him.

By this time Colonel Boyce was growing tired of his Duke of Marlborough and his State secrets, and seeking diversion. "Odds fish, it's a hard road that leads to fortune. You are happy, Mr. Waverton. You were born with yours."

"I conceive, sir, that every man of high spirit must needs take the road to fame."

"A dream of a shadow, Mr. Waverton," said the Colonel, with melancholy grandeur. "'Take the goods the gods provide you,'" he waved his hand at the crowded opulence of the room and then, smiling paternally, at Miss Lambourne.

Lady Waverton simpered at her son. He chose to ignore the hint. "Why, Colonel, if a man is happily placed above vulgar needs, the more reason—"

"Vulgar needs! Oh, fie, Mr. Waverton. A divine creature." Colonel Boyce looked wicked, and his easy hand designed in the air Miss Lambourne's shape.

Lady Waverton tittered. Geoffrey blushed, and "You do me too much honour sir, indeed," he stammered.

Colonel Boyce turned smiling upon Lady Waverton. "I vow, ma'am, a man hath twice the modesty of a maid."

"You are a bad fellow," said Lady Waverton, very well pleased.

"You go too fast, sir;" with so much mirth about him Geoffrey feared for his dignity. "There is nothing between me and Miss Lambourne."

The Colonel shook his head. "I confess I thought better of you, sir. What, is miss her own mistress?"

"Miss Lambourne has no father or mother, sir."

"And her face is her fortune? Egad, 'tis the prettiest romance!"

Geoffrey and his mother laughed together. "Not quite all her fortune, sir. She is the only child of Sir Thomas Lambourne."

"What! old Tom Lambourne of the India House?" Colonel Boyce whistled. He looked with a new interest at her as she stood by Harry, absorbing the lecture on medals, and as he looked his face put on a queer air of mockery. This he presented to Geoffrey. "Something of a plum, sirrah. Well, well, some folks have but to open their mouths."

Mr. Waverton, not quite certain whether the Colonel ought to be so familiar, concluded to be pleased, and laughed fatuously. During which music the butler announced "Mrs. Weston."

Lady Waverton and Geoffrey exchanged a glance of disgust. Lady Waverton murmured, "What a person!" It escaped their notice that Colonel Boyce had stiffened at the name. His full face lost all its geniality, all expression. He was for the first time singularly like his son.

Mrs. Weston was Alison's companion of the coach, a woman of middle age, inclining to be stout; but her face was thin and lined, belying her comfortable aspect,—a wistful face which had known much sorrow, and had still much tenderness to give.

Lady Waverton put out a languid and supercilious hand. "I hope you are better."

"Thank you. I have not been ill."

"Oh, I always forget."

"Your servant, ma'am." Geoffrey bowed.

"Oh,"—Lady Waverton turned on her elbow. "Colonel Boyce—Mrs. Weston, Alison's companion. Faith, duenna, I think."

"Your most obedient, ma'am." Colonel Boyce bowed low.

Mrs. Weston stared at him, seemed to try to speak, said nothing, and hurried across the room.

"Alison, dear, are you ready?" her voice sounded hoarse.

"Am I ever ready?" Alison laughed. "Weston, dear, we are finding friends here;" she pointed to Harry.

Colonel Boyce had followed. He laid his hand on Harry's shoulder: "My son, ma'am," said he.

Mrs. Weston's eyes grew wide, and her face was white and drawn, and she swayed. As Harry bowed to her, a lacquered box was swept off the table with a great clatter, and Colonel Boyce cried, "Odds life, Harry, you are a clumsy fellow. Here, man, here," and made a great commotion over picking it up.

Alison had her arm about Mrs. Weston: "Why, Weston, dear, what is it? Are you seeing a ghost?" She laughed. "Pray, Mr. Boyce, come to life."

"I ask pardon, ma'am." Harry rose with the box.

"'Bid me to live and I will live,'" said the Colonel, with a grand air.

"Come away, dear, come," Mrs. Weston gasped, in much agitation.

"Why, Weston, he is not our highwayman, you know," Alison was still laughing, and then seeing her distress real, took it in earnest. "You are shaken, poor thing. Come!" She mothered the woman away and, turning, called over her shoulder—

"*Revanche*, Mr. Boyce." There was an explanation to Lady Waverton: poor Weston had been so alarmed by the highwaymen that she was not fit to be out of her bed, and anything alarmed her; even Mr. Boyce; so dear Lady Waverton must forgive them. And Geoffrey took them to their carriage.

"What a person!" said Lady Waverton.

Mr. Hadley came out of his corner and looked Harry up and down with dislike. "Let me know when you play the next act, Mr. Boyce," he said, and turned to Lady Waverton. "My lady, I beg leave to go with my friends."

IV

A Gentleman's Purse

In a small, bare room Colonel Boyce sat himself down on a pallet bed and made a wry face at his son. "My poor, dear boy," he said, and shifted uneasily, and looked round at the stained walls and shivered. "It's damp, I vow it's damp," he complained.

"Oh yes. It's damp after rain, and it's hot after sun, and it's icy after frost. It's a very sympathetic room," said Harry.

"They are barbarians, these Wavertons. I vow they give their horses better lodging."

"Oh yes. I am not worth so much as a horse," said Harry.

"Lud, Harry, don't whine,"—his father was irritated. "Have some spirit. I hate to hear a lad meek."

"I thought you did," said Harry.

The Colonel laughed. "Oh, I am bit, am I? *Tant mieux*. But why the devil do you stay here?"

"Now why the devil do you want to know?" said Harry.

"No, that is not kind, boy."

"Oh, Oh, are we kind?"

"My dear Harry, I have not seen you for six years, and I have not come now to quarrel."

"Then why have you come?" said the affectionate son.

"You are a gracious cub." Colonel Boyce would not be ruffled. "When I saw you last, Harry—"

"You borrowed a shilling of me. I remember I was glad that I had not another."

"You can have it back with interest now. There is plenty in the purse, Harry, and half of all mine is yours."

"You have changed," Harry said. "Odds life, Harry, bear no grudges. I dare say I was hard in what you remember of me. Well, things were hard upon me and I lived hard. You shall find me mellow enough now."

"Hard? I don't know that you were hard. I thought you were as cold as ice. I believe, sir, I am still frozen."

"Egad, Harry, you must have had a curst childhood."

"Oh, must we be sympathetic?" said Harry.

"You're right, boy. The past is past. 'Tis your future which is the matter. So again—why do you stay here?"

Harry laughed. "They give me bed and board, and a shilling or two by the month."

"Bed?" His father shifted upon it. "A bag of stones, I think. And for the board—bread of affliction and water of affliction by what I saw of the remains. Egad, Harry, they are savages, these Wavertons."

"I did not hear you say so to madame. And Geoffrey is not a bad fellow as far as he has understanding."

"A dolt, eh? He might take a woman's eye, though. These big dreamy fellows, the women hanker after them queerly. Take care, Harry." He looked knowing. "Bed and board—bah, you can do better than that. Now what do you think I have been doing?"

"Something profitable, to judge by your genial splendours. Have you turned highwayman?"

"You all talk about highwaymen in this house," said the Colonel with a frown and a keen glance.

"Damme, no."

"Why, are you really a colonel?"

"Faith, you may come see my commission,"—Colonel Boyce was not annoyed,—"and, egad, share my pay." He pulled out a fat purse and thrust some guineas upon Harry. "Don't deny me now, boy," he said, with some tenderness.

"I never meant to," said Harry, and counted them. "But how long have you been a soldier? I never knew you were anything."

"I have been with his Grace of Marlborough in every campaign since Blenheim. Do you think it's a good service, Harry?" he smiled at his own opulence.

"For a versatile man," said Harry, and looked at his father curiously.

"Why, I can take the field as well as another. Egad, when Vendome fell back from Oudenarde I was commanding a battalion. But it is not in the field that my best work is done."

"Faith, I had guessed that," Harry said.

"You have a sharp tongue, Harry. It's a dangerous weakness. Be careful to grow out of it. Then I think you may do well enough."

"In your profession, sir? To be sure, you flatter me."

"In my profession—" His father looked at him keenly. "I am not sure. Maybe you can do better, which will be well enough. Now, what can you do? You can use a sword, I suppose, though you wear none?"

Harry shrugged. "I know the rigmarole, the salutes; I could begin a duel, *par exemple*. It's the other man who would end it."

"Duels—bah, only dolts are troubled with them. You must learn to hold your own in a flurry. You can ride, I suppose?"

"If the beast has a mane."

"Humph. You speak French?"

"As we speak it in England."

"Yes." His father nodded. "When a man is no fool, he finds his profit in not doing things too well. Well, Harry, are you Whig or Tory—Jacobite or Hanoverian?"

"Whichever you like, sir."

"By the Lord, you take after me mightily. Now look 'e, thus it is. The Queen grows old. She eats too well and drinks too well, and she has the gout. It's common among all who know her ways that she cannot last long. The poor soul will not be wise at dinner. But even if she should last, we are in an odd case. For Anne hath a conscience as well as a stomach, and it seems they grow together. As the old lady gets fatter, she feels remorse. When she's tearful after dinner now she asks her women what right she has to be queen and keep a good cellar while her poor half-brother Prince James lives in exile on *vin ordinaire*."

Harry shrugged his shoulders. "'Poor, dear lad,' says she, 'and to be sure I am a sad, bad woman. But I think I'll die a queen.' What then, sir?"

"I don't say you are wrong, Harry. She's more like to drown the lad in tears than right him. And meanwhile our rightful king, James the Pretender, is left to his *vin ordinaire*. Faith, it's a proper liquor, for rightful heirs which can't right themselves. And yet there is a chance. The Queen has always been religious, and when a woman hath religion she may play the devil with your reason any minute. But here is what's more likely. You know when an old fellow hath played the knave with some wardship or some matter of trust, often he holds fast to it all his life and then seeks to commend himself to the day of judgment by bequeathing his spoils to those from whom he stole them. Well, it's whispered among them that know her that Madame Anne will do her possible to make Prince James King when she is gone."

"A dead Queen is but a corpse," said Harry. "When she is gone 'twill not be for her to say who shall reign."

"That's half a truth. You know the law is so that Prince George of Hanover should be the King. About him no man knows anything save that he hath a vile taste in women. I do suspect Marlborough is in the right—he has a nose for men—when he saith there is nought to know. Well, we tried a Dutchman once for our King and liked him ill enough. Who is to say that we shall like a German better? Now Prince James—he is half an Englishman at least, though they say he has his father's weakness for priests. I'll not hide from you, Harry, that I am in the confidence of some great men. It's laid upon me to go to France with an errand to Prince James."

"I suppose that is high treason, sir."

Colonel Boyce smiled queerly. "You see how I trust you, Harry. Bah, you are not frightened of words. Who is the worse for it, if I find out what's Monsieur's temper and how he would bear himself if he were King?"

"And what he would pay any kind gentlemen who chose to turn Jacobites apropos."

"If you like." Colonel Boyce laughed. I promise you, Harry, there are great men in this. Now I need a trusty fellow to my right hand: a fellow who can talk and say nothing: a fellow who is in no service but mine: and all the better if he hath some learning to play the secretary. So I thought of you. And since it may carry you to something of note, I chose you with right good will."

"Do you wonder that you surprise me?"

"I profess you're not generous, Harry. It's true enough, I have done little for you yet. But the truth is I could do nothing. As soon as I have it in my power, I come to you—"

"And offer me—a game at hazard."

"Why, Harry, you're not a coward?"

"Faith, I can't tell. Perhaps I will go with you. But I have no expectation in it."

"I suppose you have some here," his father sneered. "What do they call you? You seem to be something better than Master Geoffrey's valet and a good deal worse than my lady's footman."

"Why, I believe you have lost your temper." Harry laughed. "Oh, admirable sight! Pray let me enjoy it! The father rages at his son's ingratitude!"

But Colonel Boyce had quickly recovered his equanimity. "They used to tell me that I was a cold fellow. But I vow you are a very fish. So you have half a mind to stay here, have you? Well, I bear no malice."

"It is only half a mind," Harry said. "Are you in a hurry?"

"Oh, you may sleep on it. Damme, I suppose there is little to do here but sleep. What does Master Geoffrey want with you? He is old to keep a tame schoolmaster."

"I listen to his poetry."

"Oh Lud!" said Colonel Boyce, with sincere sympathy. "I suppose they are wealthy folk, your Wavertons. Do they keep much company?" Harry shrugged. "Who is this Mrs. Weston?"

"I never saw her before." Harry paused, and then with a laugh added—"before yesterday."

"That's a fine woman, her mistress. Do you do anything in that quarter, sirrah?"

"Why should you think so?"

"She was willing enough that you should try."

"She is meat for my betters," said Harry meekly.

"For Master Geoffrey?" The Colonel looked knowing. "Do you know, Harry, I think Master Geoffrey is a pigeon made to be plucked. Well. What was the pretty lady's talk about highwaymen?"

Harry looked at his father for some time. "The truth is, I don't understand Benjamin," he said at last. "I wonder if you will. Faith, sir, here is a pretty piece of family life. The good son confides in his father alone of all the world."

"Go on, sir," Colonel Boyce chuckled. "I play fair."

So Harry told his tale of Benjamin and Benjamin's companion and their disaster. It was that appearance in the crisis of the fight of other gentlemen on horseback which most interested Colonel Boyce. "So they went in pursuit of the fellow who had fled and they never came back again." He looked quizzically at his son. "These be very honest gentlemen."

"Why, sir, I thought nothing of that. They were plainly travelling at speed. I suppose they missed him, and had no time to waste in searching."

"Then why o' God's name did he not come back to help his fellow? He was mounted, he was armed, and only you and your cudgel against him. Bah, Harry, do not be an innocent. Consider: these fellows went after him at speed. He cannot have been far away. It is any odds that he had his bolting horses in hand before he had gone two furlongs. Then— allow him some sense—then he must have turned and come back for his friend. And then these other honest gentlemen swept down on him. Well. Why have you heard no more of them or him?"

"Faith, sir, you are right," Harry conceived for the first time some admiration for his father. "I had missed that: and, egad, it is the chief question of the puzzle. But—"

"Puzzle! Oh Lud, there's no puzzle. They were all one gang, these fellows."

Harry laughed. "Then there was not much honour among the thieves. They abandoned their Benjamin to me with delight."

"Ah, bah, you do not suppose they were out for such small game as your pretty miss. They would not work in a gang to stop a simple, common coach, be it never so rich. Come, Harry, use your wits. Did you hear of any great folks on the road yesterday?"

Harry made an exclamation. "Odds life, sir, you would make a great thief-catcher. You have hit it. There was your friend, the Duke of Marlborough, stuck in the mud below Barnet Hill." And he told that part of the story.

"Humph. So they came too late," his father said. "You see how it is. This gang was charged to stop his Grace, and was something slow about it. The two first, your Benjamin and his friend, I suppose they should have held the Duke's fellows in play till the others came up. They missed him, or they shirked it, and instead, tried to stay their stomachs with some common game. The rest of the gang would be well enough pleased that you should baste Benjamin while they hurried on after the Duke. Did you mark any of them, what like they were?"

"Not I. I was too busy with Benjamin."

"And your pretty miss, eh? A pity. But it's well enough for your first affair."

"First? Why, am I to spend my life tumbling with gentlemen of the road?"

"And a profitable, pleasant life too, if you use your wits."

Harry opened his eyes. "Do you know it well, sir? Now, what I don't understand is why a gang of highwaymen should appoint to set upon the Duke of Marlborough. It's dangerous, to be sure—"

"You will understand why, if you come to France," said Colonel Boyce, with a queer smile. "There be many would pay high for a sight of his Grace's private papers," and he laughed to himself over some joke. "Nay, but you have done very well, Harry," he condescended. "I like this business of leaving Benjamin tied up on the road. 'Tis damned nonsense, to be sure, but it has an air, a distinction. Your pretty miss will like that. And I judge you have not told the Wavertons you were the hero, nor let miss tell them. 'Tis your little secret for yourselves. A good touch, Harry. Odds life, I begin to be proud of you. I suppose you will soon go pay your respects—to Mrs. Weston." He laughed heartily.

Harry was not amused. "Do you know, I think I like you much less than you like me," he said.

Colonel Boyce seemed very well content.

V

THE WORLD'S A MIRACLE

Colonel Boyce was established in the house, a guest of high honour. Harry, dazed at the mere fact, could not be very sure how it had happened or why. The Wavertons, mother and son, had assaulted the Colonel with hospitality—for a night—for another—for longer and longer—and he, appearing at first honestly dubious, remained with a benign condescension.

There is no doubt that, in an honourable way, Lady Waverton was fascinated by Colonel Boyce. She saw nothing coarse in his highly-coloured manners, suspected no guile in his flattery or his parade of importance. Harry, who had never supposed her a wise woman, was surprised by her complete surrender. He had credited her with too much pride to succumb to flattery, which was to his taste impudently gross. But he was not yet old enough to allow that other folks might have tastes wholly unlike his own, and he had himself—it is perhaps the only trait of much delicacy in him—a shrinking discomfort under praise.

Colonel Boyce took his victory with a complacency which Harry thought oddly fatuous in a man so acute.

"Egad, the old lady would go to church with me to-morrow if I asked her," he laughed, and seemed to think that in that at least my lady showed sense.

"You had better take her, sir," said Harry, with a sneer. "I know she has a good dower. And a fool and her money are soon parted."

"Damme, Harry, you are venomous!" For the first time in their acquaintance Colonel Boyce showed some signs of smarting. "What harm have I done you? No, sir, you have a nasty tongue. I intend the old lady no harm, neither. What if she has a tenderness for me? I suppose that does not make me a fool."

"To be sure, sir, I did not know your affection was serious." Harry laughed disagreeably.

"I believe you would not miss a chance to say a bitter thing though it ruined you, Lud, Harry, if you can't be grateful, don't be a fool too. What a pox are your Wavertons to me? I don't value them a pinch of snuff. What I am doing, I am doing for you. You know what you were when I found you—no better than a footman out of livery. Now, they treat you like a gentleman."

"And all for the *beaux yeux* of my father. Well, it's true, sir. But I don't know that I like any of us much the better for it."

To his great surprise his father looked at him with affectionate admiration. "Egad, you take that tone very well," said he. "It's a good card. Maybe it's the best with the women."

Harry had to laugh. "I think you have the easiest temper in the world, sir."

"Aye, aye. It has been the ruin of me."

And so they parted the best of friends. Indeed Harry had never liked his father so well or felt so much his superior. Thus from age to age is filial affection confirmed.

But he had to allow some adroitness in his father. Not only Lady Waverton, but Geoffrey too, succumbed to the paternal charms. That was the more surprising. Geoffrey, behind his vanity and his affectation, was no fool. He had also a temper apt to dislike any man who made a show of position or achievement beyond his own. Yet he hung upon the lips of Colonel Boyce. What they gave him was indeed a pleasing mixture—secrets about great affairs flavoured with deference to his ingenious criticisms. There was something solid about it, too. The Colonel, displaying himself as a man of much importance, perpetually hinted that only the occasion was needed for Mr. Waverton to surpass him by far, and to that occasion he could point the way. It appeared to Harry that his father had in mind to enlist Geoffrey for the proposed mission to France, or some other scheme unrevealed. And being unable to see any reason for wanting Geoffrey as a man, he suspected that his father wanted money.

He saw clearly that nobody wanted him, and was therewith very well content. At this time in his life he asked nothing better than to be left alone with his whims and the open air. He covered many a mile of sticky clay in these autumn days, placidly vacant of mind, and afterwards accounted them the most comfortable of his life.

Mr. Waverton's house was set upon a hill, at one end of a line of hills which now look over the wilderness of London, falling steeply thereto, and upon the other side, to northward and the open country, more gently. In the epoch of Harry Boyce those hills were all woodland— pleasant patches still remain,—and if the need of great walking was not upon him he was often pleased to loiter through their thickets. It was on a wild south-westerly day when the naked trees were at a loud chorus that Alison came to him.

The dainty colours of her face laughed from a russet hood, russet cloak and green skirt wind-borne against her gave him the delight of her shape.

"'Stand, sir, and throw us that you have about you,'" she cried.

"You're poetical, ma'am."

"I vow not I. I say what I mean. There's an unmaidenly trick. And, faith, I am here to rifle you, Mr. Boyce."

"Wish you joy, ma'am. What of?"

"Of your conceit, to be sure. Have you anything else?"

"I have nothing which could be of any use to Miss Lambourne. So God knows why she runs after me."

"Oh, brave!" Miss Lambourne was not out of countenance. "'Tis a shameless maid indeed which runs after a man"—she made him a curtsy. "But what is the man who runs away from a maid?"

Harry Boyce cursed her in his heart. She was by far too desirable. The rain-fraught wind had made the dawn tints of her clearer, lucent and yet more delicate. Her grey eyes danced like the sunlight ripples of deep water. Her lips were purely, brilliantly red. She fronted him and the wind, flaunting the richness of her bosom, poised and strong. She seemed the very body of life. For the first time he felt unsure of himself. "Did you come to call names, ma'am?" he growled.

"I allow you the privileges of a gentleman, Mr. Boyce."

"Gentleman? Oh Lud, no, ma'am. I am an upper servant. Rather better than the butler. Not so good as the steward."

"It won't serve you, sir. You have insulted me, and I demand satisfaction." She drew off her gauntleted glove and flicked him in the face with it. "Now will you fight?"

"Oh, must we slap and scratch then?" Harry flushed darker than the mark of the glove. "I thought we had been fighting."

Miss Lambourne laughed. "You can lose your temper then? It's something, in fact. Yes, we have been fighting, sir, and you don't fight fair."

"Who does with a woman?" Harry sneered. "I cry you mercy, ma'am. You are vastly too strong for me. Let me alone and I ask no more of you."

To which Miss Lambourne said, very innocently, "Why?" Harry looked up and saw her beautiful face meek and appealing, with something of a demure smile in the eyes. "Come, sir, what have I asked of you? You have done me something of a great service. There was a man handling me—do you know what that means?"—she made a wry face and gave herself a shaking shudder—"You rid me of him, and with some risk to your precious skin. Well, sir, I am grateful, and I want to show it. Odds life, I should be a beast did I not. I want to thank you and to sing your praises—to yourself also perhaps. And you are pleased to be a churl and a boor."

"In effect," said Harry coolly. "Egad, ma'am, let me have the luxury of hating you. For I am the Wavertons' gentleman usher and you are the nonpareil Miss Lambourne, vastly rich and—" he ended with a shrug and a rueful grin.

"And—?" Miss Lambourne softly insisted.

"And damnably lovely. Lord, you know that."

"I thank God," said Miss Lambourne devoutly.

"Is it true, Mr. Boyce—do the meek inherit the earth?" She held out her hands to him, one bare, one gloved, she swayed a little towards him, and her face was gentle and wistful. "Nay, sir, I ask your pardon. Call friends if you please and will please me."

Harry lost hold of himself at last. The blood surged in him, and he caught at her and kissed her fiercely.

It was he who was embarrassed. As he stood away from her, eyeing her with a queer defiant shame, she smiled through a small matter of a blush, and breathing quickly said: "What does it feel like, sir?"

"The world's a miracle," Harry said unsteadily and would have caught her again.

She turned, she was away light of foot, and in a moment through the wind he heard her singing to a tune of her own the child's rhyme:

"Fly away, Jack,
Fly away, Jill,
Come again, Jack,
Come again, Jill."

VI

HARRY IS NOT GRATEFUL

Where the lane from Fortis Green crosses the high road there stood an ale-house. On the wettest days, and some others, the place was Harry's resort. Not that he had a liking for ale-house company—or indeed any company. But within the precincts of the Wavertons' house tobacco was forbidden and—all the more for that—tobacco he loved with a solid devotion. The alehouse of the cross roads offered a clean floor, a clean fire, air not too foul, a tolerable chair, a landlord who did not talk, and until evening, sufficient solitude. There Harry smoked many pipes in tranquillity until the day when on his entry he found Mr. Hadley's sardonic face waiting for him. He liked Charles Hadley less than many men whom he more despised. Nobody in a position just better than menial can be expected to like the condescending mockery which was Mr. Hadley's *metier*. But Harry—it is one of his most noble qualities—bore being laughed at well enough. What most annoyed him was Mr. Hadley's parade of a surly, austere virtue. He did not doubt that it was sincere. He could more easily have forgiven it if it had been hypocritical. A man had no business to be so mighty honest.

Mr. Hadley nodded at Harry, who said it was a dirty day, and called for his pot of small ale and his pennyworth of Spanish tobacco. Mr. Hadley was civil enough to pass him a pipe from the box. Both gentlemen smoked in grave silence.

"So you are still with us," said Mr. Hadley.

"By your good leave, sir."

"I had an apprehension the Colonel was going to ravish you away."

"I hope I am still of some use to Mr. Waverton."

"Damme, you might be the old family retainer. 'Faithful service of the antique world,' egad. I suppose you will end your days with Geoffrey, and be buried at his feet like a trusty hound."

"If you please, sir."

They looked at each other. "Well, Mr. Boyce, I beg your pardon," Hadley said. "But you'll allow you are irritating to a plain man."

"I do not desire it, sir."

"I may hold my tongue and mind my own business, eh? Why not take me friendly?"

"I intend you no harm, Mr. Hadley."

"That's devilish good of you, Mr. Boyce. To be plain with you, what do you want here?"

"Here? Oh Lord, sir, I come to smoke my pipe!"

"And what if I come to smoke you? Odds life, I know you are no fool. Do me the honour to take me for none. And tell me, if you please, why do you choose to be Master Geoffrey's gentleman in waiting? You are good for better than that, Mr. Boyce."

"No doubt, sir. But it brings me bread and butter."

"You could earn that fighting in Flanders."

Harry shrugged. "I am not very brave, Mr. Hadley."

"You count upon staying here, do you?"

"If I can satisfy Mr. Waverton," said Harry meekly.

Hadley's face grew harder. "I vow I do my best to wish you well, Mr. Boyce. I should be glad to hear that you'll give up walking in the woods."

There was a moment of silence. "I did not know that I had asked for your advice, sir." Harry said. "I am not grateful for it."

"Damme, that's the first honest answer you have made," Hadley cried. "Look 'e, Mr. Boyce, I am as much your friend as I may be. I have an uncle which was the lady's guardian. If I said a word to him he would carry it to Lady Waverton in a gouty rage. There would be a swift end of Mr. Boyce the tutor. Well, I would not desire that. For all your airs, I'll believe you a man of honour. And I ask you what's to become of Mr. Boyce the tutor seeking private meetings with the Lambourne heiress? Egad, sir, you were made for better things than such a mean business."

"Honour!" Harry sneered. "Were you talking of men of honour? I suppose there is good cover in the woods, Mr. Hadley."

Hadley stared at him. "It was not good enough, you see, sir." He knocked out his pipe and stood up. "Bah, this is childish. You don't think me a knave, nor I you. I have said my say, and I mean you well."

"I believe that, Mr. Hadley"—Harry met him with level eyes—"and I am not grateful."

"You know who she is meant for."

"I know that the lady might call us both impudent."

"Would that break your bones? Come, sir, the lady hath been

destined for Master Geoffrey since she had hair and never has rebelled."

"Lord, Mr. Hadley, are you destiny?"

Mr. Hadley let that by with an impatient shrug. "So if you be fool enough to have ambitions after her, you would wear a better face in eating no more of Master Geoffrey's bread."

"It's a good day for walking, Mr. Hadley. Which way do you go? For I go the other."

"I hope so," Mr. Hadley agreed, and on that the two gentlemen parted, both something warm.

We should flatter him in supposing Harry Boyce of a chivalrous delicacy. Whether the lady's fair fame might be the worse for him was a question of which he never thought. It is certain that he did not blame himself for using his place as Geoffrey's paid servant to damage Geoffrey in his affections. And indeed you will agree that he was innocent of any designed attack upon the lady. Yet Mr. Hadley succeeded in making him very uncomfortable.

What most troubled him, I conceive, was the fear of being ridiculous. The position of a poor tutor aspiring to the favours of the heiress destined for his master invites the unkind gibe. And Harry could not be sure that Alison herself was free from the desire to make him a figure of scorn. Such a suspicion might disconcert the most ardent of lovers. Harry Boyce, whatever his abilities in the profession, was not that yet. But the very fact that he had come to feel an ache of longing for Alison made him for once dread laughter. If he had been manoeuvring for what he could get by her, or if he had been merely taken by her good looks, he might have met jeering with a brazen face. But she had engaged his most private emotions, and to have them made ludicrous would be of all possible punishments most intolerable. The precise truth of what he felt for her then was, I suppose, that he wanted to make her his own—wanted to have all of her in his power; and a gentleman whom the world—and the lady—are laughing at for an aspiring menial cannot comfortably think about his right to possess her.

There was something else. He was not meticulously delicate, but he had a complete practical sanity. He saw very well that even if Alison, by the chance of circumstance, had some infatuation for him, she might soon repent: he saw that even if the affair went with romantic success—a thing hardly possible—his position and hers might be awkward enough.

Her friends would be long in forgiving either of them, and find ways enough to hurt them both. Mr. Hadley, confound him, spoke the common sense of mankind.

There was one solution—that estimable father. By the time he came back to the house on Tether-down, Harry was resolved to enlist under the ambiguous banner of Colonel Boyce.

VII

Generosity of a Father

With grim irony Harry congratulated himself on his decision. When first he came into the house he heard Alison singing. There was indeed (as he told himself clearly) nothing wonderful about her voice—it resembled the divine only in being still and small. Yet he could not (he called himself still more clearly a fool) keep away from it, and so he slunk into Lady Waverton's drawing-room. Only duty and stated hours were wont to drag him there. Lady Waverton showed her appreciation of his unusual attendance by staring at him across the massed trifles of the room with sleepy and insolent amazement. But it was not the glassy eyes of Lady Waverton which convinced Harry that flight was the true wisdom. Over Alison at the harpsichord, Geoffrey hung tenderly: their shoulders touched, eyes answered eyes, and miss was radiant. She sang at him with a naughty archness that song of Mr. Congreve's:

> *"Thus to a ripe consenting maid,*
> *Poor old repenting Delia said,*
> *Would you long preserve your lover?*
> *Would you still his goddess reign?*
> *Never let him all discover,*
> *Never let him much obtain.*
>
> *Men will admire, adore and die*
> *While wishing at your feet they lie;*
> *But admitting their embraces*
> *Wakes 'em from the golden dream:*
> *Nothing's new besides our faces,*
> *Every woman is the same."*

She contorted her own face into smug folly by way of illustration. Then she and Geoffrey laughed together. "I vow you're the most deliciously wicked creature that ever was born a maid."

"D'ye regret it, sir? Faith, I could not well be born a wife."

"No, ma'am, that's an honour to be won by care and pains."

"Pains! Lud, yes, I believe that. But, dear sir, I reckon it the punishment for folly. Why,"—she chose to see Harry—"why, here is our knight of the rueful countenance!"

Mr. Waverton laughed. "It is related of the Egyptians—"

"God help us," Alison murmured.

He went on, giggling. "It is related of the Ancient Egyptians that they ever had a corpse among the guests at their feasts."

"Were their cooks so bad?" said Alison.

"To remind them that all men are mortal. Now you see why we keep Harry."

"I wonder if he looked as happy when he was alive," said Alison, surveying his wooden face.

"*De mortuis nil nisi bonum,*" Geoffrey laughed. "No jests about the dead, Alison. But to tell you a secret, he never was alive. He doesn't like it known."

Colonel Boyce, who had listened to the song and the first coruscations of wit with the condescending smile of a connoisseur, now exhibited some impatience. "Egad, Harry, why will you dress like a parson out at elbows?"

"His customary suit of solemn black," said Geoffrey.

"He is in mourning for himself, of course," Alison laughed.

"I have two suits of clothes, ma'am," said Harry meekly. "This is the better."

"Poor Harry!" Geoffrey granted him a look of protective affection. "I vow we are too hard on him, Alison." And then in a lower voice for her private ear. "A dear, worthy fellow, but—well, what would you have?— of no spirit." Alison bit her lip.

"Oh, Mr. Waverton," Harry protested, "indeed, I am proud to be the cause of such wit."

Colonel Boyce stared at his son with an enigmatic frown. Alison's eyes brightened. But Geoffrey suspected no guile. "Not witty thyself, dear lad, but the cause of wit in others, eh? Odds life, Harry, you are invaluable."

"'Tis your kindness for me makes you think so, Mr. Waverton. And, to be sure, I could ask no more than to amuse your lady."

Alison said tartly, "Oh, it takes little to amuse me, sir."

"I am sure, ma'am," Harry agreed meekly.

"It's a happy nature." and he bowed to Geoffrey, humbly congratulating him on a lady of such simple tastes.

Geoffrey, who had now had enough of his good tutor, eliminated him by a compliment or so on Alison's voice and the demand that she should sing again. He found her in an awkward temper. She would not sing this, she would not sing that, she found faults in every song known to Mr. Waverton. Yet in a fashion she was encouraging. For this new method of keeping him off was governed by a queer adulation of him: no song in the world could be worth his distinguished attention; her little voice must be to his accomplished ear vain and ludicrous; the kind things he was so good as to say were vastly gratifying, to be sure, but they were merely his kind condescension. And, oh Lud, it was time she was gone, or poor, dear Weston would be imagining her slaughtered on the highway.

Geoffrey could not make much of this, but was pleased to take it as flattering feminine homage to his magnificence. By way of reward, he announced an intention of riding home with her carriage. "Faith, you are too good"—her eyes were modestly hidden—"but then you are too good to everybody. Is he not, Mr. Boyce?"

"Oh, ma'am, we all practise on his kindness," Harry said.

"A good night to your mourning," she said sharply, "dear Lady Waverton." They kissed. "Colonel Boyce, I hold you to your promise."

"With all my heart, ma'am. Your devoted."

She was gone, and Harry, with a look of significance at his father, went off too. . .

In that shabby upper chamber of his, Harry again offered the Colonel a choice between the bed and the one chair. Colonel Boyce made a gesture and an exclamation of impatience, and remained standing. "Now, what the devil do you want with me?" he complained.

"I want to be very grateful. I want to enlist with you. When shall we start?"

His father frowned, and in a little while made a crooked answer, "Do you know, Harry, you are too mighty subtle. I was so at your years. It's very pretty sport, but—well, it won't butter your parsnips. The women can't tell what to make of it. Having, in general, no humour, pretty creatures."

"I am obliged for the sermon, sir. Shall we leave to-morrow?"

"Egad, you are in a fluster," his father smiled. "Well, to be sure, he is a teasing fellow, the beautiful Geoffrey."

Harry made an exclamation. "You'll forgive me, sir, if I say you are talking nonsense."

"Oh Lud, yes," his father chuckled.

"Whether I am agreeable to women, whether Mr. Waverton is agreeable to me—odds life, sir, I don't trouble my head about such things. Pray, why should you? As well sit down and cry because my eyes are not the same colour."

"No. No. There is something taking about that, Harry," his father remonstrated placidly.

"When you please to be in earnest, sir," Harry cried, "if this affair of yours is in earnest—" "Oh, you may count on that." Colonel Boyce was still enjoying himself.

"Then I am ready for it. And the sooner the better."

"Hurry is a bad horse. The truth is, something more hangs on this affair than Mr. Harry's whims. Oh, damme, I don't blame you, though. He is tiresome, our Geoffrey."

"Why, sir, if we have to waste time, we might waste it more comfortably than with the Waverton family. Shall we say to-morrow?"

Colonel Boyce tapped his still excellent teeth. "Patience, patience," he said, and considered his son gravely. "As for to-morrow, I have friends to see, and so have you. Your pretty miss engaged me to ride over with you to her house. And behind the brave Geoffrey's back, if you please. She is a sly puss, Harry." He expected so obviously an angry answer that Harry chose to disappoint him.

"I shall be happy to take leave of Miss Lambourne. And shall I ride pillion with you, sir? For I have no horse of my own."

"Bah, dear Geoffrey will lend me the best in the stable."

"I give you joy of the progress in his affections."

Colonel Boyce laughed. "You are pledged for the forenoon then," he paused. "And as to that little affair of mine—you shall know your part soon enough."

"It cannot be too soon, sir."

"No." Colonel Boyce nodded. "I think it's full time."

He took leave of his son with what the son thought superfluous affection.

Half an hour afterwards he was in Mr. Waverton's room—a place very precious. Everything in it—and there were many things—had an air of being strange. Mr. Waverton slept behind curtains of black and silver. His floor was covered with some stuff like scarlet velvet. There was a skull in the place of honour on the walls, flanked by two Venetian pictures of the Virgin, and faced by a blowsy Bacchus and Ariadne from

Flanders. The chairs were of the newest Italian mode, designed rather to carry as much gilding as possible than to comfort the human form. Colonel Boyce, regarding them with some apprehension, stood himself before the fire and waved off Geoffrey's effusive courtesy.

"I hope you have good news for me, Mr. Waverton?" So he opened the attack.

"Why, sir, I have considered my engagements," Geoffrey said magnificently. "I believe I could hold myself free for some months—if the enterprise were of weight."

"You relieve me vastly. I'll not disguise from you, Mr. Waverton, that I am something anxious to secure you. I could not find a gentleman so well equipped for this delicate business. You'll observe, 'tis of the first importance that we should have presence, an air, the *je ne sais quoi* of dignity and family."

"Sir, you are very obliging." Geoffrey swallowed it whole.

"When I came here I confess I was at my wit's end. Indeed, I had a mind to go alone. The gentlemen of my acquaintance—either they could not be trusted with an affair of such value, or they had too much of our English coarseness to be at ease with it. Faith, when I came to see my poor, dear Harry, little I thought that in his neighbourhood I should find the very man for my embassy." The two gentlemen laughed together over the incompatibility of Harry with gentlemanly diplomacy.

"Not but what Harry is a faithful, trusty fellow," said Mr. Waverton, with magnificent condescension.

"You are very good to say so. A dolt, sir, a dolt; so much the worse for me. Now, Mr. Waverton, to you I have no need of a word more on the secrecy of the affair. Though, to be sure, this very morning I had another note from Cadogan—Marlborough's *âme damnée* you know—pressing it on me that nothing should get abroad. So when we go, we'll be off without a good-bye, and if you must leave a word behind for the anxieties of my lady, let her know that you are off with me to see the army in Flanders."

"I profess, Colonel, you are mighty cautious."

"Dear sir, we cannot be too cautious in this affair. There's many a handsome scheme gone awry for the sake of some affectionate farewell. Mothers, wives, lady-loves—sweet luxuries, Mr. Waverton, but damned dangerous. Now here's my plan. We'll go riding on an afternoon and not come back again. Trust my servant to get away quietly with your baggage and mine. We must travel light, to be sure. We'll go round

London. I have too many friends there, and I want none of them asking where old Noll Boyce is off to now. Newhaven is the port for us. There is a trusty fellow there has his orders already. I look to land at Le Havre. Now, the Prince, by our latest news, is back at St. Germain. As you can guess, Mr. Waverton, to be seen in Paris would suit my health even less than to be seen in London. Too many honest Frenchmen have met me in the wars, and, what's worse, too many of them know me deep in Marlborough's business. I could not show my face without all King Louis's court talking of some great matter afoot. What I have in mind is to halt on the road—at Pontoise maybe—while you ride on with letters to Prince James. I warrant you they are such, and with such names to them, as will assure you a noble welcome. It's intended that he should quit St. Germain privately with you to conduct him to me. Then I warrant you we shall know how to deal with the lad." He paused and stared at Geoffrey intently, and gradually a grim humour stole into his eyes. He began to laugh. "Egad, I envy you, Mr. Waverton. To be in such an affair at your years—bah, I should have been crazy with pride."

"You need not doubt that I value the occasion, sir," Geoffrey said grandly. "Pray, believe that I shall do honour to your confidence."

"To be sure you will. Odds life, to chaffer with a king's son about kingdoms, to offer a realm to a prince in exile (if only he will be a good boy)—it's a fine, stately affair, sir, and you are the very man to take it in the right vein."

"Sir, you are most obliging. I profess I vaunt myself very happy in your kindness. Be sure that I shall know how to justify you."

"Egad, you do already," Colonel Boyce smiled, still with some touch of cruelty in his eyes.

"Pray, sir, when must we start?"

"When I know, maybe I shall need to start in an hour."

"I shall not fail you. I shall want, I suppose, some funds in hand?"

Colonel Boyce shrugged. "Oh Lud, yes, we'll want some money. A matter of five hundred pounds should serve."

"I will arrange for it in the morning," said Mr. Waverton, too magnificent to be startled. "Pray, what clothes shall we be able to carry?"

"Damme, that's a grave matter," said Colonel Boyce, and with becoming gravity discussed it.

VIII

Miss Lambourne Looks Sideways

Thus Colonel Boyce blandly arranged the lives of his young friends. It is believed that he had a peculiar pleasure in manoeuvring his fellow-creatures from behind a veil of secrecy. For in this he sought not merely his private profit (though it was never out of his calculations); he enjoyed his operations for their own sake; he liked his trickery as trickery; to push and pull people to the place in which he wanted them without their knowing how or why or to what end they were impelled was to him a pleasure second to none in life. And on a survey of his whole career he is to be accounted successful. Though I cannot find that he ever achieved anything of signal importance even for himself, at one time or another he brought a great number of people, some of them powerful, and some of them honourable, under his direction, he had his complete will of many of them, and was rewarded by the bitter hostility of the majority. He contrived, in fact, to live just such a life as he liked best. What more can any man have?

So he told Harry nothing of his engagement of Mr. Waverton, and Harry, you have seen, was not likely to guess that anyone would enlist his Geoffrey for a serious enterprise. On the next morning, indeed, Harry did remark that Geoffrey was more portentous than usual, but thought nothing of it. He was embarrassed by thinking about himself.

There was, as Colonel Boyce predicted, no difficulty about a horse for Harry. When the Colonel suggested it, Geoffrey showed some satirical surprise at Harry's daring, but (advising one of the older carriage horses) bade him take what he would. Colonel Boyce spoke only of riding with his son. He said nothing of where they were going. Harry wondered whether Geoffrey would have been so gracious if he had known that Alison was their destination, and, a new experience for him, felt some qualms of conscience. It was uncomfortable to use a favour from Geoffrey, even a trifling favour granted with a sneer, for meeting his lady; still more uncomfortable to go seek the lady out secretly. But if he announced what he was doing, there would be instantly something ridiculous about it, and he would have to swallow much of Geoffrey's humour. Geoffrey might even come with them, and Alison and he be humorous together—a fate intolerable. There was indeed an easy way of escape. He had but to stay away from the lady. But, though he despised himself for it, he desired infinitely to see her again. She compelled him, as he had never believed anything outside his own will could compel. After all, it was no such matter, for he would soon be gone with his father to France. He might well hope never to see her again.

So on that ride through the steep wooded lanes to Highgate, his father found him morose, and complained of it. "Damme, for a young fellow that's off to his lady-love you are a mighty poor thing, Harry."

"My lady-love! I have no taste for rich food. I thought it was your lady we were going to see."

"What the devil do you mean by that?" Colonel Boyce stared.

"Oh, fie, sir! Why be ashamed of her?"

"God knows what you are talking about." Colonel Boyce was extraordinarily irritated. "Ashamed of whom?"

"Of the peerless Miss Lambourne, to be sure. Oh, sir, why be so innocent? How could she resist your charms? And indeed—"

"Miss Lambourne! What damned nonsense you talk, Harry."

"I followed your lead, sir," said Harry meekly. "But if we are to talk sense—when shall we start for France?"

"You shall know when I know."

And on that they came to the top of the hill and the gates of the Hall. The wet weather had yielded to St. Martin's summer. It was a day of gentle silver-gold sunlight and benign air. With her companion, Mrs. Weston, Miss Lambourne was walking in the garden. She met the gentlemen at a turn of the drive by rampant sweetbriers. "Here's our knight of the rueful countenance, and faith, on Rosinante, poor jade," she patted Harry's aged carriage horse. "Oh, and he has brought with him Solomon in all his glory," she made a wonderful curtsy to the splendours of Colonel Boyce. "Now, who would have dreamt Don Quixote's father was Solomon?"

"I suppose I take after my mother, ma'am," Harry said meekly. "It's a hope which often consoles me."

"Why, they say Solomon had something of a variety in wives, and among them—"

Colonel Boyce dismounted with so much noise that the jest was hardly heard and the end of it altogether lost.

"You did not tell me"—Mrs. Weston was speaking and seemed to find it difficult—"Alison, you did not tell me the gentlemen were coming." It occurred to Harry that she looked very pale and ill.

"Why, Weston; dear, I could not tell if they would keep troth." She began to hum:

> *"Men were deceivers ever,*
> *One foot on sea, and one on shore,*
> *To one thing constant never."*

"Nay, ma'am, sigh no more for here are we," Colonel Boyce said brusquely.

"Oh Lud, he overwhelms us with the honour." She laughed. "How can we entertain him worthily? Sir, will you walk? My poor house and I await your pleasure."

"I am vastly honoured, ma'am. I have never had a lady-in-waiting."

"Oh, celibate virtue!" quoth Miss Lambourne. And so to the house Colonel Boyce led her and his horse, and a little way behind Harry followed with his and Mrs. Weston.

She had nothing to say for herself. She looked so wan, she walked so slowly, and with such an air of pain that Harry had to say something about fearing she was not well. Then he felt a fool for his pains; as she turned in answer and shook her head he saw such a sad, wistful dignity in her eyes that the small coin of courtesy seemed an absurd offering. A fancy, to be sure, in itself absurd. Yet he could not make the woman out. There was something odd and baffling in the way she looked at him.

She led off with an odd question, "Pray, have you lived much with Colonel Boyce?"

"Not I, ma'am." Harry laughed. "If I were not a very wise child I should hardly know my own father. Lived with him? Not much more than with my mother, whom I never saw."

"Oh, did you not?" Her eyes dwelt upon him. After a little while, "Who brought you up then?"

"Schools. Half a dozen schools between Taunton and London, and Westminster at last."

"Were you happy?"

"When I had sixpence."

"But Colonel Boyce is rich!" she cried.

"I have no evidence of it, ma'am."

"I cannot understand. You hardly know him. But he comes to you at Lady Waverton's; he stays with you; he brings you here. I believe you are closer with him than you say."

"Why, ma'am, it's mighty kind in you to concern yourself so with my affairs. And if you can't understand them, faith, no more can I."

She showed no shame at this rebuke of impertinence. In a minute Harry was sorry he had amused himself by giving it. There was something strangely affecting in the woman. Middle-aged, stout, faded, bound in manner and speech by a shy clumsiness, she refused to be insignificant, she made an appeal to him which he puzzled over in vain. Her simplicity was with power, as of a nature which had cared only for the greater things. He felt himself meeting one who had more than he of human quality, richer in suffering, richer in all emotion, and (what was vastly surprising) under her dullness, her feebleness, of fuller and deeper life.

From vague, intriguing, bewildering fancies, her voice brought him back with a start. "He brought you here?" she was asking.

To be sure, she was wonderfully maladroit. This buzzing, futile curiosity irritated him again into a sneer. "He is no doubt captivated by the beautiful eyes of Miss Lambourne."

"He! Mr. Boyce?"—she corrected herself with a stammer and a blush—"Colonel Boyce? Oh no. Indeed, he is old enough to be her father."

"I think we ought to tell him so." Harry chuckled. "It would do him good."

"I think this is not very delicate, sir." Mrs. Weston was still blushing.

"Egad, ma'am, if you ask questions, you must expect answers," Harry snapped at her.

"Why do you sneer at her? Why should you speak coarsely of her? I suppose you come to the house of your own choice? Or does he make you come?"

Harry saw no occasion for such excitement. "Why, you take away my breath with your pronouns. He and she—she and he—pray, let's leave him and her out of the question. Here's a very pretty garden."

"Indeed, we need not quarrel, I think." She laughed nervously, and gave him an odd, shy look. "Pray, do you stay with the Wavertons?"

"Alas, ma'am, I make your acquaintance and bid you farewell all in one day."

"Make my acquaintance!" Again came a nervous laugh, and it was a moment before she went on. "We have met before to-day."

"Oh Lud, ma'am, I would desire you forget it."

"I am to forget it!" she echoed. "Oh. . . Oh, you are very proud."

"Not I, indeed. The truth is, ma'am, that silly affair with our highwayman, it embarrasses me mightily. I want to live it down. Pray, help me, and think no more about it."

"I suppose that is what you say to Alison?" For the first time there was a touch of fun in her eyes.

"Word for word, ma'am."

"Why do you come here then?"

"As I have the honour to tell you—to say good-bye."

She checked and stared at him. She was very pale. But now they were at the steps of the house, and Colonel Boyce, who had resigned his horse to a groom, turned with Alison to meet them.

"I am hot with the Colonel's compliments, Weston, dear," she announced. "I must take a turn with Mr. Boyce to cool me. 'Tis his role. A convenient family, faith. One makes you uncomfortably hot and t'other freezes you. You go get warm, my Weston. Though I vow 'tis dangerous to trust you to the Colonel. He has made very shameless love to me, and you have a tender heart."

It occurred to Harry that Mrs. Weston and his father, thus forced to look at each other, wore each an air of defiance. They amused him.

"I am not afraid," Mrs. Weston said.

"I profess I am abashed," said Colonel Boyce. "Pray, ma'am, be gentle to my disgrace," and he offered his arm. She bowed and moved away, and he followed her.

Harry and Alison, face to face, and sufficiently close, eyed each other with some amusement.

"Oh, Mr. Boyce," said she, and shook her head.

"Oh, Miss Lambourne," Harry exhorted in his turn.

"You have fallen. You have walked into my parlour."

"I am the best of sons, ma'am. I endure all things at my father's orders—even spiders."

She still eyed him steadily, searching him, and was still amused. She moved a little so that the admirable flowing lines of her shape were more marked. Then she said, "Why are you afraid of me?"

Harry shook his head, smiling. "Vainly is the net spread in the sight of the bird, ma'am. But, faith, it was a pretty question, and I make you my compliments."

"So. Will you walk, sir?" She turned into a narrow path in the shadow of arches, clothed by a great Austrian brier, on which here and there a yellow flame still glowed. "Mr. Boyce—when I meet you in company you shrink and cower detestably; when I meet you alone, you fence with me impudently enough and shrewdly; and always you avoid me while you can. I suppose there's in all this something more than the freaks of a fool. Then it's fear. Prithee, sir, why in God's name are you afraid of me?"

"Miss Lambourne got out of bed very earnest this morning," Harry grinned. "But oh, let's be grave and honest with all my heart. Why, then, ma'am, I've to say that a penniless fellow has the right to be afraid of Miss Lambourne's money bags."

"Fie, you are no such fool. If one is good company to t'other, which is rich and which is poor is no more matter than which fair and which dark."

"In a better world, ma'am, I would believe you."

"And here you believe kind folks would sneer at Harry Boyce for scenting an heiress. So you tuck your tail between your legs and go to ground. I suppose that is called honour, sir."

"Oh no, ma'am. Taste."

"La, I offend monsieur's fine taste, do I?"

"Not often, ma'am. But by all means let us be earnest. I believe I mind being sneered at no more than my betters. *Par exemple*, ma'am, when you laugh at me for being shabby, I am not much disturbed."

She blushed furiously. "I never did."

"Oh, I must have read your thoughts then," Harry laughed. "Well, what matters to me is not that folks laugh at me but why they laugh. That they mock me for being out at elbows I swallow well enough. That they should sneer at me for making love to a woman's purse would give me a nausea."

Miss Lambourne was pleased to look modest. "Indeed, sir, I did not know that you had made love to me."

"I am obliged by your honesty, ma'am."

Miss Lambourne looked up and spoke with some vehemence. "It comes to this, then, you would be beaten by what folks may say about you. Oh, brave!"

"Lud, we are all beaten by what folks might say. Would you ride into London in your shift?"

"I don't want to ride in my shift," she cried fiercely.

"Perhaps not, ma'am. But perhaps I don't want to make love to your purse."

"Od burn it, sir, am I nothing but a purse?"

"I leave it to your husband to find out, ma'am, and beg leave to take my leave. My kind father offers me occupation at a distance, and I embrace it ardently. Who knows? It may provide me with a coat."

"You are going away?"

"I have had the honour to say so."

"And why, if you please?"

Harry shrugged. "Because, ma'am, without my assistance, Mr. Waverton can very well translate Horace into his own sublime verse and Miss Lambourne into his own proud wife."

He intended her to rage. What she did was to say softly: "You do not want to see me that?"

"I have no ambition to amuse you, ma'am." Miss Lambourne looked sideways. "What if I don't want you to go away?"

"Egad, ma'am, I know you don't." Harry laughed. "You amuse yourself vastly (God knows why) with baiting me."

"Why, it amuses me." Alison still looked at him sideways. "Don't you know why?"

He did not choose to answer.

"Indeed, then, if I am nought to you why do you care what folks say of you and me?"

Harry made a step towards her. "You mean to have it again, do you?" he muttered.

"Pray, sir, what?" and still she looked sideways.

"What you dragged out of me in the wood."

"Dragged out of—oh!" She blushed, she drew back, and so had occasion to do something with her cloak which let a glimpse of white neck and bosom come into the light. "You flatter us both indeed."

"I'll tell you the truth of us both"—he, too, was flushed: "you are a curst coquette and I am a curst fool."

Now she met his eyes fairly, and in hers there was no more laughter, but she smiled with her lips: "I think you know yourself better than you know me."

Harry gripped her hands. "You go about to make me mad with desire for you, you—"

"I want you so," she breathed, and leaned back, away from him, her eyes half veiled.

He had his arms about her body, held her close. The red lips curved in a riddle of a smile. He saw dark depths in the shadowed eyes.

"*Malbrouck s'en va t'en guerre*" she murmured.

Harry exclaimed something, felt her against him, was aware of all her form—and heard footsteps.

Alison was out of his grasp, her back to him, plucking a rose. "You will see me again—you shall see me again. I ride in the wood to-morrow morning," she muttered.

"You'll pay for it," Harry growled.

His father arrived, Mrs. Weston, a servant at their heels.

Alison came round with a swirl of skirts. "Dear sir, I doubt you have burnt up dinner by your long passages with my Weston. Come in, come in," and she led the way.

For once Colonel Boyce was without an answer. Harry, who was dreading witticisms, looked at him in surprise, and with more surprise saw that he looked angry. Mrs. Weston hurried on before them all. Her eyes were red.

IX

ANGER OF AN UNCLE

It seems certain that on this day Alison wore a dress of a blue like peacock's feathers. That colour—as you may see, she wears it in both the Kneller and the Thornhill portraits—was much a favourite of hers, and indeed it set off well the rare beauty of her own hues. The clarity, the delicacy, of her cheeks were such as you may see on one of those roses which, white in full flower, have a rosy flush on the outer petals of the bud, and the same rose open may serve for the likeness of a neck and bosom which she guarded no more prudishly than her day's fashion demanded. For all the daintiness, her lips, a proud pair, were richly red (stained of raspberries, in Charles Hadley's sneer), and with the black masses of her hair and grey eyes almost as dark, gave her an aspect of, what neither man nor woman ever denied her, eager and passionate life. All this was flowering out of her peacock blue velvet, and Harry, I infer, went mad.

She never expanded into the larger extravagances of the hoop, preferring to trust to her own shape. Her waist made no pretence of fine-ladyship, but the bodice was close laced *à la mode* to parade the riches of her bosom. Strong and gloriously alive, and abundantly a woman—so she smiled at the world.

It was a delirious hour for Harry, that dinner. He knew that Alison was pleased to be in the gayest spirits, and his father, in his father's own flamboyant style, seconded her heartily. He joined in, too, and seemed to himself loud and vapid, yet had no power of restraint. It was as though his usual placid, critical mind were detached and watched himself in the happy exuberance of drunkenness—which was a state unknown to him, for excess of liquor could only move him with drowsy gloom. And in the midst of the noise Mrs. Weston sat, pale and silent, a ghost at the feast.

He was glad when his father spoke of going, though he found himself talking some folly against it, on Alison's side, who jovially mocked the Colonel for shyness. But Colonel Boyce, it appeared, had made up his mind, and Harry was surprised at the masterful ease with which, keeping the empty fun still loud, he extricated himself and his unwilling son.

They were all at the door, a noisy, laughing company, and the horses waited.

"It's no use, ma'am," Harry cried, "he knows how to get his way, *monsieur mon père*."

"Pray heaven he hath not taught his son the art!"

"Oh Lud, no, I am the very humble servant of any petticoat."

"Fie, that's far worse, sir. I see you would still be forgetting which covered your wife."

"Never believe him, Madame Alison." quoth the Colonel. "It's a strong rogue and a masterless man,"

"Why, that's better again. And yet it's not so well if he'll be mistressless too."

"Fight it out, child," the Colonel cried. "'Lay on, Macduff, and curst be she that first cries hold, enough!' Come, Harry, to horse."

"See, Weston, he deserts me, and merrily!"

There came upon the scene two other horsemen—Mr. Hadley's gaunt, one-armed frame and a big, lumbering elder with a rosy face.

Harry bowed over Alison's hand. It was she who put it to his lips, and nodding a roguish smile at the other gentlemen, "So you run away, sir?" she said.

Harry looked at her and "Give me back my head," he said in a low voice. "I have lost it somewhere here."

"Oh, your head!" She laughed. "Well, maybe it's the best part of you."

He mounted, and Colonel Boyce, already in the saddle, kissed his hand to her. They rode off, compelled to single file by the plump old gentleman who held the middle of the road and glowered at them. Mr. Hadley made an elaborate bow.

The old gentleman watched them out of sight round the curve of the drive, then sent his horse on with an oath and, dismounting heavily at Alison's toes, roared out: "What the devil's this folly, miss?" He made angry puffing noises. "I vow I heard you laughing at Finchley. Might have heard him kissing too."

"Kissing? Oh la, sir, my hand, and so may you." She held it out and made an impudent little curtsy. "I protest the gentleman is all maidenly. That is why he and I make so good a match."

The old gentleman spluttered and was still redder. "Match, miss? What, the devil!"

"Oh no, sir. Pray come in, sir. I see you are in a heat, and I fear for a chill on your gout."

"You are mighty civil, miss. You are too civil by half," the old gentleman puffed, and stalked past her.

Alison stood in the way of Charles Hadley as he made to follow. There was some pugnacity on her fair face. "It's mighty kind of Mr. Hadley to concern himself with me."

"Egad, ma'am, if I come untimely it's pure happy chance."

She whirled round on that and they went in. "Will you please to drink a dish of tea, Sir John?"

"You know I won't, miss." The old gentleman let himself down with a grunt into the largest chair in her drawing-room. "Now who the plague is this kissing fellow?"

"Sure, sir, it's the gentleman Mr. Hadley told you of," said Alison meekly. She hit both her birds. Mr. Hadley and his uncle looked at each other. Sir John snorted. Mr. Hadley shrugged and gave an acid laugh.

"What, what, that fellow of Waverton's? Od burn it, miss, he's a starveling usher."

"Oh, sir, don't be hasty. I dare say he'll be fat when he's old."

"Don't be pert, miss. D'ye know all the county's talking of you and this fellow?"

Alison paled a little. She spoke in a still small voice. "I did not know how much I was in Mr. Hadley's debt. I advise you, Sir John, don't be one of those who talk."

"You advise me, miss! Damme, ain't I your guardian?"

"I am trying to remember that you once were, sir. But you make it very hard."

"What the devil do you mean?"

"I mean—"

"I vow neither of you knows what you mean," Mr. Hadley drowned her in a drawl. "I never saw such fire-eaters. Look 'e, Alison, we come riding over in a civil way and—"

"Tell me you have been planning a scandal about me. Oh, I vow I am obliged to you."

Mr. Hadley laughed. "Lud, child, you ha' known me long enough. Do I deal in tattle? And if we have seen what we should not ha' seen, if you're hot at being caught, prithee, whose fault is it? Egad, you know well enough there's things beneath Miss Lambourne's dignity."

"Yes, indeed, and I see Mr. Hadley is one of them."

"You're a fool for your pains, Charles," John shouted. "What's sense to a wench? Now, miss, I'll have an end of this. You're old Tom

Lambourne's daughter for all your folly, and I'll not have his flesh and blood the sport of any greedy rogue from the kennel."

There was a moment of silence. Then Alison, whose colour was grown high, said quietly, "Pray, Sir John, will you go or shall I? I do not desire to see you again in my house."

"Go?" The old gentleman struggled to his feet. "Damme, Charles, the girl's mad. Yes, miss, I'll go—and go straight to my Lady Waverton. Od burn it, we'll have your fellow out of the county in an hour. Egad, miss, you're besotted. Why, what is he?—a trickster, a knight of the road. 'Stand and deliver,' that's my gentleman's trade. He's for your father's money, you fool."

"Good-bye, Sir John," Alison said, and turned away.

With unwonted agility, Mr. Hadley came between her and the door. "You are not fair to us, Alison," he said. "Prithee, be fair to yourself." She passed him without a word. Mr. Hadley turned and showed Sir John a rueful face. "We have made a bad business of it, sir."

Sir John swore. "Brazen impudence, damme, brazen, I say."

"Oh Lord! Don't make bad worse."

Sir John swore again. Upon his rage came Alison's voice singing:

"When daffodils begin to peer
With heigh! the doxy, over the dale,
Why, then comes in the sweet o' the year,
For the red blood reigns in the winter's pale."

Sir John spluttered, and went out roaring for his horse.

X

Young Blood

There is reason to believe that from the first Mr. Hadley suspected he was making a fool of himself. This sensation, the common accompaniment of an attempt to do your duty, was just of the right strength to ensure that all his actions should be disastrous. It was, as you see, not strong enough to restrain him from exciting the dull and choleric mind of Sir John Burford; it did not avail to direct the ensuing storm. And then, having first failed to be sufficient check, it developed into a very paralysis.

Startled by the furies he had roused in Alison, Mr. Hadley found that suspicion of his own folly develop into a gruesome conviction. It compelled him to labour with Sir John vehemently until that blundering knight consented to wait before exploding his alarms upon Lady Waverton. Even as the first blundering remonstrances had irritated Alison's wanton will into passionate resolution, so this ensuing vacillation and delay gave it opportunity.

If the tale had been told to Lady Waverton, no doubt but Harry would have been banished from Tetherdown that night. It is likely, indeed, that the ultimate fates of Alison and Harry would have been the same. But many antecedent adventures must have been different or superfluous.

Mr. Hadley was now full of common sense. Mr. Hadley sagely argued with his uncle that they would do more harm than good by carrying their tale to Lady Waverton. The woman was a fool in grain, and whatever she did would surely do it in the silliest way. Tell her a word, and she would swiftly give birth to a scandal which the world would not willingly let die, in which Mr. Harry Boyce, if he were indeed the knave of their hypothesis, might easily find a means to strengthen his grip of Alison. It was better to wait and (so Mr. Hadley with a sour smile) "see which way the cat jumped."

Perhaps Madame Alison, who was no kitten, might not be altogether infatuated. The shock of the afternoon, for all her heroics, might have waked in her some doubt of the charms of Mr. Boyce. The girl was shrewd enough. She had dealt with fortune-hunters before—remember the Scottish lord's son—and shown a humorous appreciation of the tribe. She was not a chit with the green sickness; she was neither so young nor so old that she must needs fall into the arms of any man who made eyes at her. After all, likely enough she was but amusing herself with Mr. Boyce. Not a very delicate business, but they were full-blooded folk, the Lambournes. Remember old Tom, her father: there was a jolly bluff rogue. Well, if miss was but having her fling, it would do no good to tease her.

Thus Mr. Hadley, cautiously recoiling, doubting or hoping he was making the best of things, brought Sir John, in spite of some boilings over, safe back to his home and his jovial daughter.

When Harry and his father rode away from Alison, for once in a while Harry found his father's mood in tune with his own. Colonel Boyce suddenly relapsed from hilarity into a perfect silence. He soon reined his horse to a walk, and his wonted alert, soldierly bearing suffered eclipse. He gave at the back, he was thoughtful, he was melancholy—a very comfortable companion.

"Pray, sir, when do we start for France?" said Harry at length.

"What's that? Egad, you're in a hurry, ain't you? Not to-night nor yet to-morrow. Time enough, time enough. Make the best of it, Harry." It occurred to Harry that his father was preoccupied.

But with that he did not concern himself. He was in too much tumult. It appeared that he would be able to meet Alison in the morning. He did not know whether he was glad. He had been telling himself that he would have snatched at the excuse to fail her, and yet was not sure that if his father had announced instant departure he would not have bidden his father to the devil. But still in a fashion he was angry, in a degree he was frightened. He knew that he would go meet the girl now; he could not help himself—an exasperating state. And when he was with her—her presence now set all his nature rioting—with other folk by, it was hard enough to be sane; when he was alone with her in the wood, what would the wild wench be to him before they parted? There was no love in him. He had no tenderness for her, he did not want to cherish her, serve her, glorify her. Only she made him mad with passion. But, according to his private lights, he was honest, and wished to be, and was therefore commanded to try to save the girl from his wicked will and hers. He despised himself for the gleam of cautious duty. What in the world was worth so much as the rose petals of her face, the round swell of her breast?

"Damme, Harry, a man's a fool to be ambitious," so his father broke in upon this tumult. "Why do we fret and trick after a place, or a purse, or a trifle of power?"

Harry stared at him. "Lord, sir, why are you so moral?"

And then Colonel Boyce began to laugh. "I grow old, I think. Oh, the devil, I never had regrets worse than the morning's headache for last night's wine. I suppose if you live long enough, life's a procession of morning headaches. Well, I vow I've not lived long enough yet, Harry."

"I dare say you are the best judge," Harry admitted.

"There's a higher court, eh? Who knows? Maybe we are all the toys of chance." He shrugged. "Why then, damme, I have never been afraid to take what I chose and wait for the bill. Dodge it, or pay it. Odso, there is no other way for a hungry man."

"Lord, sir, now you are philosophical! What's the matter?"

"Humph, I suppose my stomach is weakening," said Colonel Boyce. "I don't digest things as I did."

In this pensive temper they came back to Tetherdown. The Colonel's servant was waiting for him with letters, and he was seen no more that night. Harry did not know till afterwards that Mr. Waverton, as well as letters, was taken to the Colonel's room.

Madame Alison was left by the exhortations of her anxious friends feeling defiant of all the world. It is a comfortable condition, but, for a passionate girl of twenty-two, fruitful of delusions.

Alison was so far happier than Harry in that she knew what she wanted. You may wonder if you will how Harry Boyce, with nothing handsome about him but his legs, could rouse in the girl just such a wild longing as her beauty set ablaze in him. These problems, comforting to the conceit of man, are numerous. And, as usual, madame had dreamed her gentleman into a wonderful fellow. The overthrow of the highwayman became from the first a splendid achievement. Sure, Mr. Boyce must be of rare courage and strength, even as he was deliciously adroit, and that insolent air with which he did his devoir gave one a sweet thrill.

Afterwards, he progressed in her imagination from victory to victory. What served him best was his capacity for puzzling her. That its hero should want to keep such a gallant affair secret proved him of amazing modesty or amazing pride—perhaps both—a titillating combination. It surprised her more that he should dare rebuff the advances of Miss Lambourne. Madame knew very well the power of her beauty over men. If she gave one half an inch she expected that he should be instantly mad to get an ell of her. But here was Mr. Boyce, though she gave him a good many inches, as supercilious about her as if he were a woman. It was incredible that the creature had no warm blood in him. Indeed, she had proof—she could still make herself feel the ache of his grasp in the wood—that he was on occasion as fierce as any woman need want a man. Why, then, monsieur must be defying her out of wanton pride. A marvellous fellow, who dared think himself too good for her.

She made no account of all his wise, honest talk about being poor while she was rich. To her temper it was impossible that a man who wanted her in his arms should stop to weigh his purse and hers, or to consider what the world would say of him for wooing her. All that must be mere fencing, mere mockery.

To be sure, he fenced mighty cleverly. The smug meekness which he put on when she attacked him before others was bewildering. If she had never seen him in action she must have been deceived. And, faith, it seemed certain that he wanted to deceive her, to put her off, to put her aside. The haughty gentleman dared believe that he could be very comfortable without Miss Lambourne. It must not be allowed. He was by far too fine a fellow to be let go his way. Faith, it was mighty noble, this self-sufficient power of his, capable of anything, caring for nothing, hiding itself behind an impenetrable mask, and living a secret life of its own. She was on fire to enter into him and take possession, and use him for herself.

So she was driven by a double need, knew it, and was not the least ashamed. She longed to have Harry Boyce in her arms and his grip cruel upon her. But also she wanted to conquer him and hold his mind at her order. She imagined him under her direction winning all manner of fame. And she believed herself mightily in love. . .

There is a moss on the birch trunks which makes a colour of singular charm, a soft, delicate, grey green. A hood of that colour embraced Alison's black hair and the glow of the dark eyes and her raspberry lips. The cloak of the same colour she drew close about her with one gauntleted hand, so that it confessed her shape.

The birches could still show a few golden leaves, though each moment another went whirling away as the crests bowed and tossed before the wind. In the brown bracken beneath Harry Boyce stood waiting. His graces were set off with his customary rusty black. His hat was well down upon his bobwig, and he hunched his shoulders against the wind, making a picture of melancholy discomfort. He rocked to and fro a little, according to a habit of his when he was excited.

Alison was very close to him before she stopped.

"What have you come for?" he growled.

She drew a breath, and then, very quietly, "For you," she said.

"You have had enough fun with me, ma'am."

Her breast was touching him, and he did not draw back.

"Then why did you come?" She laughed.

"Because I'm a fool."

"A fool to want me?"

"By God, yes. You know that, you slut."

"No. You would be a fool if you didn't, you—man."

"Be careful." Harry flushed.

"Oh Lud, was I made to be careful?"

He gripped her hand, and, after a moment, "Take off your hood," he muttered.

"Is that all?" She laughed, and let it fall from hair and neck, and looked as though sunlight had flashed out at her. "Honest gentleman, you are lightly satisfied."

"So are not you, I vow."

She was pleased to answer that with a scrap of a song:

> *"Jog on, jog on the footpath way,*
> *And merrily hent the stile-a!*
> *A merry heart goes all the way,*
> *A sad one tires in a mile-a."*

"Faith, yours is a mighty sad one, Harry. Pray, what are you the better for stripping me of this?" She flirted the hood.

"I can see those wicked colours of yours. Lord, what a fool is a man to go mad for a show of pink and white!"

"And is that all I am?"

Harry shrugged. "Item—a pair of eyes that look sideways; item—a woman's body with arms and sufficient legs."

"Lud, it's an inventory! I'm for sale, then. Well, what's your bid?"

"I've a shilling in my pocket ma'am and want it to buy tobacco."

"Oh, silly, what does a man pay for a woman?"

Harry laughed. "Why, nothing, if she's worth buying."

Then Alison said softly, "Going—going—gone," and clapped her hands and laughed.

"You go beyond me at least," Harry said in a moment.

She put her hands behind her and leaned forward till her bosom pressed upon him lightly, and then, with her head tilted back so that he saw the white curve from under her chin, and the line of the blue vein in it, "You want me, Harry," she said.

"You know that too well, by God."

"Too well for what, sir?"

"Too well for my peace, ma'am." He flushed.

"His peace!" She laughed. "Oh Lud, the dear man wants peace!"

He flung himself upon her, holding her to him as she staggered back, and kissed her till she was gasping for breath, gripped her head to hold it against his kisses, buried his face in the fragrance of her neck. She gave herself, her arms still behind her, offering the swell of her breasts to him, her eyes gay. . .

"You are mine, now. You're mine, do you hear?" he said unsteadily.

"I want you," she smiled, and was crushed again.

When he let her go, it was to step back and look at her, wondering and intent. She stood something less than her full height, her bosom beating fast. She was all flushed and smiling, but now her eyes were dim and they met his shyly.

"Egad, you're exalting," he said with a wry smile.

"I feel all power when you grasp at me so—power—just power."

"No, faith, you are not. When I hold you to me, when you yield for me, I am all the power there is. Damme, the very life of the world."

"So then," she looked at him through her eyelashes, "and have it so. For it's I who give you all."

"In effect," Harry said: and then, "go to, you make us both mad."

"I am content."

"Yes, and for how long?"

She made an exclamation. "Have I worn out the poor gentleman already?"

"Would you keep yourself for me? Will you wait?"

"Why, what have we to wait for now?"

"Till I am something more than this shabby usher."

"I despise you when you talk so." Her face flamed. "Fie, what's a word and a coat? You have lived with me in your arms. You are what I make of you then. Is it enough, Harry, is it not enough?"

"I'll come to your arms something better before I come again. I am off to France."

"Ah!" Then she studied him for a little while. "You meant to run away, then. Oh, brave Harry! Oh, wise! Pray, are you not ashamed?"

"Yes, shame's the only wear."

"I'll not spare you, I vow."

"Egad, ma'am, mercy never was a virtue of yours."

"Is it mercy you want in a woman?"

"I'll take what I want, not ask for it."

"Why, now you brag! And if there is not in me what monsieur wants?"

"So much the worse for us both. But you should have thought of that before."

"Faith, Harry, you take it sombrely." She made a wry mouth at him. "Pluck up heart. I vow I'll satisfy you."

"You'll not deny me anything you have."

She paused a moment. "Amen, so be it. And must we never smile again?"

"I wonder"—he took her hands; "I wonder, will you be smiling to-morrow when I am away to France."

"Oh, are you still set on that fancy?" She gave a contemptuous laugh. "Prithee, Harry, shall I like you the better for waiting till you have French lace at your neck and a frenchified air?"

"You'll please to wait till I bring Miss Lambourne a fellow who has done something more than snuffle over a servitor's books. I want to prove myself, Alison."

"You have proved yourself on me, sir. What, am I a lean wench in despair to hunger for a snuffling servitor? If you were that, I were not for you. But I know you better, God help me, my Lord Lucifer. Why then, take the goods the gods provide you and say grace over me." Harry shook his head, smiling. "Lord, it's a mule! Pray what do you look to do in France?"

"I am pledged to my father and his policies—to go poking behind the curtains of the war and deal with the go-betweens of princes."

"So. You talk big. Well, I like to hear it. What is the business?"

"My father, if you believe him, has Marlborough's secrets in his pocket and is sent to chaffer for him. You may guess where and why. Queen Anne hath a brother."

Her eyes sparkled. "You like the adventure, Harry?"

"Egad, I begin to think so."

"I love you for that!" she cried, and it was the first time she spoke the word. "Why then, first go with me to church and call me wife!"

He drew in his breath. "By God, do you mean that?"

"Why, don't you mean me honourably?" She gave an unsteady laugh, her eyes mistily kind.

He sprang at her.

XI

Absence of Mr. Waverton

It was always in after life alleged by Mr. Hadley that his steady interest in the family of his uncle was nothing but a desire to keep the old gentleman out of mischief. Sir John Burford was indeed of a temper too irascible to be safe with his bucolically English mind: a man who in throwing tankards at his servants and challenges at his friends was a source of continuous anxiety to his reasonable kinsfolk. But he had also a daughter.

She received the benevolent Mr. Hadley when on the morning after the explosions in Alison's house he came to see whether Sir John was still dangerous or his daughter any thinner. It was the latter purpose which he professed to Susan Burford. She was not annoyed. In her cradle she had been instructed that she was a jolly, fat girl, and through life she accepted the status, like every other which was given her, with great good humour. She was, in fact, no fatter than serves to give a tall woman an air of genial well-being. It was conjectured by her friends that her father, needing all his irascibility for himself, had allowed her to inherit only his physical qualities. She had indeed the largeness of Sir John and his open countenance. Her supreme equanimity perhaps came from her mother. She was by a dozen years at least younger than Mr. Hadley, and always thought him a very clever boy.

"Sir John is gone out to the pigs, Mr. Hadley. Perhaps you'll go too," she said, and looked innocent.

"Well, they are peaceful company, Susan. And you're so surly."

"I thought you would find some joke in that," said Susan, with kindly satisfaction.

"Damme, don't be so maternal. It's cloying to the male. Be discreet, Susan. You will talk as though you had weaned me but a year or two, and still wanted me at the breast."

Susan was not disconcerted. "Will you drink a tankard?" said she. "Or Sir John has some Spanish wine which he makes much of."

"Susan, you despise men. It is a vile infidel habit." He paused, and Susan dutifully smiled. "Why now, what are you laughing at? You! You don't know what I mean."

"To be sure, no," said Susan. "Does it matter?"

"Oh Lud, your repartees! Bludgeons and broadswords! I mean, ma'am, you think men are nought but casks—things to fill with drink and victuals. Is it not true?" Susan considered this, her head a little on one side and smiling. She wore a dress of dark blue velvet cut low about the neck, and so, nature having made her sumptuous, was very well suited. "Egad, now I know what you're like," Mr. Hadley cried. "You're one of Rubens' women, Susan; just one of those plump, spacious dames as healthy as milk and peaches, and blandly jolly about it."

Susan looked down at herself with her usual amiable satisfaction and patted the heavy coils of her yellow hair and said: "Sir John often talks of having me painted. But that's after dinner. Will you stay dinner, Mr. Hadley?"

"Damme, Susan, what should I say after dinner, if I say so much now?"

Susan smiled upon him with perfect calm. "Why, I never can tell what you will say. Can you?"

"You're a hypocrite, Susan. You look as simple as a baby, and the truth is you're deep, devilish deep. Here!" He fumbled in his pocket. "Here's a guinea for your thoughts if you tell them true. Now what are you thinking, ma'am?"

"Why, I am thinking that you came to see my father, and yet you stay here talking to me;" she gurgled pleasant laughter and held out her hand for the guinea.

Mr. Hadley still retained it. "That pleases you, does it?"

"Yes, indeed. You're so comical."

Mr. Hadley surrendered the guinea, looked at his empty left sleeve and made a wry face. "Lord, yes, I am comical enough. A lop-sided grotesque."

"That's not fair!" He had at last made her blush. "You know well I did not mean that. I think it makes you look—noble."

"It makes me feel a fool," said Mr. Hadley. "Lord, Susan, one arm's not enough to go round you."

"So we'll kill the Elstree hog for Christmas;" that apposite interruption came in her father's robust voice. Sir John strode rolling in. "What, Charles! In very good time, egad. You can come with me."

"What, sir, back to the swine? I profess Susan makes as pretty company."

Sir John was pleased to laugh. "Ay, the wench pays for her victuals, too. Damme, Sue, you look good enough to eat." He chucked her chin paternally. "Well, my lad, I ha' thought over that business and I'm taking horse to ride over to Tetherdown."

"Oh Lord," said Mr. Hadley. "And what then, sir?"

"I'll talk to Master Geoffrey."

"Oh Lord," said Mr. Hadley again. "Do it delicately."

"Delicate be damned," said Sir John.

"I had better ride with you," said Mr. Hadley.

"Good boy. Here, Roger—Mr. Hadley's horse."

Susan stood up. "Lud, sir, you will not be here to dinner then?"

Sir John shook his head. Mr. Hadley scratched his chin. "I am not so sure that Geoffrey will give us a dinner," said he.

"Why, sir," Susan was interested, "what's your business with Mr. Waverton?"

"To tell him he's a fool, wench," quoth Sir John.

"Oh. And will Mr. Waverton like that?"

"Like it! Odso, he'll like it well enough if he has sense."

Mr. Hadley grinned. "That's logic, faith. Well, sir, have with you."

So off they rode. On the way Sir John was pleased to expound to Mr. Hadley the profound sagacity of his new plan. He would rally Geoffrey on his flaccidity; accuse him of being an oaf; and, describing all the while in an inflammatory manner the charms of Alison, hint that Geoffrey's tutor had ambitions after them. "And if that don't wake up my gentleman, he may go to the devil for me and deserve it."

It crossed Mr. Hadley's lucid mind that a gentleman who required so much waking up did not deserve Miss Lambourne. But she was quite capable of discovering that for herself, if indeed she had not already. And certainly it would do Geoffrey no harm to be made uncomfortable. So Mr. Hadley rode on with right good will.

But when they came to Tetherdown it was announced that Mr. Waverton had gone riding. "Why, then we'll wait for him." Sir John strode in. The butler looked dubious. Mr. Waverton had said nothing of when he would come back.

"Why the devil should he?" Sir John stretched his legs before the fire. "He'll dine, won't he?"

The butler bowed.

"Prithee, William," says Mr. Hadley, "is Mr. Boyce in the house?"

"Mr. Boyce, sir, is gone walking."

Mr. Hadley shrugged. "Odso, away with you," Sir John waved the man off. "Let my lady know we are here."

The butler coughed. "My lady is in bed, Sir John."

"What, still?" quoth Sir John, for it was close upon noon.

"Hath been afoot, Sir John. But took to her bed half an hour since."

"What, what? Is she ailing?"

The butler could not say, but looked a volume of secrets, so that Sir John swore him out of the room.

"Vaporous old wench, Charles," Sir John snorted. And a second time Mr. Hadley shrugged.

In a little while the butler came back even more puffed up. Her ladyship hoped to receive the gentlemen in half an hour.

XII

In Haste

"Oh, Harry, Harry, I give in. I am the weaker vessel. At least, I have the shorter legs."

"What, you're asking me to spare you already? Lord, how will you bear me as a husband?"

They were under the great beeches in Hampstead Lane, breasting the rise to the heath, on their march for that kindly chapel, where, if you dined in the tavern annexed, the incumbent would marry you for nothing, charge but the five shillings, cost price of the Queen's licence, and ask no questions.

Harry shortened his stride, and looked down with grim amusement at Alison's breathless bosom.

"I believe you mean to make an end of me before you have begun with me," she panted. "Lord, sir, what a figure you'll cut if you bring me to church too faint to say, 'I will.'"

"Why, the Levite would but take it for maiden modesty. Not knowing you."

"You are trying to play the brute. It won't save you, Harry. I shan't be frightened."

"You! No, faith, it's I. I am beside myself with terror."

"I do believe that's true!" She laughed at him. "But, oh, dear sir, why?"

"Lest I should not fulfil the heroical expectations of Miss Lambourne. Confess it, ma'am; you count on me to exalt you into heavens of ecstasy, to bewilder the world with my glories, and be shaved by breakfast-time."

"To be sure, I'll always expect the impossible of you."

"There it is. I suppose you expect me to begin by creating a wedding-ring."

"Why, you have created me."

"Oh, no, no, no. You're a splendid iniquity, but not mine, I vow."

"This woman of yours never lived till you made her. I profess Miss Lambourne was ever known for a dull cold thing born 'to suckle fools and chronicle small beer.'"

"So she wrote me down her property. Egad, ma'am, it was very natural."

"You know what you have made of me," Alison said.

"God knows what you'll make of me. And now in the matter of the ring—"

"Oh Lud, what a trivial thing is a man!" She drew off her glove and held out a hand with two rings on it. "Marry me with which you will." One was a plain piece of gold, paler than the common, carved into an odd device of a snake biting its tail.

"With thine own ring I thee wed," Harry said, and took it off. "I take you to witness, Mrs. Alison, the snake was in your paradise before I came."

They were across the heath now and going down the steep, narrow lane beyond. The chapel of the Hampstead marriages stood raw red beside a garden with lawns and arbours shaggy in winter's untidiness. Even the tavern at the gate, a spreading one-story place of timber, looked dead and desolate.

Harry forced open the sticking door and strode in, Madame Alison loitering behind. He was met by a dirty lad whose gaping clothes were half hidden by a leather apron, and whose shoes protruded straw—a lad who smelt of the stable and small beer.

"Where's the priest?" said Harry.

"In the tap," said the boy, and shuffled off.

There came out into the passage, wheezing and wiping his chops, a little bloated man in a cassock, with his bands under his right ear. He leered at Harry and tried to look round him at Alison.

"You're out of season, my lord," said he. "These chill rains, they play the mischief with lusty blood. Go to, you'll not be denied, won't you? Do you dine here?"

"We have no time for it."

"What, you're hasty, ain't you?" He gave a hoarse laugh. "There's my fee to pay then."

"Here's a guinea to pay for all," said Harry.

The dirty fist took it, the little red eyes peered at it closely, the dirty mouth bit it and was satisfied. "Go you round to the chapel door and wait. Lord, but man and wench never had to wait for me." He waddled off.

Harry turned upon Alison. "So with all my worldly goods I thee endow," he said, with a crooked smile. "God give you joy of them. I vow I was never so frightened of spending a guinea."

"Why, d'ye doubt if I'm worth it? Nay, sir, I'm honest stuff and challenge any trial."

Harry looked down at her and was met by eyes as bold as his own.

The chapel door opened, and the little priest beckoned them in. A pair of witnesses were already posted by the altar, the dirty lad of the tavern and a shock-headed wench.

"Licence first, licence first." The parson bustled off to a table in a corner. "I warrant you we do things decently in Sion. Aye, and tightly, my pretty. Never a lawyer can undo my knots, never fear."

He scratched laboriously over their names, while the dank smell of the place sank into them.

They were marched to the altar. A hoarse muttering poured from the priest. He made no pretence of solemnity or even of meaning. He was concerned only to make an end and have done with them. Of all the service they heard nothing clearly but what they said themselves, and while they were deliberate over that the little priest grunted and puffed at them.

He ended with a leer and drove them before him back to the table. There was more scratching in his register. The two uncouth witnesses scrawled something for their names and shambled off.

"Let's breathe some free air," said Harry, and laid hold of his wife.

The parson chuckled. "Free? You'll never be free again, my lord. I can see that in madame's eye. What, you ha' sold your birthright for a mess of pottage, ain't you? And mighty savoury pottage, too, says you." He rolled his eyes and smacked his lips. "Softly now, softly, madame wants her certificate. Madame wants to warrant herself a lawful married wife, if you don't. . . There, my lady. And happy to marry you again any day at the same price."

They were away from him at last and in clean air stretching their legs up the hill again.

"Poor Harry!" Alison laughed. "Before you looked like a man fighting for his life. Now you look like a man going to be hanged. Dear lad! Pray how much would you give to escape me now?" She put her arm into his. He let her shorten his stride a little, but made no other confession of her existence. "Fie, Harry, it's over early to repent. In all reason you should first be sure of your sin. Who knows? I may not be deadly after all. 'Alack,' says he, 'I will not be comforted. Egad, the world's a cheat. A fool and his folly are soon parted they told me, and here am I tied to her till death us do part. So, a halter, gratis, for God's sake.'"

"You're full of other folks' nonsense, Mrs. Boyce," said Harry with a grim look at her.

"Oh, noble name!" She bobbed a curtsy. "Full? I am full of nothing but fasting, aye," she sighed, and turned up her eyes—"fasting from all but our sacrament."

They were upon the ridge of the heath and Harry checked her, and stood looking away over the wide prospect of mist-veiled meadow and dim blue woods. She was beginning her mocking chatter again when he broke in with, "Ods life, ha' done!" and turned to look deep into her eyes. "There's mystery in this, and I think you see nothing of it."

"Why, yes, faith. If you were no mystery, should I want you? If you had discovered all of me, would you want me?"

"Bah, what do we know of living, you and I, or—or of love?"

She laughed, with a scrap of twisted song:

> *Most living is feigning.*
> *Most loving mere folly,*
> *Then heigho the holly,*
> *This life is most jolly.*"

He shrugged and marched her on again.

"Pray, sir, will you dine at home?" she said demurely.

Harry flushed. "I must go tell my father and all," he growled. "I'll be with you soon enough, madame wife."

"Oh brave! Dear sir, have with you. I must see Geoffrey's face."

"Egad, let's be decent!" Harry cried.

"Decent! For shame, sir! What's more decent than man and wife?"

"Man and wife!" Harry echoed it with a sour laugh. "Do you feel a wife? I never felt less of a man."

"You shall be satisfied," she said, and looked at him gravely. "And I—I am not afraid, Harry."

XIII

Distress of a Mother

M r. Hadley and Sir John Burford in the hall at Tetherdown looked at each other across the fire. "Would you call for a pipe now, Charles?" says Sir John, fidgeting.

"There'll be none in the house, sir. Geoffrey has no stomach for tobacco."

"Damme, if I know what he hath a stomach for," Sir John grumbled, and kicked at the burning logs. "He don't eat no more than an old woman, nor drink so much as a young miss. Ain't the half-hour gone, Charles?"

"That's a poetic phrase, sir. It means a year or so—while she's tiring her hair."

"What and painting her face, too? Same as Jezebel."

My lady's waiting-woman, Arabella, came in. She minced in the manner of her mistress, but, being a foot shorter, with different effect. She stood before Sir John, who had the largest chair, and stared at him, with languid insolence. "Ods my life, don't ogle me, woman," says he.

"At your leisure, sir, if you please." She tossed her head.

"Leisure! Oh Lord, I'm at leisure, thank 'e."

Arabella sniffed.

"I think you are in madame's chair, sir," Mr. Hadley explained.

"What, then? She ain't here, nor I don't carry the plague."

"The lady-in-waiting wants to compose it for madame."

"Compose!" Sir John exploded an oath, and jumped up. "I ha'n't decomposed it."

Arabella dusted the chair, wheeled it a little this way and that, put two footstools before it, and three cushions into it, contemplated them for some time, and then shifted them a little. After which she minced out with a great sigh.

"Good God!" says Sir John.

"I wonder," says Mr. Hadley—"I wonder if we've come to take the breeks off a Highlander?"

"What's your will?" Sir John gasped.

"I wonder if my lady knows all we can tell her. It might have made her hypochondriac."

"Hip who? Odso, I am hipped myself."

My lady came. She had so much flowing drapery about her that she seemed all robes. She moved very slowly, she was bowed, and she leaned upon the shoulder of Arabella. With care she deposited herself in the big chair. Arabella arranged her draperies, arranged the cushion, and stood aside. My lady lay back, put back the lace about her head, and showed them her large pale face and sighed. "You are welcome, gentlemen," said she. "You are vastly kind."

"Odso, ma'am, what's the matter?" Sir John cried.

"Why, have you not heard? Arabella, he has not heard!" My lady was convulsed, and clutched at the maid, who comforted her with a scent-bottle. "He has gone!" she sighed. "He has gone."

"What the devil! Who the devil?"

My lady recovered herself. From somewhere in her voluminous folds she produced a letter. "If it would please you, be patient with me. My unhappy eyes." She dabbed at them with a handful of lace, and read:

"My lady, my mother,—I have but time for these few unkempt lines, wherein to bid you for a while farewell. My good friend, Colonel Boyce, has favoured me with an occasion to go see something of the warring world beyond the sea. And I, since the inglorious leisure of the hearth irks my blood, heartily company with him. It needs not that you indulge in tears, save such as must fall for my absence. I seek honour. So, with a son's kiss, I leave you, my mother. G.W."

On which his mother's voice broke, and she wept.

"Lord, what a fop!" said Sir John. My lady swelled in her draperies. "So he's gone to the war, has he? Odso, I didn't think he had it in him."

"Sir, if you jeer at my bereavement!" my lady sobbed.

"And where's Harry Boyce?" says Mr. Hadley.

Sir John stared at him. "Why, seeking honour too, ain't he? What's in your head, Charles?"

"This is rude," my lady sobbed; "this is brutal. The tutor! Oh, heaven, what is the tutor to me? I would to God I had never seen him—him nor his wicked father."

Sir John tugged at Mr. Hadley's empty sleeve and drew him aside. "What are you pointing at, Charles? D'ye mean the two rogues have took Geoffrey off to make away with him between 'em?"

"Lord, sir, you've a villainous imagination." Mr. Hadley grinned. "I mean no such matter. Nay, I'll lay a guinea, Harry Boyce is not gone at all."

"Sir John"—my lady raised herself and was shrill—"what are you whispering there?"

"What, what? You mean the old fellow took Geoffrey off to leave the young fellow a clear field with Ally Lambourne? Odso, that's devilish deep, ain't it? But we can set the young fellow packing, my lad. We—"

"Sir John!" my lady's voice rose higher yet.

"Coming, ma'am, coming. Od burn my heart and soul!" That last invocation was not directed at her but an invading tumult.

The butler entered backwards, protesting, between two men who did not take off their hats. They were in riding-boots and cloaks, and splashed from the road. They had pistol butts ostentatious in their side pockets, and one carried some papers in his hand.

"Stand back, my bully, stand back, or you'll smell Newgate," says he to the butler.

"Burn your impudence," Sir John roared, and strode forward.

"In the Queen's name. Messengers of the Secretary of State, with his warrant." The man waved his papers under Sir John's nose. "Master of the house, are you?"

"I am Sir John Burford of Finchley, and be hanged to you."

"There is the mistress of the house, sirrah," says Mr. Hadley

"Thank'e. In the Queen's name, ma'am. Warrants to take Oliver Boyce, Colonel, and Geoffrey Waverton, Esquire."

My lady shrieked, fell back, and was understood to be fainting.

"You come too late, sirrah," says Mr. Hadley. "Your foxes be gone away."

The man tapped his nose and grinned. "That won't do, sir. Set about it, Joe," and he nudged his fellow.

"What's the charge against them?" says Mr. Hadley.

The man laughed. "Come, sir, you know better than that. I ain't here to answer questions." Mr. Hadley put his hand in his pocket. The man grinned and shook his head, and went out pushing his comrade in front of him. Mr. Hadley followed them. As soon as they were out in the corridor and the door was shut behind them, the man turned and held out his hand to Mr. Hadley, who dropped into it a couple of guineas. "Lord, now, what did you think it was?" says the messenger genially. "Treasonable correspondence—Pretender—Lewis le Grand and so forth. Quite gentleman-like, d'ye smoke me?"

"Prithee, who set you on?" says Mr. Hadley.

"Now you go too far, ecod, you do. I don't mind obliging a gentleman, but you want to lose me my place. We'll be searching the house, by your leave."

Off they went, and Mr. Hadley went back to my lady. She had been revived, and the air was heavy with scent. She fluttered her hands at the ministering Arabella and said faintly, "What is it, Charles?"

"It seems there's some talk of their having dealings with the Pretender."

"Lord bless my soul," Sir John puffed.

"The Pretender?" Lady Waverton smiled through her powder. "La, now, Geoffrey's father always had a kindness for the young Prince."

"I vow, ma'am, you take it with a fine spirit," says Mr. Hadley in some surprise.

"You'll find, Mr. Hadley, that such families as ours, the older families, know how to bear themselves in this cause."

Sir John stared at her and puffed the louder, and muttered very audibly, "Here's a turnabout!"

"Oh, ma'am, to be sure it's a well-born party," Mr. Hadley shrugged. "D'ye give us leave to remain and see that these fellows show no impudence?"

"Oh, sir, you are very obliging," says my lady superciliously.

Mr. Hadley bowed, and withdrew to the recess of a window with Sir John following. "Here's a queer thing, Charles. Did ever you know Master Geoffrey was a Jacobite?" Mr. Hadley shook his head. "Nor this Colonel Boyce neither?"

"I never saw a Jacobite in so good a coat, and I never thought Geoffrey would risk his coat for any king. And thirdly and lastly, I never knew Whitehall put itself out in these days whether a man was Jacobite or no. Why, damme, they be all half Jacobites themselves, from the Queen down."

"Aye, aye," says Sir John sagely. "A devilish queer thing indeed."

And on that came Alison and Harry—Alison rosy and smiling, Harry a pale and deliberate appendage. "Dear Lady Waverton, let me present my husband."

Lady Waverton sat up straight. Lady Waverton embraced the pair of them with a bewildered glare.

"I married him this morning," Alison laughed.

"Alison, this is unmaidenly jesting," said my lady feebly.

"Why, if it were, so it might be. But the truth is, it's unmaidenly truth. For I am Mrs. Harry Boyce. Give me joy."

"Joy!" my lady gasped. "It's unworthy! It's cruel! Oh, Geoffrey, Geoffrey! How dare you?" She was again understood to faint.

Through the rustle of Arabella and the odours of scent came the explosions of Sir John, swearing.

Mr. Hadley moved forward, and, ignoring Alison, addressed himself to Harry. "Pray, sir, did you know that Mr. Waverton this morning left Tetherdown in your father's company, your father taking him, as he says in a letter, to the wars?"

"Knew?" Lady Waverton chose to speak out of her swoon. "To be sure they knew. They would not have dared else. Dear Geoffrey! A villain! And you, miss—you whom he trusted! Oh!" She again took scent.

"La, ma'am, he trusted me no more than I him. You are not well, I think."

"You give me news, Mr. Hadley," Harry said. "I knew that my father meant to go abroad, and understood that I was to go with him."

"Perhaps you'll go after him." Mr. Hadley shrugged and turned away.

"Why, what's all this, Harry?" Alison laughed. "Your wise father hath chosen to take Geoffrey instead of you?"

"In spite of my modesty, I'm surprised, ma'am," says Harry.

"Burn your impudent face," quoth Sir John from the background.

"Well, sir, if you were in your father's plans, maybe you'll pay your father's debts," quoth Mr. Hadley.

"What do I owe you, Mr. Hadley?" says Harry, bristling.

The two messengers came back again. "Right enough, sir, gone away." The spokesman nodded at Mr. Hadley. "We'll be riding. Trust no offence?" He looked hopeful.

"Here's Colonel Boyce's son, wishing to answer for his father."

The man looked Harry up and down and chuckled.

"Lord, and mighty like. Servant, sir," he winked at Harry. "Tell the Colonel, sorry we missed him," He winked again and laughed.

"What's this comedy of yours, Mr. Hadley?" says Harry.

"Your friends have warrants to arrest your father and Mr. Waverton for treasonable correspondence with the Pretender. But none for you, I fear, Mr. Boyce."

"Devil a one," the man laughed. "Come, Ned, we'll be jogging," Out they swung.

A bewildered company, full of suspicions, stared at one another.

"Come, Harry, let us go home," Alison said.

"Home!" Lady Waverton gasped with an hysterical laugh. "Hear her!"

"My lady"—Alison made her a curtsy—"gentlemen—all the friends of Mr. Boyce will be very welcome to me."

Sir John swore. "You for a fool and he for a knave, damme, you're well matched."

"When you were younger, sir, I suppose you were less of a boor," says Harry. "Mr. Hadley—my lady—" he made two stiff bows and gave his arm to Alison.

"Humph, they go off with the honours." Mr. Hadley shrugged, and held out his arm in front of Sir John, who was plunging after them.

"Be hanged to you. What did the rogue mean, telling me I was old?"

"Why, he meant that a man who is too old to fight should be civil."

"Too old?" Sir John fumed. "Burn him for a coward."

"I think not," says Mr. Hadley. "But for the rest—God be with you. My lady—sincerely your servant."

My lady was now weeping. "You never loved him," she complained. "You were never his friend," and she became speechless.

The two men looked at each other. "Well, Charles, we'll to horse," Sir John concluded. "Servant, ma'am." They left her in the scented embraces of Arabella.

To Harry as he went out came the butler, who, with something of a furtive manner, produced and gave him a letter. Harry looked at the writing and thrust it into his coat. Alison saw and took no notice.

They walked on for some way before silence was broken. Then Harry said: "Well, madame wife, so you feel you've been bit."

"Who—I? What do you know of what I feel?"

"Oh, I can tell hot from cold. I know when you are thinking you ought to have thought twice. Egad, I agree with you. You've been badly bit. Here you were told that I was just off out of the country; that you must catch me at once if you wanted to catch me; that if you took me you would soon have me off your hands. And now we're tied up, you find I'm not going at all. I vow it's disheartening. But if you'll believe me, I did honestly believe my old rogue of a father. I did think he meant to take me."

"And now you can't be comforted because you have to stay with me. Oh, Harry, you're a gloomy fellow to own a new wife. But why did the good man take Geoffrey when he might have had you? I should have thought he knew a goose when he saw one."

"I can't tell. I never saw much meaning in the old gentleman."

"You might as well look at his letter."

Harry stared. "How did you know that was his?"

"You like doing things mysteriously, the family of Boyce."

The letter said this:

MR. HARRY,

I flatter myself that you will be offended. But 'tis all for
your good. When I came after you I did not know that you
were so clever a fellow. No more did I expect that I should
have to like you. But since I do, I prefer that I should do
without you. And since you have some of my wits, you may
very well do without me. But I believe you will do the better
without friend Geoffrey. Therefore I take him, who will
indeed do my business much more sincerely than your worthy
self. With the dear fellow safe out of the way, I count upon
you to push on bravely with Mrs. Alison. You'll not find two
such chances in one life. If you were master of her you could
promise yourself anything in decent reason you please to
want. For all your wits you are not the man to make his own
way out of nothing. So don't be haughty. Why should you?
It's a mighty pretty thing, Harry, and (trust an old fellow who
hath made some use of the sex in his day) as tender as you
may hope for in an heiress. She has looked your way already,
and in her pique at the good Geoffrey deserting her, you'll
find her warmer for you. If you don't make her warm enough
for wiving, you're an oaf, which is not in my blood—nor your
mother's, to be honest. Nor if I was young again and played
your hand, I wouldn't let her grow cold when I had her
safe. . . So be a man, and I give you my blessing.

O. BOYCE

Harry held it out to Alison. "We're a noble family—the family of
Boyce," said he.

But Alison read it without a blush or a sneer, and when she gave it
back she was laughing. "Oh, he's more cunning than any beast of the
field! Oh, he knows the world! Poor, dear fellow."

"Oh Lud, yes, he's a fool for his wisdom. But he's my father."

"Well, sir?" Harry scowled at the ground. "Oh, what does he matter?
Harry, what does anything matter to-day—or to-morrow, or to-
morrow's to-morrow?"

"I had no guess of all this." Harry crushed the paper. "You believe that?"

"Oh, silly, silly."

"You're still content?"

"Not yet," Alison said.

XIV

Spectators of Paradise

I n the old house on the hill Mrs. Weston sat alone. She was looking out of the oriel window at a garden of wintry emptiness and wind swept. The westerly gale roared and moaned, the heavy earth was sodden and beaten into hollows and pools through which broke tiny pale points of snowdrops. Away beyond the first terrace of lawn the roses bowed and tossed wild arms. A silvery gleam of sunlight fell on the turf, glistened, and was gone. Mrs. Weston sat with her hands in her lap and her needle at rest in a half-worked piece of linen. A veil of languor had fallen upon the wistfulness of her face. Her bosom hardly stirred. The sound of the opening door broke her dream, and she picked up her work and began to sew eagerly. It was Susan Burford who came in, royally neat in her riding-habit, for all the storm. She walked in her leisurely, spacious fashion to Mrs. Weston, who started and stood up, laughing nervously. "Indeed Alison will be pleased. You are kind. I know she has been longing to see you."

Susan laughed and, a large young goddess of health, stooped to kiss the worn face. "You always talk about somebody else. Are you pleased?"

"My dear!" Mrs. Weston protested. "You know I am."

"We match very well. You never want to talk, and I never have anything to say." Susan sat down, and for some time the only sound was from Mrs. Weston's needle. At last, "You are still here, then," Susan said.

"My dear! Why not, indeed?"

"Oh. But you would always stay by Alison if she needed you."

"Why, she never has needed me. And now less than ever."

"Oh." Susan considered that. "And is he kind to you?"

Mrs. Weston flushed. "Indeed he has been very good to me."

"That is all I wanted to ask you," said Susan, and again there was silence.

After a little while Mrs. Weston dropped her sewing and looked anxiously at Susan. "Have you ever seen him?"

"Only his back. He used to keep in the corners at Tetherdown."

"I suppose people—talk about him."

"I don't listen," said Susan, "People are always in such a hurry. I can't keep up."

"I suppose you think Alison was in a great hurry."

"Only Alison knows about that."

"Yes." Mrs. Weston looked at her with affectionate admiration, as though she had been endowed with rare understanding of the human heart. "Do you know you are the only one of the people Alison liked who has come here—since?"

"Oh." (Susan's favourite eloquent reply.) "I don't mind about people."

"He doesn't mind at all. She doesn't mind yet."

"What is that you are working?" said Susan.

"But indeed they are most perfectly happy," said Mrs. Weston, in a hurry.

"Is it for a tucker?" said Susan.

In a greater hurry, Mrs. Weston began to explain. She was still at it when Alison and Harry came back.

They too had been riding. The storm had granted Alison none of Susan's majestic neatness. She looked a wild creature of the hills, her wet habit clinging about her, black ringlets broken loose curling about her, brown eyes fierce with life, and all the dainty colours of her face very clear and bright. She saw Susan and cried out, "Oh, my child, I love you."

Susan rose leisurely to her majestic height and smiled down upon her. "I think you are the loveliest thing that ever was made," said she. Alison laughed, and they kissed.

"I am quite of your mind, ma'am," said Harry. "Or I was," he made Susan a bow, "till this moment."

"I was going to ask her if she was happy, sir," Susan said. "I shan't ask her." She held out her hand.

"But I want you to ask me a thousand things." Alison put an arm round her, "Come away, come. At least I am going to tell you"—she shot a wicked glance at Harry—"everything." Off they went.

"What's this mean, ma'am?" Harry stood over Mrs. Weston. "Is our wise Sir John sending to spy out the land?"

"I wish you would not talk so." Mrs. Weston shivered. "It is like your father. Oh, sure, you have no need to be suspicious of every one."

"Suspicious? Faith, I don't trouble myself." Harry laughed. "All the world may go hang for me. But you'll not expect me to believe in it."

"I think you need fear no one's ill will. You are fortunate enough now."

"Miraculously beyond my deserts, ma'am. As you say. But there's the wisdom of twenty years' shabbiness in me. And I wonder if the good Sir John wants to be meddling."

"You need not be shabby now."

"Lord, I bear him no malice. For he can do nought. Only I would not have him plague Alison."

At last Mrs. Weston smiled upon him. "Aye, you are very careful of her."

"I vow I would not so insult her." Harry laughed.

"But you need not be afraid. Susan is here for herself. She is like that. She is the most independent woman ever I knew. She has come because she loves Alison."

"Why, then, I love her. And egad it will be easy. She's a splendid piece."

Mrs. Weston gave him an anxious glance. "She is very loyal," said she, with some emphasis.

"It's a virtue. To be sure it's a virtue of the stupid." Harry cocked a teasing eye at her. "And I—well, ma'am, you wouldn't call me stupid."

"I don't think it clever to jeer at what's good—and true—and noble."

"Egad, ma'am, you are very parental!" Harry grinned. "You will be talking to me like a mother—and a stern mother, I protest."

"Am I stern?" Mrs. Weston looked at him with eyes penitent and tender.

"Only to yourself, I think. Lud, ma'am, why take me to heart?"

"What now, Harry?" Alison and Susan close linked came back again. "Whose heart are you taking?"

"Why, madame's," said Harry, with a flourish. "You see, ma'am," he turned to Susan, "I've a gift for making folks cry."

"Oh. Like an onion," says she, in her slow, grave fashion.

"Susan dear! How perfect," Alison laughed. "Now I know why I am growing tired of him. A little, you know, was piquant. But a whole onion to myself—God help us!"

"Yet your onion goes well with a goose," Harry said.

"Alack, Harry, but there's nothing sage about you and me."

"Oh, fie! See there she sits, our domestic sage"—he waved at Mrs. Weston.

"To be sure we couldn't do without her." Alison caressed the grey hair.

"I must be riding, Alison," Susan said.

Alison began to protest affectionate hospitality. Harry shook his head. "I have warned you of this, Alison. We are too conjugal. It embarasses the polite."

"I am not embarassed," said Susan, with her placid gravity. "I want to come again."

"By the fifth or sixth time, ma'am, I may feel that I am forgiven."

"I have nothing to forgive you, Mr. Boyce."

"Then you can do it the more heartily." Harry smiled and held out his hand.

"Oh." There was a faint shadow of a blush. "I did not think I should like you." She turned. "I beg your pardon, Alison."

"I beg, ma'am, you'll come teach my wife to be kind. She also is frank. But for kindness—well, we are all sinners."

"There it is, Mr. Boyce," said Susan, holding out her hand.

And when she was gone. "Now, why did I not marry her first?" said Harry pensively.

"Because she would never have married you, child. Being of those who like the man to ask."

As Susan rode down the north slope of the hill, she was met by Mr. Hadley, gaunt upon a white horse, like death in the Revelation. The comparison did not occur to Susan, who had a fresh mind, but she did think white unbecoming to Mr. Hadley, and said, gurgling, "Where did you find that horse? Or why did you find it?"

"He was a bad debt. But he has a great soul. And don't prevaricate, Susan. Where have you been?" Mr. Hadley bent his sardonic brows.

"To gossip with Alison."

"Odso, I guessed you would turn traitor."

"No. I haven't turned at all, Mr. Hadley."

"She has declared war on us. Your dear father fizzes and fumes like a grenade all day. And you go gossip with her. It's flat treason, miss. Come, did you tell Sir John you were going?"

"No. But he would guess. He is so clever about me. Like you."

"Humph. If he guesses you're a woman, it's all he does. And, damme, I suppose it's enough. So your curious sex bade you go and pry. Well, and what did you see in Mr. Harry Boyce?"

"I suppose you are scolding me," said Susan placidly.

"With all my heart."

"Oh. Why do you ride that horse?"

"Damme, miss, don't wriggle. You had no business at Highgate!"

"He looks as if he had the gout."

Mr. Hadley grinned. "But as you went, let's hear what you saw."

"I always loved Alison."

"Your business is to love your father, Susan—till some other man asks you."

"I love her better now. She is so happy."

"Damn her impudence," said Mr. Hadley.

"Why did you lose your temper with her?"

"I never lose my temper with any one but you."

"Well. You made my father lose his."

"Ods life, Susan, don't you know it's a man's right to tell women how they ought to live? Dear Alison wouldn't listen."

Susan laughed. "She has made you look very foolish."

"If she has I'll forgive her."

"Oh. You do then," said Susan.

"On your honour, miss, what did you think of Mr. Harry Boyce?"

"I wondered Alison should love him."

"Ods life, yes. But what's this you're saying?"

"He is so quiet and simple."

"Simple! Damme, the fellow's an incarnate mask."

"Oh. I think I know all about him. I never thought I knew all about Alison. She wants so much."

"And she hasn't got all she wants, eh?"

"Yes, I believe," said Susan, after a moment.

"Pray God you're right."

"Oh. I like to hear you say that. You have been so"—for once her placid words stumbled—"so sordid about this."

"Damme, Susan, don't be a saint." Mr. Hadley grinned. "They die virgins."

XV

Mrs. Boyce

It was a time of wild plots. The long war of Marlborough had left England impregnably triumphant, and France ambitious of nothing but peace. No fear remained that foreign arms would carry James, the Pretender by right divine, to his sister's throne. Who should reign when Anne's growing weakness ended in death was for England alone to decide, and English law gave the succession to Prince George of Hanover. But there was a party, or at least the leaders of a party, who saw more profit to themselves in importing the Pretender.

Harley and Bolingbroke, they had thrust out of the Queen's confidence and the government the friends of Hanover. They had undermined the authority of Marlborough at home and abroad, and were now ready, honourably or dishonourably, to put an end to the war which made him necessary. If he were dispatched into ignominy or exile, there could be no one strong enough, they believed, to prevent them driving England the way they chose. What that way would be no one clearly knew, themselves, perhaps, least of all. But together and singly they set going many strange secret schemes which were to make a new king, a new England, and new magnificence for themselves, singly or together. All which the mass of England watched with shrewd, incurious eyes. It could not long be a secret that plots were afoot. To shoulder out of power all who were committed friends of the lawful order was a confession of designs against it. As if that were not enough, Bolingbroke and Harley so managed their business that everything they did was wrapped in a mist of trickery and intrigue. And yet, though they were vastly mysterious over what could have borne the light without much shame, they contrived to let the agents of their deeper treachery blunder into notice and fill the air with rumours of untimely truth. Still England gave no sign.

"Under which King"—Hanoverian or Pretender—perhaps there were few in England who cared. If the Pretender was bred French and a Papist, Prince George was a German born. Some of those who had joined heartily in driving out his father began to put it about that the son would be a better king for that lesson. George of Hanover had the right of law, but the Parliament of to-morrow might undo what the Parliament of yesterday had done. Who could be ardent for the right of an unknown foreigner over England? And few were ardent, but there were many who, caring nothing for Pretender or Hanoverian, had a solid resolution that England should not be torn in the cause of either. Whatever was done, must be done quietly and in good order. Since it seemed that the Hanoverian had no need to change anything in law or State or Church, best that he should be king. As for the devious politics, the tricks, and the mystery of Harley and Bolingbroke, they were of no account to plain men.

There was yet another party not content to watch and wait till the plotters lost themselves in their own mysteries. The men whom Harley and Bolingbroke had driven from power had no mind to submit to impotence. They well knew what they wanted: the Hanoverian, the lawful, limited king upon the throne and themselves as his ministers. They were not delicate about the means they used. Since there were treason and plots, they too turned their hands to plotting and with a vigour and ruthless resolution of which the other camp was innocent.

So the wise and eminent were busy while Harry Boyce and his Alison made trial of their marriage. Harry lived in a dream of bewildered happiness. He had counted on nothing but the need of his passion, hoped for nothing but its ecstasy in her beauty, and at its wildest the strain of gloom in him had bade him dread what lay beyond. She gave him a miracle of mad delight. A new force of life was born in him while he enjoyed her joy. It was a discovery of intoxicating power that he could wake that rare, consummate creature to such eager exultation as his own. In those wonderful hours it seemed that they passed out of themselves into a world where every part of their being was one and in the happiness of unbounded strength. So passion and she kept faith with him and something more. But the miracle of passion in her arms had less enchantment than the joy of the quiet hours. It was with this that she bewildered him. Before she yielded to him, he would have jeered at the hope that she might bring the gift of peace in her bosom. As the first days of marriage passed he learnt that all his placid loneliness had been the mere endurance of hunger. He had stayed himself with the husk of life. She satisfied him with the fruit. For she too could be calm, delighting in the little daily things, utterly happy with nonsense. To share all that with her was to find in it a strange, lulling enchantment of content.

His fortune seemed too good to be real. For he possessed all that ever fancy had pretended was worth coveting: his life was a perfect happiness. No doubts from within, no troubles from without, had power to assail him. All the old, reasonable, practical fears were become ludicrous cowardice, only remembered for Alison to tease with. As for other people, and what they said and thought and did, some folks were kind and were welcome, no folks were of account. He and she deliciously sufficed themselves. And there was no dread of change, save in age and death, infinitely distant and insignificant—no matter but to glorify the power of life. Sometimes he was aware that the wonder of passion must grow faint and fail, but he saw nothing which could take from him the quiet, exquisite, daily joys. Was it real, or a charmed dream, this perfect fortune of content? Indeed, nothing was real in those days but the delight in being with her.

Alison had her share. He did not deceive himself. She had her ecstasies and her exultations, she thought herself even madder than he was. And in these days, perhaps, her passion was deeper and stronger than his. She was satisfied, she felt herself accomplished, and gloried in her new power with a more profound, a more secret delight than his. She had given him eagerly all that she had, and in the giving found herself more than ever her own. For all the union, the deepest, truest self in her stood aloof in a mystery. It was not of her will, for she desired to deny him nothing. She did not reckon him weak in failing to take all of her. This must needs be the way of life. No man's passion could be stronger than his. Doubtless he too had his secret soul apart. And indeed it was glorious not to lose self in love, to stay always, through the ecstasies, aloof, to give always anew of will and choice—never to merge helpless in some unknown double being and become only half a body, half a soul, capitulating always to the rest, to the other.

This self-glorious pride of hers gave her for a while that zest in all the trivial common things which made her a companion so delightful to Harry's temper. But she enjoyed them in a spirit different from his. All the bread-and-butter business of living was to him delightful in itself and for itself. He was born to want no better bread than is made of wheat. She played with it, made a dainty mock of it, amused herself with it, and at the back of her mind despised it.

So they lived, and you imagine Mrs. Weston's dim, wistful eyes watching them with a great tenderness. For she understood them no better than they themselves.

H.C. BAILEY

It was Alison who first grew tired. Not of love or passion, but of the trivialities and the quiet life at Highgate. She had ambitions, or thought she had. It had been just rediscovered that women could be leaders in the world—at least in politics and the tricks of statecraft. Women were the fiercest partisans and their voices powerful in the warring parties. It was a woman, his termagant duchess, who had given Marlborough his ascendancy in England, made him dominate all Europe. It was a clever woman who had contrived Marlborough's downfall and given his enemies the government of England. It was a woman—another duchess—who beat Swift. You need not suspect Alison, who had some humour, of imagining Harry Boyce a Marlborough. But he did believe him able to make a noise in the world, and coveted much the sensation of owning him while the world listened. She did not see herself controlling queens and kings and parties, but she was well aware of her beauty and its power, and had a mind to use it widely. She was hungry for excitement.

So Mrs. Alison determined to set her man upon a larger, busier stage. The decree went forth that old Tom Lambourne's house in the Lincoln's Inn Fields was again to be inhabited. Harry was asked for his advice afterwards. Perhaps he would have been wiser if he had begun their first quarrel then. But he was enjoying her too much to deny her her ways or her whims, and he only laughed at her. He was not pleased, to be sure. He had a taste, which cannot have come from his father, for copse and field. He never found anything in the town which was worth the living in other folk's smoke. He disliked crowds and in particular crowds of fine ladies and gentlemen. So with some horror he saw before him a vista of polite splendours, and said so.

"Oh Lud, sir," says she, "if I had wanted to sleep my life away I should not have married you. And if you wanted to sleep out yours you should not have married me."

"I was born for innocence and green fields. You'll make me a bull in a china shop."

"I'll love you the better, child. Faith, Harry, I would be very glad to have you break something."

"Madame's heart, *par exemple*?"

"That would be an adventure."

So you find them arrived in the Lincoln's Inn Fields as the first step to the conquest of the world. The world was not as excited as Alison thought fit. Her father, old Tom Lambourne, had commanded reverence in the City and some respect even as far west as St. James's by sheer weight of wealth. A rare capacity for living hard had won him an army of diverse friends. But neither his business nor his pleasures provided him with many who could be bequeathed to his daughter. Her mother, born a baker's daughter in Shoe Lane, having died in giving Alison birth, had left her nothing besides her admirable body but some grumbling objects of charity. It remained for Alison to make her own way in the world of fine ladies and gentlemen. Since she was by certain fame an heiress of great possessions, her way might have been easy if she had not found herself a husband. The taint of the city, if she had borne herself humbly, need not have made her quite intolerable to people of birth. But since her money was already married she could only be reckoned as a city goodwife; pretty enough, indeed, to be game for fine gentlemen, but to fine ladies a nobody.

Folks were slow in coming to the grand house in Lincoln's Inn Fields; slower still, if they had houses of elegance, to ask Mrs. Alison back. It suited Harry very well. He would, as his wife complained, go mooning across the fields to Islington almost as happily as through the woods at Highgate. His books had almost as good a savour in town as in the country. When she dragged him to hear Nicolini or Wilks or the Bracegirdle, he could console himself by gentle jeering over the fact that in a playhouse where everybody knew everybody not a creature had a bow for him or her. Of course she smarted. Day by day he chose to affect astonishment over her failures, believing with infatuated content that he was slowly driving her back to the country and sanity, though he was but driving her away from him. And she, choosing to feel humiliated, blamed him for the shame of it.

"Why, child," says he in his supercilious way, "'tis not failing to be in the *beau monde* that's ridiculous, but wanting to be."

To such monitions she began not to answer back—a symptom very dangerous.

She set up a basset table. That, if anything could, must proclaim her a woman of fashion—a woman, indeed, who had a fancy to be a trifle daring. There's no doubt that Alison about this time and afterwards did want to dabble in danger. She was not her father's daughter for nothing. She encouraged high play. For herself, she enjoyed the excitement of it, having no need to care if she lost. She wanted to have about her people who affected heavy stakes, believing in the innocence of her heart that they were exhilarating company. So she made for herself a queer society, which Harry to her angry disgust defined as a mixture of sheep and wolves. There were good wives and lads from the city anxious to make a jingling show with the funds of the family counting-house, there were hungry beaux and madames from the other end of the town seeking their fortune impudently wherever it might be found.

To one of these happy parties there was introduced a Mrs. Boyce. She was a faded, handsome creature much jewelled about lean shoulders. Alison, who hardly heard her name in the rout, took no account of it and little of her. But on the next day this Mrs. Boyce came early and caught Alison alone.

She began with such a fuss about apologizing for her earliness that Alison set her down for an ill-bred, tiresome creature. She had a high voice which, like the rest of her, was a trifle faded. "I protest, ma'am, I have long desired to know you better." Alison languidly muttered something civil. "Let me make myself known first, I beg. I am the niece of Sir Gilbert Heathcote."

Alison, of course, had heard of Sir Gilly—one of the chiefs of high finance—but cared nothing about him. "I am vastly honoured, ma'am. I was only born Thomas Lambourne's daughter."

"There is no need; ma'am." A long, lean hand was waved. "I wonder if we are in some fashion connected. We are both called Mrs. Boyce. The Boyces of Oxfordshire, ma'am?"

Alison's laugh had something of a sneer in it, "Of nowhere that I know, ma'am. My husband is Mr. Harry Boyce, son of Colonel Oliver Boyce."

The lady fluttered her fan, settled herself afresh in her chair, rearranged her close-fitting lips. Alison was reminded of a hen preening itself. "I had heard so, ma'am. And my husband is Colonel Oliver Boyce."

"La, ma'am, do you mean the same?" Alison cried.

Mrs. Oliver Boyce gave a lifeless smile. "That is why I did myself the honour of giving you my confidence, ma'am. I think there are not two Colonel Oliver Boyces. The younger son of one of the Oxfordshire family."

"Oh Lud, how should I know? I never looked into the grandfathers."

"No, ma'am?" The tone was patronizing contempt. "You might have been the wiser of it. Colonel Oliver Boyce—he has taken the title lately—when I knew him he was something in the service of the Duke of Marlborough. Oh, a fine man to the eye, ma'am, and very splendid in his talk."

"Why, that's his likeness," Alison laughed. "And what then, ma'am? Have you come seeking the Colonel? He is the Lord knows where. Or is it—faith, you don't tell me Harry is your son?"

"No, ma'am. At least I was spared bearing children."

"Oh—why, give you joy if you would have it so. But how can I serve you? Maybe your Colonel is not my Colonel after all. At least he and Harry are father and son heartily enough."

"It may be so, ma'am," said the lady heavily, and here Harry came in.

Alison looked up laughing and then frowned. Harry would not ever dress fine. His wig was still unfashionably small, he wore some sombre stuff, and to her eye (as she said) looked like a mole. "Here's Mr. Boyce, ma'am. Harry, Mrs. Oliver Boyce, who is come to say that you never had father nor mother."

"Your obliged servant, ma'am." Harry opened his eyes. "Pray, has my father married again?"

"You'll find, sir, that Colonel Boyce has only been married once."

"If you please, ma'am," said Harry blandly. "Pray, are you blaming him? Or—" a gesture expressed his complete ignorance of what she was doing.

The lady seemed to force herself to laugh. "Oh, fie, sir. Sure it is not for me to blame him."

"No, ma'am?" Harry was first interrogative then acquiescent. "No, ma'am. I wonder if you could give me the Colonel's direction."

"I, sir? You are pleased to amuse yourself."

"I vow, ma'am, I was never less amused."

"Colonel Boyce was pleased to leave me five years ago. I have not forgotten it, if you have."

"Faith, this is very distressing," Harry protested in bewilderment. "But you do me injustice, ma'am. I have forgotten nothing about my father. For I never knew anything."

"As you please, sir," the lady drawled. "I was talking, by your leave, to Mrs. Boyce."

"Oh, ma'am, a hundred pardons," Harry took himself off in a hurry. His chief emotion over the lady seems to have been satisfaction that she wanted nothing to do with him. As for her story of being his father's deserted wife, he had long supposed his father capable of anything. As for the lady herself, he wrote her down a tiresome busybody and perhaps he was not far wrong.

Alison too was much of the same opinion, but it was unfortunately hampered by a natural curiosity to hear what the lady could tell about the mystery of Harry and his father. "You had something to say to me, ma'am?"

"I count it my duty, ma'am, to give you warning of Colonel Boyce."

Alison stood up. "Duty? I know nothing of your duty, ma'am. But I think it is mine not to listen to you."

"I protest, I should have said the same," the lady drawled. "I too had spirit once, child. That was before I suffered. I would I had known you earlier. And yet perhaps I may do something to save you even now."

"I cannot tell how, ma'am."

"Listen, if you please!" the lady said dramatically. "I was something of an heiress as you are and maybe something of a toast too. The worse for me. I choose to believe it was not only my money which brought Oliver Boyce upon me. He took all I could give him and very soon gave me nothing, not even common courtesy. When I began to be careful he began to be brutal. But for my family—I told you that Sir Gilbert Heathcote was my uncle—he would have stripped me of every penny. When they stepped in to save me some rag of my fortune, my good Mr. Boyce left me. I have never had a word from him since. Pray, child, take warning."

"If it is so, I am sorry for it," said Alison coldly, "I believe I hear company." She began to walk to the outer room.

Behind her, "As for your Harry Boyce," said the lady, "oh, I make no doubt he's Oliver's son, though certainly he is none of mine."

Alison made as if she did not hear, and she was spared more by the coming of some of her guests. The card tables filled. There was no more danger of being private with Mrs. Oliver Boyce. Indeed, the lady, as if she had done all she wanted, took her leave early. She was affectionate about it, for which Alison liked her none the better. Through most of that evening, amid the flutter of cards and the clatter—"Spadillio, on my life! What, it's Basto, is it? Did you hear of Mrs. Prue? She'll not show for a month. We win the Codille, ma'am. They say the Duchess and she pulled caps"—Alison was telling herself over and over that the creature was a detestable low thing who only wanted to make mischief. It should, you think, have needed no effort to believe that. But the obvious malice had power to annoy a mind already discontented. Alison could not stop wondering what the mystery was about Harry's birth and his father. Perhaps Harry knew more than the little he professed. Perhaps he was not the careless, indolent fellow he chose to seem, but something more cunning and less lofty. What if he were just such another as the woman painted his father—a fellow on the hunt for an heiress, who, once he had her and her money, cared no more about her? To be sure there was some evidence for that. Since they had come to town, he was always off by himself. If she wanted him with her, she had to plead and plague him. A proud office! Why, that very night monsieur did not please to appear at the card tables. He was too fine for her and her company. So she fretted and rubbed the poison in. And naturally, she fared ill at the card table. Her cards were bad and she made the worst of them. She was not a good loser and it was a wife much inflamed who, when her guests were gone, sought out her husband.

Harry sat with Mrs. Weston, who was at needlework and, if Alison had been able to see, looked very benign. But it was he who demanded all the wife's angry eyes. His wig was on the table beside him. He had a pipe in his mouth. He was lolling in the deeps of a chair and smiling to himself over a book. "You might be in an ale-house, you look so slovenly."

Harry grinned up at her. "Oh, madame wife hasn't been winning to-night. Tell me all about it."

"Faugh! Your pipe," Alison coughed. "For God's sake keep it to the tavern. It's enough that you reek of it without making my house reek too."

Harry gave a great sigh and put the pipe down. "We were so comfortable till you came. I am glad to see you, dear."

"I was comfortable till you came." Alison snapped.

"Pray, mother Weston," says Harry, "forgive our public caresses. We have not long been married."

Alison looked ice at him. "Weston dear, would you leave us? I have something to say to Harry." Harry opened his eyes. Mrs. Weston looked at her anxiously, bade them a nervous good-night, and hurried out.

"Harry—who was your mother?" Alison stood stern over the lolling husband.

"Egad, what's this? Have you been brooding over your bony friend? Who is she?"

"She says she is your father's wife; and says he left her."

"Well, if she is his wife, I wager he did leave her. Faith, she was made to be deserted."

"What do you know of her?"

"Nothing, by the grace of God. Why should I? If my father got drunk and married her, he would not want to talk about it when he was sober."

"I despise you when you talk so," Alison cried.

"And yet you listened to her, child."

"She says that he took all her money before he left her."

"Oh! Pray, why has she so much to say, and to you?"

"She wanted to warn me against Colonel Boyce."

"And against his son, I think. And you were so kind as to listen. Egad, ma'am, I am obliged to you. Well, now you know what to do. You have the money and I have none. Pray, lock up your purse to-night."

"You are childish," said Alison with lofty scorn. "Harry—who was your mother?"

"Oh, I thought your kind friend told you I had none. I dare say it's as true as the rest."

"You don't know?"

"I never saw her."

"She said—" Alison hesitated.

"Oh Lud, don't be squeamish now."

"She said your father had never been married except to her."

"Odso! That is what you had to tell me. I am a bastard, am I?" He laughed and turned in his chair. "Give you good-night, madame wife."

"Harry—"

"Oh, God save you!" He took up his pipe. "I am no company for you. And, by God, you are no company for me."

She looked at him a moment, hesitated, went slowly out.

XVI

The Affair of Sir George

The irruption of Mrs. Oliver Boyce could not easily have been foretold. That the past life of Colonel Boyce was likely to throw shadows over his son Harry might have considered, but the nature of the lady and her care and the successful opportunity of her malice were hardly to be calculated. There is less excuse for him in the affair of Sir George Anville. Given the conditions of that hasty marriage and the state into which it had brought them and the society about them, some Sir George or other was a natural consequence.

The ugly quarrel which Mrs. Oliver Boyce had made for them was never composed. When they met again in the morning they were coldly and haughtily civil, and so they chose to remain. Mrs. Weston, not being blind, saw that something was amiss and tried with blundering motherly affection to push them back into one another's arms. She hardened, as is usual, their hostility. Each was mortally afraid of weakening, each suspected the other at once of softness and of guile and so held aloof and fed upon scorn. They had both enough of that pride of sex which gives one pleasure in the sufferings of the other. And of course the quarrel was poisoned with a sordid taint. The colder, the haughtier Harry was, the more Alison inclined to believe that he had wanted nothing of her but her money. The haughtier, the colder Alison was, the more Harry raged against her for a mean creature who desired to make him feel his dependence upon her money bags.

In himself Sir George Anville was of no importance. If Harry had been comfortable he could never have taken the trouble to be angry over the man. It is certain that Alison never thought him worth any thought of hers, still less worth one finger's surrender. And yet Sir George contrived to be disastrous to the pair of them.

That was not, as Lady Mary Wortley Montagu said of him in another matter, altogether his fault. "The fool has excuses," quoth she, "which others have not. He is so great a fool that you hardly believe his folly is but folly." Sir George was a man born without impulse or capacity for anything. Lady Mary, who was fond of using him for her wit, made a grammarian's jest on him, "The creature's an anomaly:

active in form, passive in meaning." He was bred in a society which made it a fashion to be vicious. He affected to follow the fashion. If vice must needs be something active, or at least, something of the will, Sir George Anville must escape punishment. But he was to a wholesome taste more offensive than sinners who did more damage. It was Harry's worst blunder in the affair that he treated Alison as if she did not feel that.

Sir George knew no other way of passing his life than in dangling about women. He was generally tolerated as a butt, and being impervious to contempt, supposed that his fascinations procured him immunity. He did—it must be reckoned the first of his two accomplishments—he did know a pretty woman from a plain one, and therefore as soon as he knew Alison much resorted to her. His other accomplishment was to dress well. He was lean and had an air of languor which was not affected, but a natural lack of vigour. It may be believed that Alison tolerated him because he made a not disagreeable decoration to her rooms. But at this era she was cynical, and perhaps told herself that Sir George was as good a man as another.

He began to come at hours when she could be found alone and was sometimes admitted. So Harry caught him once or twice, was ironically obsequious to him (which Sir George took for solemn earnest), and afterwards amused himself by congratulating Mrs. Alison on the power of her charms. "Odds fish, I can't tell where you'll stop, ma'am. You'll have a corpse on his knees to you yet. Maybe the corpse of a lord. I vow I'm proud of you." Which was not likely to get the door shut on Sir George.

So that dangling gentleman became convinced that Alison was yielding to his embraces. He was, in a limp way, gratified. A devilish fine woman to be sure. She might be a trifle exhausting to a man of *ton*. But what would you? Women were greedy and must be satisfied with what one could spare them. And it was pleasant to see the pretty creatures pining. He would lure madame on with a few tit-bits. In this kindly mood he went to her on a wet April day when Alison was fretting for a wild walk or a wilder ride in wind and rain. But even to herself she would not confess that she was tired of the town. It would have assimilated her to Harry.

Sir George sat himself down by Alison's side, simpered at her, sniffed, put his thin hands on his thin knees and ogled them. Alison held out to him a cup of tea. He arranged his rings before he took it and then again simpered at her. After some humming and hawing, "D'ye go to the play to-night, ma'am?" he drawled.

"What play is it?"

"Ah—some curst play or other," said Sir George; and exhausted by that effort relapsed for a while into silence.

Alison did not help him out. It is possible that she was wondering how a creature so vapid could go on existing. She looked Sir George over with an odd, close inspection. Sir George, who had some perceptions, became aware of it and according to his nature misunderstood it. He sniffed again, and "Pray, ma'am, what perfume do you use?" Alison stared at him. "I am delicate in such things," said he, and smelt his own handkerchief.

Alison hesitated between disgust and amusement. To be sure the creature was such a fool that it was not fair to think of him save as a buffoon. So unfortunately she chose amusement. "Oh, I vow, Sir George, your delicacy is rare," she laughed.

The poor creature took it for a compliment. He leered at her: "But you are exquisite, my Indamora."

"Who?"

"It's an amorous lady in a play," Sir George explained. "Pretty creature," he patted Alison's arm, and leaned upon her to kiss her neck.

She was so surprised that his lips had almost time to reach her. "Lord, sir, are you mad?" she cried, as she thrust him off.

"Pretty creature," Sir George giggled, and clung to her.

"Your carriage is at the door, Sir George." Harry stood over them. His face was as much a mask as ever, his voice placid.

Alison started up and stood to face him with a lowering brow. He did not appear to see her. Sir George shook down his ruffles. "Carriage? What d'ye mean?" says he. "I ha' had no carriage this year. I came in a hackney coach."

Harry turned away from him and opened the door.

"Eh? Oh, stap me!" Sir George giggled and got on to his feet, "Madame, your eternally devoted." He went out with a strut, waving his scented handkerchief in the direction of Harry.

Then Alison spoke. Her eyes were furious. "You—oh, you boor! How dare you?"

"Egad, that's very good!" Harry laughed.

She beat her foot on the floor. "Oh, you are not to be borne! To make a noise of it! To make a scandal of me and that—that creature!"

"To be sure, I came untimely. Well, ma'am, if you wanted to be quiet about it, I had rather it made a noise."

"My God!" she was white. "You dare say that to me! Be careful, Harry."

"Pray, ma'am, no heroics."

"I warn you, there are things I'll not bear."

"Is it possible?" Harry sneered.

She swept past him and away.

XVII

RETURN OF MR. WAVERTON

It seems that, years afterwards, Harry and Alison were afflicted with a dreary and remorseful wonder at these wars. Both, as they grew older, had something of a turn for moralising, and in their copious letters to their several children is evidence of much penitence and puzzling over the disasters of their youth. Each plainly took all the blame. Each is eloquent about the sins of pride and hardness. Harry preaches the duty of trust; Alison the folly of easy intimacies. Both of them, in those latter days when they could calmly estimate what they had lost, still wondered with a gloomy scorn how they had come to let the ugly, ridiculous affair of Sir George set them against each other. You find them both trying to recall (or guess) what exactly it was that, in the time of crisis, they felt and believed.

When it was all part of their history, Harry could hardly persuade himself that ever he had fancied Alison untrue, even disloyal; or Alison believe that she had stormed against him for driving out of the house a man who had been impudent to her. Yet it is not to be doubted that Harry did let suspicions of her honesty poison him. He could not, at the worst of his anger, believe that she would play false with such a husk of a fop; but he told himself that she wanted to make the fellow into a waiting gentleman, a servant, and a toy at once—a thing more nauseous than a lover. And Alison, though at the back of her brain she was aware that Harry had excuse for what he had done, raged the more against him for the intolerable things he had said. His suspicions made her despise him. For his assumption of authority she hated him.

There were almost from the first the usual sage and kindly friends to tell them that it was all a misunderstanding, that they had only to be frank with each other and commonly reasonable and there would be no quarrel left. But it is doubtful whether this sagacious advice could have done them much good if they had taken it. "Talk things over like rational creatures," was (as usual) the prescription. But if they had really been rational, they would only have come to the conclusion that they ought not to be married. The force of their passion, to be sure, was real enough and still moved in them. To hold them together they had nothing else. There was no consciousness of other need, no longing for a common life, no desire to help or give. If they had been most calmly wise and wisely calm in a dozen conversations, they would but have made this all the clearer.

Still it is true, as the sagacious friends guessed, that they did not try to compose the quarrel. Each was by far too proud. Harry was pleased to consider that he had done his duty by a flighty wife, and would take no more account of her unless she were penitent—or provoked him again. Alison, reckoning herself meanly insulted, was resolved that he could never again be more than an unwelcome guest in her house. They were, to be sure, ridiculous. In private they avoided each other. In public they continued to meet, for each was too proud to confess to the world the failure of their marriage. You imagine how poor Mrs. Weston enjoyed life in an icy atmosphere, the temperature of which she was not permitted to notice.

Such were their relations when the final blow fell upon them. They dined late in the Lincoln Inn Fields. It was as much as six o'clock and they were still at table—as jovial as usual. The butler came to Alison with an elaborate whispering. "Pray him come up," she said aloud, and looked defiance down the table at Harry. "It is Mr. Waverton."

"Lord, Lord, is he still alive?" Harry grinned. "That's heroic."

"Back from France? Is Colonel Boyce come back?" Mrs. Weston cried.

"I know nothing of Colonel Boyce," said Alison coldly.

"You couldn't please him better," Harry laughed. "Dear Geoffrey! I wonder if he knows anything? Well I It would be a new experience."

Mr. Waverton came. He was more stately than ever—browner also, but not changed otherwise. His large and handsome face affected all the old melancholy.

"Oh, Mr. Waverton!" Harry grinned. "You do honour me. Pray let me present you to my poor wife."

Geoffrey took no notice of him. "Madame, your obedient," he bowed to Alison. "I beg leave to have some speech with you."

"There's still some dinner. Draw up a chair," said Harry.

"I did not come to dine, sir."

"Oh, that's a sad stomach of yours. A glass of wine, then?"

"I do not take wine with you, Mr. Boyce."

"I wonder if you have made a mistake. For you have come into my house."

"I will answer for all my mistakes, sir, with hearty goodwill."

"Egad, you'll be busy."

"Oh, be silent!" Alison cried. "You are welcome, Mr. Waverton. How can I serve you?"

"I understand the gentleman's desire to hurry me into a quarrel, ma'am. Be sure that I shall not permit it." Harry laughed disagreeably. "It's very well, sir. But I choose first that you should listen to what I have to say."

"Listen I Oh Lud, is it a poem?"

Mr. Waverton flushed. "You are impertinent, sir. It shall not serve you. I intend that madame shall know the truth of your father's treachery and yours."

Harry stood up. "Are we to stay for more of this, ma'am?"

"I shall stay," Alison said.

"You remark the gentleman's impatience to silence me, ma'am. I promise you that I shall tell you nothing which he or any man can deny."

"It's a dull tale, then," Harry muttered.

"I think it will excite you enough, ma'am. You are advised that I went to France with Colonel Boyce. The office which he offered me was to negotiate with Prince James. This I undertook readily, for to his party my family hath ever had an inclination, nay, an affection, and I saw in the affair duties of honour and moment."

"To the greater glory of Geoffrey, first Duke of Waverton, whom God preserve," quoth Harry.

"I did not, I will avow, foresee that the thing was but a trick to take me away from my house and out of the country. Though I may regret, ma'am"—he bowed magnificently to Alison—"I do not even now blame myself for my blindness, for I have ever accounted it unworthy of a man of honour to fear treachery in his servants"—he glared at Harry—"or weakness—ah—weakness in those to whom he gives his devotion"—he made melancholy eyes at Alison. "No more of that. In fine, I did not suspect that a fellow who was taking wages from my hand had plotted to rob me of what was my dearest hope, or that another—another—would surrender herself a prey to his crafty greed."

"Damme, it is a poem after all," Harry groaned.

"You said you had something to tell me, sir," said Alison coldly.

"Nay, ma'am, be patient. I give you no reproaches. But what is, is. If it irks you that I remind you of it, do not give the blame to me."

"I shall blame you for being tedious, by your leave." Alison yawned.

"Wait till all's told. Well, ma'am, I left Tetherdown with Colonel Boyce, and we rode posthaste to Newhaven. He was there joined by some half-dozen fellows, low fellows to my eye. This much surprised me, and I took occasion to tell him so, for he had given out that his was a very secret errand of Marlborough's privy policy, into which he would admit none but me. He made out that these fellows were but messengers and escort, and I permitted myself to be satisfied, though I remarked that he was on familiar terms with them. But that gave me little concern, for I had from the first remarked in Colonel Boyce a coarse habit of intimacy with the vulgar."

"Aye, aye, you and he took to each other famously," says Harry.

"Lud, sir, must you be so wordy?" Alison cried.

"You will find that every word has its import, ma'am. From some of these fellows Colonel Boyce learnt that there was a warrant out against him for treasonable practices with the Pretender. This affected him to great indignation, in which, as I frankly told him, I found matter for bewilderment. Since he was, as he professed, about to deal with the Pretender, it was but fair that the Government should arraign him on that charge. Over which he was pleased to laugh at me, and then, to explain his mirth, averred that the Government, and in particular Mr. Secretary St. John, was much more Jacobite than he, and so had no title to meddle with him. Then he said that what irked him was that they should have heard of his dealings with France, which must be done secretly or fail. So we went in a hurry aboard the schooner which was ready for him, and crossed to Dieppe, landing by night beyond the town. I make no doubt from his adroitness that Colonel Boyce hath done business in France before, but of what kind I leave you to guess when you have heard all. We were well furnished with horses and upon the road to Paris before noon. He gave out to some officers which questioned him that we were of Prince James's service upon our way to St. Germain. We rode to Pontoise, and there, as it had been planned from the first, Colonel Boyce stayed while I rode on to the Prince. He dared not, as he said, go himself to Paris, for fear that some of the French officers should recognize him as Marlborough's man and denounce him for a spy. Therefore was I to go with letters to the Prince, and messages which should persuade him to ride out to Pontoise and come to business with Colonel Boyce. I went on then alone, save that Colonel Boyce gave me one of his fellows to be my guide and servant, and he stayed with the rest at Pontoise. Thus far, I beg you remark, I had no cause to apprehend treachery. Upon the face, the scheme was fair enough, and all had been done even as Colonel Boyce proposed to me in England. I will maintain myself honourably free of any blame in the affair against any man whomsoever."

"God bless you," said Harry heartily.

Mr. Waverton visibly laboured with a repartee.

"Oh, sir, a prayer from you is a rare honour," he said at length. "You're to understand, ma'am, that I was furnished with letters of credence from certain of the Jacobite agents in England—John Rogers and Mrs. White, I remember. How they were come by, I cannot now tell, though I may guess, for it is plain that there was no stint of money in the affair. So I came easily to speech with the Prince and his secretary, my Lord Middleton. And I will ever maintain that His Royal Highness is altogether such as a prince should be. Being of a dark complexion and a melancholy dignity, there is in him no lightness of thought or word. To me he was, I profess, very flattering, showing me courtesies beyond my rights or expectations. He received me, in a word, most favourably, and being influenced, as I regret I cannot doubt, by my person and address, was easily inclined to ride out to Pontoise. Only my Lord Middleton made difficulties. He is of a sardonic turn, and permits his wit to outrun his civility. He set me questions in a fashion which my honour could not brook. Yet I can relate that in the end I prevailed over my Lord Middleton's jealousy. For he said to the Prince: '*Enfin*, sir, I can tell no reason why you should not go see this Colonel if you choose. If there were any guile in the business, faith, they would never have trusted it to this fellow!'

"So the thing was agreed. In the morning we rode for Pontoise, the Prince, my Lord Middleton, myself. His Royal Highness was pleased to limit himself to one servant. The man with whom Colonel Boyce had provided me went on to carry advice of our coming. We came to Pontoise towards evening. Colonel Boyce had put up at the Lion d'Or. He was waiting for us in the courtyard and received us, as I thought, something shortly, hurrying us into the house. But once inside, he made ceremony enough, with endless speeches about the condescension of His Royal Highness. All this too obsequious, in a boorish taste, so that the Prince bade him have done and come to business. Therewith Colonel Boyce was as full of apologies as he had been of servilities. I vow I never heard him so copious as that night.

"He took us, you are to understand, to an upper room. And what first moved my suspicion was that he bade me be gone. Then my Lord Middleton countered him with, 'I believe, sir, the gentleman had best stay.' Immediately Colonel Boyce was all smiles over his blunder, and we sat down about the table in that upper room and came to the substance of his negotiation. He kept, I'll allow, to the purposes which, from the first, he had pretended to me: whether Prince James, if assured of support from Marlborough and his friends, would choose to avow himself Protestant; but he made so many conditions over it, he was so vague and wary that 'twas hard to tell what he would be at. When my Lord Middleton tried to pin him to something plain and certain he would ever evade, till it began to grow late and the Prince talked of supper and bed. This Colonel Boyce took up very heartily, and was indeed giving his orders when there came a noise in the courtyard and he ran to the window and looked out.

"My Lord Middleton was behind him, with a 'What's your anxiety, sir?'

"'Why, my lord, I would not have these roysterers break upon the Prince's incognito. Pray, sir, this way and you'll be secure'; he points to an inner door.

"'I believe we are as safe here, sir,' says my Lord Middleton.

"'Egad, sir, come away,' says Colonel Boyce; and he was in fact dragging the Prince across the room when the door bursts open and in comes a stranger, a little man. He flung himself across the room upon Colonel Boyce, making some play with a pistol. There was some grappling and wrestling. I recall that they gasped and breathed hard. But it's odd, I believe, that there was no word spoken. Then Colonel Boyce freed himself and bolted through that inner door. The stranger fired a shot after him, and while we were all deaf and sneezing with it and utterly amazed he turns on us. 'That's a miss,' says he. 'Please God they'll bag him below. Eh, Charles,' he wags his head at my Lord Middleton, 'I thought you had more sense,'

"'Damme,' says my lord, 'it's Hector McBean. And prithee what's all this ruffling, Mac?'

"'Why, you have let His Majesty walk into a stinking trap. That fellow Boyce, he hath been Marlborough's spy, Sunderland's spy, the devil's spy this twenty year.'

"'Why, I thought he had something the smack of it,' says my lord. 'And yet—'

"'Who's this now?' Captain McBean turned on me. 'Yours or his?'

"'His ambassador in fact,' My lord looked me over and took snuff. 'You won't tell me that hath any guile in it. Prithee, what is it you have against the man Boyce?'

"'Eh, did ye see him run?' says Captain McBean. 'A man's not in that hurry if he hath a good conscience. If ye'll please to have him up, maybe we'll hear a tale.'

"But as he spoke there came into the room a French officer of dragoons, who, saluting the Prince, asked Captain McBean if he had found his rogue. On which 'Have I found him?' Captain McBean cries out, 'Eh, sir, did he not run into your arms?' But it appeared that Colonel Boyce had not been caught, and they determined at last that he must have made his way out by a door at the back of the inn and won clear away. But I am sorry to tell you, ma'am, that he hath not yet been found. For if they catch him in France, he may count on a hanging."

"Pray, sir, how did you dodge the rope?" Harry said. "Did you talk them to death, your Pretender and his tail?"

"You're too eloquent for me, Mr. Waverton," Alison yawned. "I can't tell what you want to say. What is this mighty crime which you and Colonel Boyce were compassing?"

"Sneers become you ill, ma'am," says Mr. Waverton magnificently. "I repudiate any charge whatsoever; and tell my story my own way. Some hot words passed between Captain McBean and the Frenchman, each blaming the other for Colonel Boyce's escape. Then Captain McBean says 'The fellows that were drinking in the tap, I suppose you've let them dodge you too? No? Well, that's a wonder. Tie this rogue up with them and have them in guard.' So he mocked at me, but the Prince brought him up roundly.

"'You go too fast for me, my good captain,' quoth he. 'What's your charge against the gentleman?—who is to my mind a very simple gentleman.' So His Royal Highness was pleased to honour me."

"Egad, he was right, Waverton," Harry laughed.

"I think I know how to value your fair words now, sir," says Mr. Waverton grandly. "Be pleased to spare them. Upon that, as I was saying, Captain McBean lost command of himself and was grossly violent. Roaring that I was none the less a knave because I was so natural a fool, and the like empty insolence. Accusing me of being art and part in a vile plot with Colonel Boyce to kidnap and murder His Royal Highness."

"Now we have it," Alison murmured and looked at Harry strangely.

"Aye, ma'am. Now, perhaps (though late enough) your eyes are opened," said Mr. Waverton with relish. "Well, I let the man run on. He was indeed not to be stopped. A rude, vehement fellow. When he was exhausted, I addressed His Royal Highness."

"Lack a day, I believe you," says Harry.

"I made it clear to him, sir, that my birth and position must warrant me innocent of any treachery, and though I might well disdain to answer these reckless charges I owed it to myself to remark to His Royal Highness that, but for my desire to serve him, I had never meddled in the affair. So that when I had done, my Lord Middleton says, laughing, 'Egad, sir, it seems you owe this fine gentleman thanks for his kindly condescension to you'; and the Prince was pleased to answer, 'We are too small for his notice, faith. But is he finished yet?' Then I bowed to His Royal Highness and sat down, well enough pleased, as you may believe.

"But this Captain McBean called out in his rude fashion, 'Eh, sir, he may e'en be the booby he pretends. The better decoy, I allow. But by your leave, we'll look into it more narrowly. Would Your Majesty please to permit me have up the other rogues?'

"This, in a word, they did, and Captain McBean and my Lord Middleton (who is to my mind something more of the attorney than becomes a man of rank) questioning the fellows shrewdly, it was made put—I crave your attention, madam—it was made out that Colonel Boyce had undertaken for the service of the Hanoverian junto here to kidnap or kill Prince James. And the plan was to bring the Prince out to Pontoise and so drag out affairs that he passed the night there. Then in the night they were to invade his room and command him to follow them. They pretended indeed that they meant only to carry him off. But 'tis not to be doubted that they looked for resistance and a bloody issue to the affair. So, ma'am, here is the trade of the family of Boyce—to procure murder, and the murder of a prince of the blood royal, of our lawful king. I give you joy of the name you bear."

Alison bent her head. "You may well be proud of your part, Mr. Waverton."

"They let you go, did they?" says Harry; "your captain and your lord and your prince?"

"Let me go, sir? There is nothing against me. I defy your impudence. Nay, I thank you, I thank you. You lead me gracefully to the end of my story."

"Good God! It has an end!"

"When these rogues were questioned about me, not a man of them could pretend to have anything against me. They openly confessed that Colonel Boyce had warned them that I must be kept in innocence of the affair lest I should thwart it. For he said that he had brought me into it to show a good face to the Prince as one beyond suspicion of treachery. Nay and moreover—and here's my last word to you, ma'am—he avowed that he chose me because he wanted me out of England where I stood between his own son and a pretty heiress. At which, as I remember, my Lord Middleton chose to be amused."

"Damme, I like that man," says Harry.

"So, ma'am," Mr. Waverton tossed his head. "Here you have it. I am drawn into a murderous, vile, base treason that I may be kept out of the way while Mr. Boyce prosecutes his designs upon you. I give you joy of the loyal fidelity which yielded to him. I leave you to enjoy him with what appetite you may."

He made a majestic bow, he turned and was gone.

Harry and Alison were left staring at each other.

From behind came a small strained voice: "Colonel Boyce—he—he is safe, then?" It was Mrs. Weston.

The two turned with a start, surprised by her existence.

Harry laughed. "Oh aye, he is safe. He would be."

Mrs. Weston rose slowly and then made a rush for the door.

The husband and wife were left alone.

XVIII

Harry is Dismissed

A lison turned and stared into the fire. Harry filled himself a glass of port and drank it and laughed. She looked round at him. "Faith, Mr. Waverton is mighty good entertainment," he explained.

"Is that all you want to say?"

Harry would not be awed by that ominous voice. "Oh Lud, how could I dare talk after him? Our poetic orator!" He made flourishes in the air after Mr. Waverton's manner. "Nay, but I would give my new wig to have been in that upper chamber at Pontoise. Dear Geoffrey on his defence booming noble periods—and the Prince, poor gentleman, with his fingers in his ears! If dear Geoffrey was telling the truth. I wonder."

"Oh, is that what you'll pretend?"

"Pretend? I pretend nothing, ma'am. Why, to be sure, our Geoffrey always means to tell the truth—having, God bless him, no imagination. But you'll remark what when he tells a tale, it's Mr. Waverton has always the *beau rôle*. He sees the world like that, dear lad. So I should be glad to hear the Caledonian gentleman's notion of what happened."

"I see. You'll make that your defence. Geoffrey imagined it all."

"Egad, ma'am, you may lower your tone. I have nothing to defend, nor are you set in judgment."

Alison started up. "Do you suppose all this is to make no change?" she cried.

"You're a splendid creature, by heaven," says Harry, tilting his chair back and watching her with a little epicurean smile, the proud vigour of her, the blood in her cheeks, the flash of her eyes, and the sweep of the white arm.

"I could hate you for that," she said, and her lips set.

"Yes. I think you're in a fair way to it," says Harry. "I wonder if you know why."

"Because I have come to despise you," she cried sharply.

"You will be solemn, will you?" says Harry. "Much good may it do you. And so, egad, have at you heartily. For you have said things which both of us will find it hard to forget."

"Oh, you can feel that?"

"Look 'e, ma'am, if we are to be in earnest, we had best not snap at each other like a pair of puppies. Now, what's happened?"

"You have to ask that? My God, if you have to ask, there's no use in words between you and me."

"Oh Lud, don't be mystical. Mr. Waverton comes here to do his poor possible to make mischief between us. I suppose you saw that. He tells us that he went blundering with my father into a muddle of a plot."

"He tells us that your father planned a vile base murder and sought to make him, a man of honour, part in it. Pray, sir, is that not infamous?"

"Egad, if you haven't caught his style! You believe all that, do you?"

"Yes."

"We shall go far to-night, I think," Harry shrugged. "And shall I tell you why you believe it, ma'am? It's because you are looking about to find matter for blackening me."

Alison hesitated a moment. "You cannot deny it. It is proved. Your father would not stay to face them."

"Face a pistol and a furious Scot? Well, I never said he was a hero."

"Do you pretend it was only a fight he feared? Do you dare tell me it was an honest, honourable plan? Nay, come, let me see if there's anything you think shameful."

Harry shrugged. "I know my father not much better than you do, ma'am. I never thought him a Bayard. Some plot there was, I think, and these political plots are all dirty enough. But, Lord, who is clean of them? And I'm not ready to write my father off a murderer because Mr. Waverton went blundering into a business which, on his own confession, he does not understand."

"He went in your place. You should have gone with your father."

"Should have gone? D'ye wish I had, ma'am?"

"Perhaps."

Harry started up. "Oh, say it out. I knew we should go far to-night."

They stood close, fronting each other fiercely. "My God, is it strange if I wish you had gone? Your father is a base wretch who should be on the gallows, and I am to be his son's wife and bear the name, and the while he goes bragging that he took Geoffrey Waverton off so that you should be free to come at me."

"Aye, that. To be sure, that rankles. But you have known it long. I showed you the letter he left me which said he had taken Geoffrey out of my way and bade me snatch my chance of you. And you made light of that, ma'am. Oh, it was a base thing, if you will, but you know well enough it went for nought. We had done our work before. By God, Alison, Geoffrey there or Geoffrey here, you would have come to me."

"Ah!" It was like a cry of pain. "You brag of it. I forced myself on you, I suppose." Harry exclaimed something, made a gesture. "Oh yes, you were all cold virtue and chastity and honour, and I—what was I?" She shuddered and drew back from him. "Yes, you would turn on me. You would taunt me with that."

"Egad, you're in a frenzy," says Harry. "You cry aloud and cut yourself with knives. You will be hurting yourself."

"I loathe you for that calm way of yours," she cried. "You mock me till I am mad, and then you please to be grave and lofty. You—I took you out of the gutter."

"What now, ma'am?" Harry stiffened.

"It's all a mask!" she cried. "Nothing of you shows in your voice or your face—your face, bah, it's always the same, when you kiss and when you strike. A mask! You're always in a mask. That's how you took me. I was a fool, and thought there must be something fine behind it." She laughed. "You were clever enough. You knew the trick and the mystery of it would take a woman. A mask! Yes, faith, that is the wear for a highwayman. I remember how Charles Hadley used to laugh at your 'Curst stand-and-deliver stare.' I liked it, I liked the challenge of it. But he knew you better. That's your trade, the highwayman, faith, the highwayman! You trick us all and prey upon us, as you dare. So you marked me down, who was rich and a girl, and you have caught me, and you have rifled me, and, for what you care I may now go hang. I ask you for my pride again, my honour, and you mock at me. Oh, I am ashamed for a fool and worse, and you know it, God help me, but you—you—"

Harry shrugged. "I suppose we have come to the end now," he said coolly. "Well, ma'am, to be sure we married in haste, and it seems we have both come to repentance. As for wrong that I have done you— why, I can't make you a maid again, and, if you please, more's the pity. My apologies and regrets. For the rest, all of your money that hath been spent on me will go in a small purse, and, I promise you, you shall spend no more. So you may sleep sound, and I wish you good night."

She watched him cross the room, and, as he was opening the door, cried out, "What do you mean?"

He turned. "Why, would you still be talking?" Their eyes met in defiance. "You can go," she said.

"I have had the honour to tell you so," he said, and was gone.

XIX

ALISON FINDS FRIENDS

I t was on the second day after that Susan Burford and Mr. Hadley rode in to the Lincoln's Inn Fields. They found Alison and Mrs. Weston together, and both sewing—a fact which failed to interest Mr. Hadley, but surprised Susan, who knew Alison, without a taste for needlework.

"My dear," says Susan, embracing Alison physically and spiritually in her large, buxom, genial way.

"You have been a long time finding me," says Alison and put her off. "I suppose I know why you kindly come to me now."

"B-r-r-r-r!" Mr. Hadley made the sound of one who comes into a cold draught. "The truth is, Susan has been so busy improving herself that she has had no time for her friends. In fine, she has been trying to make herself worthy the honour of my affections and large enough to support the burden of my dignity. I don't say she satisfies me, but she does her best." He propelled Susan forward with his one hand. "'A poor thing, ma'am, but mine own.'"

"Oh, he is amusing himself, you see," says Susan, in her leisurely fashion.

"Damme, Susan, you're so mighty innocent that sometimes I believe you are innocent."

"But you have known me so long," Susan protested.

Alison stood up with an air of ceremony. Her pale face constrained itself at last to smile at them. "My dear, I wish you may be very happy," says she, and gave Susan a matronly kiss. "Mr. Hadley, you're a fortunate man." She put out a stately hand.

Having bowed over it. "B-r-r-r," says Mr. Hadley.

"Damn these east winds. Susan, you're a plague with your affections. You will have me talk about you, and I can't make you interesting, I hope, ma'am, we find Mr. Boyce well?"

Alison drew back. "Why do you ask that? You have seen Mr. Waverton, of course."

Mrs. Weston put down her work and folded her hands upon it.

"Why, yes, I have seen Geoffrey; and what's worse, heard him. I hope he did not plague you too long."

"Pray, Mr. Hadley, don't be ironical. You can spare me that. Mr. Waverton told us his story the night before last. Thereupon Mr. Boyce and I parted company. He left my house immediately and I do not know where he is."

Mr. Hadley distinguished himself by containing an oath. Susan said, "Oh, my dear," in that slow, calm way which might mean anything.

It was Mrs. Weston who cried out, "Alison, you never told me."

"You asked once or twice where he was, and I told you I did not know. What does it matter?"

"You quarrelled with him?"

"Quarrelled!"

"Because of what this Mr. Waverton said?"

"Do you think it could make no difference?"

Mrs. Weston clasped her hands and swayed in her chair.

"Alison; we had no guess of this. I am sorry. I am so sorry," Susan said.

"There is no need." Alison held her head high.

"If we have, in some sort, forced your confidence, I beg you believe, ma'am, it was not meant," So Mr. Hadley in the grand style. "For I protest it never came into my head that Geoffrey would make mischief between you and Mr. Boyce."

"You say that?" Alison stared at him. "Oh, you mean I was so besotted with him."

Mr. Hadley relapsed to his ordinary manner. "Damme, d'ye think we came for nothing but to jeer at you? I promise you we have pleasanter matter to hand. Neither to jeer at you, nor to meddle with you, Alison, but friendly. So take us friendly in God's name. If you will go about to find a sneer in every word, why, a sneer you'll find, but not of my making. We bring you nothing but goodwill, and want nothing more of you. But if we irk you, why, let us go and we'll see you again in good time."

"That's a pretty speech to begin with an oath," Alison said, through the flicker of a smile. "And, faith, I should be slow to take offence at you. For we quarrelled before, because you were at pains to warn me. Well, sir, I humble myself before your wisdom."

There was a pause. "Oh. Now we are all ill at ease," says Susan.

"Odso, ma'am, it's not fair," Mr. Hadley cried. "I am not here to say, 'I told you so,' I am not so proud of it. Well, damme, I have no temptation to be meddling in your affairs. But I think you will have to know. It is with Mr. Waverton I have fallen out now."

"With Mr. Waverton?" Alison repeated. "What is there between you and him?"

"I believe he had the impertinence to expect my sympathetic admiration. While I was thinking him a low fellow. Which I took occasion to tell him. Without result." Mr. Hadley shrugged. "But I believe he did not feel it. It's a thick hide."

"And what was your difference?"

"Why, this precious story of his."

There was some little time of silence. "You don't believe it," Alison said slowly. "Come, you must say more than that."

"I profess, ma'am, I have no will to say anything. Whatever I say, I'll be impertinent."

"Oh. Shall we mark it in you?" Susan said.

"Well, sir, you were not always so shy of scolding me," says Alison, and again with a faint smile.

"Scold you! God warn us, I have no commission. I can tell you what I thought of Waverton and his tale. Did I believe it? Ods fish, I never remember believing Geoffrey. If he had to tell you two and two was four, he would pretend that his genius first discovered it. So I don't know what happened at Pontoise. Likely the old Colonel did mix him up in some plot which some other fellows smoked. Maybe it was even such as Geoffrey said, kidnapping and murder to follow. These plots, they grow nastier and nastier the longer they are afoot. And Colonel Boyce—well, by your leave, I don't think him delicate. But for the rest of it, I'll wager that's Geoffrey's sprightly invention. You know very well, ma'am, I have no kindness for your Mr. Boyce. But, damme, he never thought of tricking Geoffrey out of the way to give himself a free hand with you. And it's a low trick in Geoffrey to go about with that tale."

"Oh! But he is stupid," Susan said.

"What if Colonel Boyce thought of the trick?" says Alison.

"Egad, Mr. Boyce is unfortunate in his father. Maybe he knows that as well as we. But—damme, ma'am, you will have it—I believe there was not much trick in his affair with you."

"I believe you once warned me of his tricks," Alison said coldly. "It's no matter now. I tease you with my affairs."

"If I can serve you, I'm heartily at your command."

"Oh, you have worked hard to make the best of a bad business. But I can do that for myself, and I like my own way of it."

Mr. Hadley bowed.

"Oh! Let us go home," Susan said.

Alison looked at her in some surprise, and, as she stood up, came quickly to kiss her. "Have I been rude?" she whispered.

"That would be no matter," Susan said, "You choose to be angry with me?" Alison stiffened.

"Oh! One isn't angry. One is sorry," Susan said.

Alison let her go, and Mr. Hadley, ceremonious but with visible relief, went after her.

Then Mrs. Weston said suddenly, quickly, "Where is he?"

"He?" Alison chose to be slow. "Mr. Boyce? I have no notion."

"You drove him out?"

"I could not endure him longer. Or he could endure me no longer. He went heartily enough. I think we were both glad it was over."

"You taunted him till he had to go?"

"Weston, dear!" Alison laughed at the sudden fierceness of the meek. "What's the matter?"

"I have heard you mocking him."

"Maybe. We both have sharp enough tongues."

"You used to jeer at him for being poor."

"Good lack, are you calling me to account, ma'am?"

"Yes, you may well be ashamed! Where is he?"

"Ashamed? What do you mean, Weston? What is the man to you?"

"I am his mother," Mrs. Weston said.

"You! . . . You! Oh, but this is mad!"

"I am not mad."

"But, Weston, dear, you knew nothing about him till he came; nor he of you. How could he be your son?"

"I had never seen him since he was a baby. I was not married."

"That is why you would not tell me? Oh, Weston, dear!"

"I did not mean to tell you now. I knew it would hurt him with you. But I suppose it's no matter now. But these are my affairs, not yours."

"My dear—"

"You need not pity me."

"What am I to say?" Alison held out her arms.

"You have nothing to say now. You are not his wife now. You have never been anything but a bad wife." She gathered up her work with unsteady hands and turned away.

"Where are you going?"

"I am going out of your house. Away from you."

"But, Weston—not now, not to-night. Where can you go? What can you do?"

"I can do well enough without you, as he can. . . Why don't you tell me that I have been living on your money? You told him so often enough."

"Oh. . . you're cruel," Alison said.

"What does it matter? You'll not be hurt. You are too hard." She hurried to the door.

"Ah, don't go like this," Alison cried. "Weston, let's part kindly. I could not know. I have done nothing against you." Mrs. Weston laughed. "Stay a moment at least. I want to know. Harry's father—is Colonel Boyce—?"

"Yes, there it is. That is all you want—to pry into all the story. It is nothing to you. He is nothing to you now."

The door closed behind her.

XX

RETURN OF CAPTAIN MCBEAN

Harry was not gone far. In Long Acre stood a tavern calling itself 'The Hand of Pork.' This had always tempted Harry, whose tastes were of the people. While still a domesticated husband, he had tried its ale with satisfaction. When he left Alison it was to 'The Hand of Pork' that he brought his small, battered box.

He had a few guineas in his pocket, and made a wry face over them. "Ill-gotten gains," says he, for some were the scraped savings of Geoffrey Waverton's tutor and some the pocket money of Alison's husband. But he was in no case to be delicate. Beef and bread had to be paid for, and, in fact, his scruples were little more than a joke. It is not to be concealed that in minor things Harry Boyce was not nicely honest. If you can imagine him seriously arguing over that money—a thing impossible—he would have said that the guineas were of consequence to him and none to Geoffrey and Alison, that whether he had dealt honestly by them or not, it would not better his case to pay them back a few shillings. You have seen that he had qualms of conscience over the rights of Geoffrey's service and Alison's arms. But the ugly, awkward details gave him no trouble. He may, if you please, have swallowed a camel or so, but he never strained at a gnat.

Now that he was done with Geoffrey and Alison, both, his first feeling was comfort. It was a huge relief to be his own man again. He told himself indeed that he was mighty grateful to Geoffrey for bringing on the final explosion. For one thing, it wiped off all Geoffrey's score. If Master Geoffrey had been treated shabbily, Master Geoffrey had played a shabby trick. They could call quits—a pleasant sensation. It would have been awkward if Geoffrey had chosen to be magnanimous nobility. But he was never intelligent, the poor Geoffrey.

He had done his best to be damaging, bless him, and in all ways had been a benefactor. For, in fact, it was a great relief to be done with Alison. What with her fretful discontent, her rages, her industrious hate, she had made herself intolerable. I do not suppose that he forgot, even in the heat of the divorce, the exquisite pleasure which for a while she had given him. I think he was always ready to acknowledge that to himself, for it is certain that he bore her no malice, and if he blamed her for their catastrophe, blamed himself as much. He might make the most or more of all the taunts, of her zeal to find occasions for despising him. He forgot nothing and forgave her nothing; he wrote her down a cruel enemy. But he did not pay her back with equal hate; he dismissed all the warfare and the wounds with a shrug of sagacious cynicism.

She hated him? She had the right, she was his wife. And perhaps she was in the right too. He must fairly be reckoned a very poor match for her beauty and her wealth and her not insignificant brains. After all, he was essentially a nobody—a nobody in every department, body, mind, and soul. She might even claim that she had been cheated, for if she ought to have known that she was marrying a nobody, she could not guess that he had a bar-sinister or a disreputable father. Certainly Madame Alison could plead something of a case.

You are not to suppose Harry in an ecstasy of meek devotion. He was quite sure that she had behaved to him very badly. He admitted no excuse for her eagerness to hurt him as soon as she was tired of him. She might hate him; but after all there were obligations of courtesy, of decency, of womanhood, and her venomous temper had broken them all. He was well rid of her. In fine, she and he could call quits as well as he and Geoffrey. There was no occasion to rage against her. She had treated him badly, but, first, he had brought her into an awkward mess. Faith, she ought not to have hurried into a marriage for passion if passion was so soon to sate her. But then, what man would blame a woman for marrying for passion? Not the man she married, who might rather humble himself because he had not been able to keep her passion alive. Well, it was over, and since it was over, nothing for it but to part. God be with her! She had given him his hour. And he—why, at least she had lived with him moments she would not forget. A glorious woman. It is probable that in these first hours of their parting he began to love her.

So much for his emotions. But you will not suppose that Harry Boyce was wholly occupied with emotions. He could not indeed afford it. He had to make some provision for keeping alive. Perhaps you will be surprised to hear that he had a friend or two. There was an usher at Westminster, and a hack writer of Lintot's in Little Britain. He did not propose to live on them, who had hardly enough to feed themselves. But he looked for them to put him in the way of some pittance, and they did. The usher had news that, after Ascension-Day, Westminster would be wanting a writing master, for the man in possession hoped by then to marry the dean's cook and set up an ale-house. The author procured a commission to write two lampoons and a pamphlet against French wines. In the intervals of this occupation, Harry looked for his father.

It would be hard to guess—Harry himself could not have told—what he hoped to gain by that. He wanted, of course, to find out the truth of the mission to France. Whether his father was likely to tell it, he could not make up his mind. What he would do with the truth if ever he learnt it, he did not know in the least. Suppose the best event: suppose his father could declare excellent intentions and Geoffrey a liar. Harry imagined himself going to Alison with the news and demanding to be taken on again. A nightmare joke.

Yet to come at the truth seemed the most important task in life. The first step, though you think it impossibly difficult, did not dismay him. He had no doubt of discovering his father. That Colonel Boyce should have been killed or even caught was incredible. He was not the man so to oblige his enemies. It was incredible, too, that he would go long into hiding. Away from the importance of bustle and intrigue he could not exist. Therefore he would certainly come back to London: therefore sooner or later he would be found at one of the coffee-houses favoured by the brisk fellows in the underworld of politics—at Tom's, or the British, or Diggory's by the Seven Dials. He might be heard of among the fire-eating Jacobites of Sam's. There were not so many likely places, but Harry laid down more pennies than he could spare at the bars, and all in vain.

He sat in Sam's on an afternoon chopping Greek tags with a jolly, fanatical old parson. The days were fast lengthening, and for one reason or another—the company at Sam's were not too fond of light—only a candle here and there was burning. A little man came in with a party very obsequious to him. As he walked up to the bar Harry had a glimpse of a lean, brown face. He remembered it and yet no more than faintly, and could not tell where he had seen it. It did not much engage him, and he went on with his Greek and his parson. The little man made some noise with the pretty girl behind the bar, claiming the privileges of an old friend and a good deal of liquor, and it was a little while before he was established at a table with his party. Harry chose to mouth out something Homeric and sounding. The little man stopped in the middle of lighting his pipe. "I know that roll, *pardieu!*"

he muttered, and in a florid fashion declaimed, "Fol de rol de row," and laughed alcoholically. "Who's talking Hebrew here?"

One of his party pointed out Harry and the parson. The little man blinked through the smoky twilight. He stood up, took his candle and lurched across the room to Harry. Down under Harry's nose he put the candle with a bang. Harry jerked back and glared at him, and he, rocking a little and blinking, said thickly, "It's a filthy likeness, after all, it is."

"No, sir, there's only one of me," said Harry. "If you see two, give God the glory and go to bed."

"I'm saying, bully, I'm saying," the little man's accent became more Caledonian and he clutched at Harry's shoulder. "I'm saying, my laddie—"

"Damme, that's what I complain of."

"I'm saying I do not like your complexion. It's yellow, my jo, it's a wee rotten orange, it is so." His company, a faithful tail, shook with laughter.

"Sleep it off, sir," says Harry, with a shrug.

"What's your will? Clip it off, do ye say so? Losh, you would have a face or two to spare. Eh, but I'm doubting you know too much o' clipping. There's clippit ears, and maybe you have a pair." He twitched Harry's bob wig awry; and with singular luck reeled out of the reach of Harry's answering blow. "Ay, and there's clippit shillings and maybe ye make your filthy living by their parings and shavings. Well a well, and there's clippit wings; and I'll clip yours, my bonny goose, the night." He clutched at the wig again and tossed it into the fire.

Harry sprang up and struck at him. He flung himself backwards into the arms of his friends and with a surprising adroitness plucked out his sword. "Have at ye, my man;" he giggled and made a pass.

"Easy, Captain," says one of his company. "The boy hath no sword."

"Oh ay, 'tis the Lord that's a man of war. The devil was aye for peace. Well, what ails ye not to lend the imp a bodkin?"

The fat old keeper of the coffee-house waddled into the midst. "Sure, Captain, you don't mean it. I would need to set my lads upon you. 'Tis disorderly homicide, indeed. Ye can't mean it. Not downstairs. I'll not deny there's the elegant parlour on the first floor."

"Ye're a canting old devil, Sam," says the little man. "But I'll oblige you. Come up, my bully, and I'll show you a thing."

"Here's for you, cully." One of the company thrust upon Harry a sword.

"Oh, by your leave,"—Harry waved it oft—"I don't fight a drunken man."

"Drunk!" the little man screamed. "Ods blades, there's a naughty way to mock a gentleman. I'll school you, bully; fou or fasting, I'll school you. What, you'll not lug out, like a bonny lad should? I jaloused it. I'm thinking you would take a beating like a lamb, laddie. Well a well. I'll be blithe to rub you down with an oaken towel. Here, Patrick, give us your staff."

"Oh, I see you must be let blood." Harry shrugged. "Well, sir, do I fight the whole platoon?"

"You're peevish, do you know, you're peevish. Here, Fraser, give him your hanger. Do you second the bairn, Donald? Come, Patrick, I'll have you. There's one for you and one for me, my man, and damn all favours."

It seemed to Harry that the little man's company were something surprised at this turn, but they took it in a disciplined silence. So the party of four marched up the stairs. You will believe that Harry liked the business ill enough. He shot glances at the two chosen for seconds. There was nothing sottish about them. They were very soberly alert, they had the tan and the vigour of open-air life. They looked anything but the fit comrades for a swashbuckling tavern hero. They were as stiff as pokers, they said not a word, they showed not a sign of interest in the affair—rather like two soldiers on guard than ready seconds in a drunken brawl. Once in the upper room they made their arrangements with solemn care, locking the door, clearing a sufficient space, and setting the candles so that the light fell fairly. Harry was taken aside, helped out of his coat, asked if he needed anything, gravely advised to risk nothing and play close.

"We are at your service, Mr. O'Connor," says Donald.

"At your pleasure, Mr. Mackenzie," says the other.

Harry was set against the little man and the swords crossed. It then occurred to him that the little man was very suddenly recovered from his liquor. The blustering chatter had been cut off as soon as they started up the stairs. Since then the little man had spoken not one word. Of the unsteadiness, the blinking, the rocking to and fro, nothing remained. He had marched to his place with a formal precision. There was the same manner, a correctness exact and staccato, about this sword play.

The knave can never have been drunk, Harry said to himself as he sweated and was the more embarrassed by bewilderment. But he dared not let himself think. The little man was urgently dangerous, and Harry knew enough to know it. Harry had no pretensions to science. All he could use was the rudiments. He had kept his head at singlestick, held his own with the foil against other lads, and never before faced a point. The little man had the speed and certainty of a *maitre d'armes*. So Harry fought, breathing hard, every muscle aching, mind numb and dazed under the strain, expecting—hoping—every moment the thrust that would make an end.

It did not come. The ache and fever of the fight went on and on. Still the little man was masterful and precise. Still he demanded all Harry's vigour and more than all, kept him struggling desperately, beset by fear on the edge of death. Harry felt himself weakening, faltering, and still the opposing blade searched his defence sharply, still the little man was an exemplar of easy precision. And yet Harry's maladroitness always sufficed to save his skin. He was puzzled, and blundered and fumbled the more. The play grew slower and slower, and he was the more tortured, enduring many times the shame and the pain of defeat.

At last he had hit upon the truth. He was wondering in a dazed fashion why that other sword seemed always to wait on him when he made a gross mistake. Visibly, palpably, the little man's blade halted to give him time for a parry. Harry dropped his point and gasped out, "Damme, sir, you are playing with me."

"What's your will? I fight my own way. At your convenience, sir."

"The Captain's within his right, sir," says Harry's solemn second.

"Damn you, for a pack of mountebanks!" Harry cried.

"On guard, sir," says the little man.

Harry gave him an oath and dashed at him. There was a moment's wild fighting and then the little man forced it back to order. They were at the old game again, precise scientific thrust, pause, and blundering parry, when to Harry's amazement the little man's sword wavered and flew from his hand.

Through a long minute Harry stood staring at him, and he waiting unarmed for Harry's thrust. Again Harry lowered his sword. At once the little man stooped and picked up his. "Do you demand to continue, Captain?" says his second.

"You're a fool, Patrick," quoth the little man.

The impenetrable second saluted and turned to his fellow. "Another bout, if you please, Mr. Mackenzie."

"Would you grant it, sir?" says Harry's solemn Scot.

"Egad, we are all mad here," Harry wiped his brow. "Oh, play it out to hell."

The little man saluted formally and again they engaged. And now Harry was enveloped in another kind of fighting. Scientific it might be, but science far beyond his understanding. The little man's point was everywhere upon him and he thrusting blindly at the air. He might have been pinked a score times over, he was for all he knew. And then on a sudden his own point touched something. Next moment it was struck up to the ceiling. Some one called out "A hit." He saw the two seconds standing between the swords and a red scratch on the little man's cheek.

"*Touché*," says he with a bow. "My compliments, if you please. It's some while since a man marked me. I am glad to know you, sir. Pray, what's your name?"

"Harry Boyce, sir."

"Egad, it's wonderful!" says the little man, with a laugh which appealed to Harry. "Hector McBean, at your service." Harry stared. "Aye, aye, I'm thinking we'll explain ourselves. Will you walk, sir?"

"If you please."

Captain McBean took his arm, said over his shoulder to the two seconds "To-morrow," and marched off with him. Once they were out in the street, "So you are Colonel Noll Boyce's son," says Captain McBean with an odd look.

"He has often told me so."

"If you had not such a look of him I wouldn't believe it. Oh, pardon, monsieur, *mille pardons, ma foi.* I have been insolent to you in all this affair. You'll please to observe that the whole of it, and the issue, is to your honour. Will I have to say more?"

"Oh Lud, no. Pray, let's talk sense."

"I take to you marvellously, *mon enfant.* Well now, have you heard of me?"

"Enough to want much more."

"What, has father been talking?"

"D'ye know where he is, Captain McBean?"

"I wish I did."

"So do I. It was Mr. Waverton who told the tale. Now you know why I am eager to hear what you can say of my father or my father of you."

"Are you a good son, Mr. Boyce?"

"I pay my debts."

"There's a crooked answer. Are you in the Colonel's secrets?"

"I have no reason to think so."

"I guess he did not trust you. I guess he was right. Do you remember where you met me first?"

"I remember that I can't remember."

"And me that thought I was a beauty! Well, but you were busy. You were making mud pies with Ben."

"I have it. You were his captain on the horse. Pray, sir, what was my Benjamin's mystery?"

"I am going to trust you, Mr. Boyce. I shall not require you to trust me unless you choose. I tell you frankly I hope for it. And so—come in with you."

They turned out of the Strand into Bow Street. Captain McBean let himself into a house, and took Harry up to a room very neat and cosy. "D'ye drink usquebaugh? A pity. It's the cleanest liquor. Well, draw up." He pushed a tobacco-box across the table. "That's right Spanish. Now, *mon cher*, are you Jacobite or Hanoverian?"

"I never could tell."

"Oh, look you, I ask no confidences. And I make no doubt of your honour. If you had a mind to play tricks you would have tried one on me to-night. Well, I have proved you. Your pardon again. But when I saw Noll Boyce's son lurking in Sam's, how could I know he was without guile? Now there is something I must say to you. But how much I say is a question. I have no desire to embarrass you with awkward knowledge. So which is your king, *mon enfant*, James or George?"

"I care not a puff of smoke for either."

"So. I suppose there is something you care for. Well—you asked about Ben's mystery. It's a good beginning. The rascal should have stopped the Duke of Marlborough's coach and held it till I came up with my fellows. Instead of which he went about some private thieving. I am your debtor for giving the knave his gruel. What's Marlborough to me? It's not his dirty guineas I was after, but his papers. He was then pretending to negotiate with St. Germain. There were those of us who doubted the old villain had some black design in his head again, and it was thought that if we could turn over his private papers, we should know where to have him. It was certified that he had with him something from his agents abroad. Well, we missed him, and how deep he is dipped in this business, I know no more than you.

"Now I come to your father, *mon enfant*, and I promise you I will be as delicate as I may. Do you know, *par exemple*, how Colonel Boyce is in the mouths of gentlemen?"

"Oh, sir, that's another of the matters for which I care nothing."

"*Tenez donc*. You were born old, I think. Well, Colonel Boyce has been in some few plots, devices, and manoeuvres. No man ever denied him wit, nor will I, *mordieu*. But it's his virtue that neither his friends nor his enemies were ever sure of him. I believe, Mr. Boyce, that if he heard me he would thank me for a compliment. *Bien*—I come back to my tale.

"It was known to us poor Jacobites in England that Colonel Boyce was making salutes to St. Germain. Which much intrigued us, for we would not, by your leave, have him of our side. They don't know him there as we do, and King James, God save him! is young and honourable and sanguine."

"Poor lad," says Harry with a shrug.

"You may keep your pity, Mr. Boyce," McBean said stiffly. "I would have him so, by your leave. Now we heard that letters went to St. Germain from Colonel Boyce full of windy promises—*verbosa et grandis epistola*. D'ye keep up your humanities?—in the name of my Lord Sunderland and my Lord Stair. Black names both. But they were vastly intrigued at St. Germain. If Sunderland and Stair were ready to turn honest, then *pardieu*, there was hope of the devil himself. Oh, I don't blame the King nor even Charles Middleton, though he is old enough to be slow. The times are changing, and maybe Stair and Sunderland they see it as well as we, and mean to find salvation. I can't tell. But the thing looked ill. Stair and Sunderland—there is no treachery too foul for those names. And if they meant honestly, why—saving your presence, *mon enfant*—why did they choose Colonel Boyce for their agent? It was no good warranty. So we adventured a counter. We have friends enough now in the Government, *mon cher*, and it was arranged that the Colonel should be arrested as a Jacobite. A good stroke, I think. It was mine. Only the old gentleman dodged it."

"Pray, what did you know of Mr. Waverton?"

"That sheep's-head!" McBean laughed. "Why, a letter came to hand in which the Colonel talked of taking the pretty gentleman to France. So he was joined in the warrant. *D'ailleurs*—it made a good appearance. However, we missed him; but we found something in his papers which made me queasy. So I e'en was off to France after him.

"The Colonel stayed at Pontoise and sent your Waverton off to St. Germain with a mighty plausible letter about secret proposals from the chiefs of the Whigs, which brought the King out to hear them secretly. *Ma foi*! I think Charles Middleton should have smelt a rat. But it was a clever trick, and to choose your Waverton to play it was masterly. For who could think that peacock would be in anything crafty? At Pontoise I tumbled in upon them, and your father, *mon cher*, he ran off on sight of me. Observe, I press nothing against him. I allow that the best evidence I have against him is just that—he ran away when he saw me. Secondly, he had with him some three-four rascals whose faces would hang them. And thirdly and lastly, beloved brethren, these fellows, when put to it and charged with a plot to murder King James, were frightened for their lives and babbled wildly, of which the sum was that they had been brought but to kidnap him. I grant ye, they may have lied, and I would not hang a dog (who was not a Whig) upon their word. But confess, *mon cher*, the thing is black enough. What did the Colonel want with King James alone? Why did he need his bullies? Why did he run away? I leave it with you."

Harry knocked out his pipe. "I am obliged for the story, sir. Why did you tell it?"

"You have a cold blood in you, *mon enfant*" says Captain MacBean. "Observe, I look for nothing wonderful from you. I allow your position is very difficult to a man of honour. And with all my heart—"

"Oh Lud, sir, let's have nothing pathetic."

"Aye, aye," McBean bowed. "Mr. Boyce! I do profess I feel the delicacy of the affair, and I detest it, *pardieu*. But I dare not absolve ye from your duty."

"Oh, sir, you are very sublime."

"Hear me out, Mr. Boyce. I have shown you cause to fear that your father has it in mind to compass a vile treachery, perhaps a murder. Would you deny it?"

"Damme, sir, I am not the day of judgment."

"*Bien*. I believe that is an answer. I declare to you there is yet a chance that he may succeed, aye, here in London."

Harry swore. "If your friends must go walking into traps what is it to me?"

"Well, sir, though you will own no loyalty to king or queen or country, I'll not be deceived. I call on you for your aid. It's believed your father is in London. It is likely he will seek you out, as he did before. Maybe at this hour you know where he is."

"If I did, should I betray him to you, sir?"

"I ask no treachery. But I do call on you, discover his purpose if you can, and if he intends violence to the King, prevent it. Lord, sir, it's to save your father from infamy, and your own name."

"The King? The Pretender is in London?" Harry cried.

"I told you that I should trust you far, Mr. Boyce."

Harry stared at him, and after a moment stood up. "I can do nothing," he said. "It is of all things most unlikely that I should do anything. For what I know, my father is dead. He has been nothing else to me all my life. But I believe I should thank you."

"Well!" quoth McBean. "God help you. I ha' drawn a bow at a venture. I think I have hit something, Mr. Boyce."

XXI

Consolations by a Father

Do you remember how frightened Swift was of the Mohocks? How he came home early, and even (that was bitter) spent some pence on being carried in a sedan chair to avoid the "race of rakes that play the devil about this town every night, slit people's noses," and so forth? He had some reason to fear.

> *"Was there a Watchman took his hourly rounds*
> *Safe from their blows or new invented wounds"*

in these last days of Queen Anne? Their way was to gather and take plenty of liquor, "then make a general sally and attack all that are so unfortunate as to walk the streets through which they patrol. Some are knocked down, others stabbed, others cut and carbonadoed." The women would be turned upside down or clapped into barrels and rolled over the stones.

It was a dark night with but a glimpse of the new moon when Harry left Captain McBean. From Bow Street to the "Hand of Pork" in Long Acre was only a few hundred yards, but murky enough, and Harry took Mr. Gay's advice for such night walking:

> *"Let constant Vigilance thy footsteps guide,*
> *And wary Circumspection guard thy side."*

Nevertheless, as he was coming by the corner into Long Acre, he was surprised by a sound at his heels. He stepped quickly aside and turned upon it, felt a blow upon his head, saw flashes of light and the street, whirling round, rose up to meet him, and he knew no more.

When he came to himself he was in a room with fire and lights. He raised himself and heard voices. Then some one was standing over him. He looked up into his father's face. "Who was that?" he said feebly.

"Don't you see yet, Harry? It will soon pass off."

"Lord, I know you. Who are the others?"

"There is none here but me," said Colonel Boyce.

Harry looked painfully round the room and saw that it had become empty. "What was it? A pistol?" said he, and began to feel his head.

"Egad, nothing so gentlemanly. A cudgel, by the look of the bruise. A Mohock's club, I suppose. I found you lying in the kennel as I was coming home."

"Oh, you're at home are you?" Harry laughed stupidly. "And where is home?"

"These are my lodgings in Martin's Lane, Harry, and you are welcome. But what have you to do in town? Young husbands should not be night walkers."

Harry stared at him for a moment. "I thought you knew everything," he said. Then, beginning to scramble up, he became aware that his clothes were all undone—coat, shirt, even breeches. "Odso, why were you stripping me?"

"I found you so. They shave you close, the Mohocks."

"They are a queer crew, your Mohocks." Harry looked at his father. "What should I carry inside my shirt?" Then he thrust his hands into his pockets. "Well, I had not much, but all's gone."

"Damned rogues," said his father with honest indignation. "How much have you lost, Harry?"

"Five guineas or so."

"I can make that good at least. But what is it to you? You are a warm fellow now. What, you've made no hole in Madame Alison's money bags yet."

"You're offensive, do you know?" Harry said. "I have been itching to tell you so."

Colonel Boyce's face set. "What now? Are you against me, sirrah?"

"Ods fish, you're a martyr, ain't you?" Harry laughed. But we are beginning at the end, I think. If you remember, sir, you promised to take me to France and went off without me."

"D'ye quarrel with that? Why, you had a fatter fish to fry than you could catch with me. So I left you at her and you ha' dined upon her. What's the matter then?"

"You were not honest with me—"

Colonel Boyce laughed, "Ah, bah, you will be a Puritan. It must be your mother in you."

"My mother! Thank you. We'll come to her. But one tale at a time. You let me think I was to go with you till you were gone without me. You took Waverton and told me nothing of that till you had him safe away."

"Egad, boy, it was all for your good."

"Perhaps you did think so," said Harry after a moment. "In fact it's what I complain of. You want to play Providence to me. Pray, sir, go about your business."

Colonel Boyce shrugged. "You're a proper grateful son. So be it. You have your wealthy wench and want no more of me. Well, go to the devil your own way, Harry."

"By your leave, I prefer it. But there's more, sir. Now comes Mr. Waverton and declares to my wife and me that you enticed him into a vile plot: for your pretence of a mission to the Pretender was nothing but a device for murder."

"Mr. Waverton said that to Mrs. Harry Boyce? Egad, it wasn't civil of Mr. Waverton. And what did the lady say to him?"

"That's no matter. What do you say to him, sir? Did you intend murder?"

"Lud, Harry, you talk like a ranting parson. It was not your way. Who has put this buzz of morality into your head? I suppose your pretty wife would have you break with your father. He's a low, coarse fellow, faith, who might want some of her money."

"We will leave my wife out, if you please. She will not trouble you. She and I have parted."

"God's my life! What's the quarrel?"

Harry shrugged. "Does one ever know? I was not good enough for her, I believe. And perhaps she was not good enough for me."

"Damn you for a prig," says his father.

"If you like. But you'll remark that I do not complain of her."

"Bah, you make me sick, sir! Not complain of her! That luscious piece! Egad, you should be drunk with her. But you're not a man, Harry, you're a parson."

"Oh, command your emotions! She rebelled against being wed to a man whose father ran about the world compassing murder, to a man who was withal a low fellow, a bastard. So far, it is your affair."

"I see you are no hand with a woman."

"Do I take after you, sir? We came upon a woman who said she was Mrs. Oliver Boyce and could not live with him, and boasted vehemently that she was no mother of mine."

Colonel Boyce plucked at his mouth. "So dear Rachel has got her finger into the pie. Why, Harry, you have had no luck."

"She is your wife, then. Oh, I admire your taste, sir. And pray, who was my mother?"

Colonel Boyce began to say something and stopped. "It's no matter. I believe she would not wish you to know. Why, Harry, I profess I am sorry. If we had been married, better for us all."

"Oh, you will be mysterious still. I suppose you are as tender of her honour as of mine or your own. And this matter of murdering the Pretender, pray, is that a mystery too?"

Colonel Boyce became restless. "Ods life, sirrah, there is no matter of murder. Who told you so? The fool Waverton. And where did he get the tale?"

"A gentleman who runs away tells his own tale."

"Now mark, Harry. The plan was but to bring Prince James to England—"

"Dead or alive," Harry laughed.

"Pshaw. I had him at Pontoise and was doing well with him. Then in comes a swashbuckling Scots Jacobite which is my private enemy, and a dozen bullies at his tail. Well, I had no mind to have him stick me or turn me over to the French as a spy of Marlborough's, so I went off. The fool Waverton let himself be taken. I make no doubt the Scot filled him to the brim with slanders of me. But is that my fault?"

"So you're done with the Pretender?"

Colonel Boyce gave his son a queer look. "Why, there's not much to be done with him in Martin's Lane, boy."

"Then what are you doing?"

"Egad, Harry, I should think you want to lay an information against me. Waiting for better times is all my business now. My bolt's shot. And pray, sirrah, what may be your business now you've cut loose from Mrs. Alison?"

Harry laughed. "Living on my means."

"Why, does she settle something on you?"

Harry looked at his father without affection. "Do you know, sir, I am not always proud of your name."

"Egad, but you must have money somehow."

"The family motto, I suppose. Well, sir, I write for the Press."

"Good God, not for the newspapers? You have not fallen to that?"

"Oh, sir, the shillings are clean by comparison."

They looked at each other for a minute or two. "You walk abroad late, Mr. Author," says Colonel Boyce. "Do you make friends in your profession?"

"I believe I have two in the town—a hack writer for Lintot and an usher at Westminster. And what then, pray?"

"You were with them to-night?"

"You are paternal on a sudden, sir. Do you think of putting me out to nurse again?"

"So." Colonel Boyce stood up as if he had finished and then forced a laugh and slapped his son's shoulder, "Come, Harry, why quarrel? There's room enough for you here. I allow I owe you something. Join in with me."

"I have no luck in mysteries, sir. I'll wish you goodnight."

"Now you bear me a grudge," his father protested.

"What, for getting me born? Sometimes, perhaps."

"Egad, Harry, I should like to do something for you."

"Then give me a sword."

"A sword? And what for i' God's name?"

"In case I meet any more of your Mohocks."

Colonel Boyce was taken aback for a moment. Then he cried out heartily: "Damme, the rogues took five guineas from you too. Here, fill your purse, child." He shot out gold on the table.

"I'll take back my five guineas," said Harry, and counted them, while his father watched with a frown.

"There are swords of mine below," said Colonel Boyce.

They went down and from a rack of arms Harry chose a plain black hanger with an agate hilt. As he did it on he saw below it some heavy staves loaded with lead—just such as the Mohocks used.

"And where do you lodge?" says Colonel Boyce.

"At the 'Hand of Pork' in Long Acre. Goodbye, sir."

Colonel Boyce nodded, and for some time after he had gone stood at the door, watching.

XXII

Two's Company

Alison was gone back to her house at Highgate—and immediately regretted it. She took her adventures in a youthful, egoistic fashion: saw herself as a lovely woman made the prey of man and robbed of her right to her own life, a tender, confiding soul deceived and tortured into despair. The Lincoln's Inn Fields became the abomination of desolation, her fine society was dust and ashes and mankind in general all mocking villainy. So it was natural that she should retire from the world and become a recluse of tragic dignity. What other part is there for the deserted wife to play?

But she came upon awkward difficulties. The world would not be left behind. It was much more closely about her among the woods and meadows of Highgate than in her London drawing-room. The would-be fine ladies and gentlemen of her routs and her card parties, so the sweetmeats and the wines and strong waters were good enough, cared nothing whether she had a husband upstairs or somewhere else. Out in the country every one, gentle and simple, had a curious eye upon her. The very woods and meadows must be jogging her memory and putting her questions. Every one had known Miss Lambourne of the Hall and gone whispering about her strange, passionate marriage. Each pleasant path and lane had seen something of that first wild happiness. All day long she was driven back upon herself and what she had lost.

There is no doubt that she suffered. Of course she still told her heart wonderful tales about the shame that she had to bear and her torturing wrongs, and beyond doubt she believed most of them. For she could still profess to herself a miserable degradation in being married to a man of no name: she would be gloomily convinced that Harry was by his father's villainy a proven knave. But what hurt her most was the growing suspicion that she was much to blame for her own plight. Alison Lambourne, who acknowledged no law but her own will, who had never dreamed that she could be wrong in her desires, driven to confess a ruinous blunder! Imagine her distress. At first she chose to pretend that she had been overthrown by passion. The more she tried to despise Harry, the more that fancy shamed her. But there was in her a strength which refused to be content with that. She would still boast to herself that she was not the woman to be swept away by a gust of longing for the man who chanced to take her eye. And so she brought down on herself the inexorable question—if Harry were man enough to wake passion in her and deserve her magnificence, why had she driven him off? For all her selfishness and her insolent pride, she had a vehement desire, a part perhaps of her very pride in her womanhood, to owe him nothing, to play him fair, to give him all that a man could ask. Little by little she forced herself to believe that she had failed of that. After all, he had offered her nothing but himself, poor, friendless, of no repute, indolent, careless of all the world—and she had professed content. What his father might do was no matter to that. He had offered her what he was and given it faithfully. And she had not played fair. When she found herself confessing that, she discovered a new power of being wretched. All the romantic, egoistic melancholy went down the wind. The finest, proudest of her, her own honour, told of a torturing wound.

"I'll satisfy you"—that had been the boast before the wild marriage was done. And after all she had chosen to deny him. Nothing else could matter. There could be no excuse. It was he that she had taken, not his name or what he might be, and he had not changed. It was herself that she had promised—what other honour for woman or man than to give like for like?—and she had broken faith. She was humiliated—a state of all others the most dolorous for Alison.

To it came on a merry spring day Mr. Waverton. She was in two minds whether to let him see her, and then—too proud to hide from him or greedy of a chance to hurt him—had him in.

Mr. Waverton had decorated himself for a house of mourning. His large form was all black and silver and drooped sympathetically. His handsome face was set in a chastened melancholy as of one who grieves for another's trouble with a modest satisfaction. "Dear lady," says he tenderly, and bowed over her hand.

"Dear Geoffrey," says she. "Here's a new song."

"Madame?"

"'Vengeance is mine' was the refrain last time. Now it's weeping over the penitent prodigal. How I love you, Geoffrey."

Mr. Waverton made a gesture of emotion, an exclamation. "I wronged you, Alison," he said in a deep voice. "Nay, but you must forgive me. I have suffered too. Remember! I had lost all."

"Ah, no," says Alison tragically, "you had still yourself, Geoffrey."

His emotion was understood to be too much for Mr. Waverton. In a little while, "We have both been the sport of villainy," he said. "Forgive me, Alison. I remember that I spoke bitterly. Can you wonder? I had dreamed of you in his arms. To see you there in that knave's power—ah, I was beside myself. And he laughed, do you remember, he laughed!"

"He never would take you to heart, in fact."

"A treacherous hound!" said Mr. Waverton with startling vehemence.

"Oh, he was honest when he laughed."

Mr. Waverton swept Harry out of the conversation. "Forgive me, Alison, I should have known. My heart should have told me."

"Oh Lud, and is your heart to give tongue now?"

"My heart," said Mr. Waverton with dignity, "my heart is always crying to you. And now—now that the first agony is past, I know all."

"I wish I did," said Alison and looked in his eyes.

"But even then—ah, Alison, I have blamed myself cruelly—even then I should have known that when your eyes were opened, when you knew the truth, you would have no more of him."

"You might have known," Alison said slowly. "You might have judged me by yourself."

"Aye, that indeed," says Mr. Waverton heartily. "For we are very like, Alison, we are of the same spirit, you and I."

"You make me proud."

"It's our tragedy: we so like, so made to answer each other, should be betrayed to our ruin by this same vile trickster. Oh, I blame you no more than myself."

"This is too generous."

"No," says Mr. Waverton. "No. When I came on that woman of yours, that Mrs. Weston—faith, I am glad that you have cut her off too. I never liked that woman."

"Yes, she is poor."

"There it is! I doubt she was in Boyce's pay."

Alison opened her eyes at him. "Oh, Geoffrey, you surpass yourself to-day. Go on, go on."

"If you please," says Mr. Waverton, something ruffled. "I believe he hired her to play his game with you. Had you a suspicion of it when you sent her packing?"

"By God, Geoffrey, I could suspect anyone when you talk to me."

"She is bitter against you. When I heard from her that you had driven the fellow away from you, I was on fire to come to you."

"To forgive the prodigal! Oh, your nobility, Geoffrey. And pray where did you meet Mrs. Weston?"

"Why, in the High Street here. She lodges in one of those wretched cottages behind the street."

"She is here?" Alison shivered a little.

"Perhaps she has some game to play yet. She may be his spy. Be warned against her."

Alison leant forward in her chair. Her face was hidden from him. "You are giving me a lesson, Geoffrey. I'll profit by it, I promise you!"

"Alison!" Mr. Waverton gave a laugh of triumph. "I fight for us both. And I promise you I am eager enough. As soon as I learnt that you had left him, why, he was delivered into my hand. By heaven, he shall find no mercy now. Already I have him watched. I went to an attorney much practised in these treasonous cheating plots, and of him I have hired trusty fellows who know all the rogues in London and their hiding-holes. You said something?"

But Alison was laughing.

"I believe there is some humour in it," Mr. Waverton conceded grandly. "Well, they have tracked him down. Our gentleman lies at a filthy tavern in the Long Acre. The 'Leg of Pork,' or some such lewd name. He haunts Jacobite coffeehouses and the like low places. They believe that he makes some dirty money by scribbling for the Press. A writer in the newspapers! He is sunk almost to his right depth. They make no doubt that before long we shall catch him dabbling in some new treasonous matter. And then—" he made gestures of doom.

"Well? And then?"

"The law may revenge us on the treacherous rogue," said Mr. Waverton with majesty.

Alison stood up. Mr. Waverton, always polite, started up too. "I give you joy, Geoffrey," she said very quietly.

"Not yet! Not yet!" Mr. Waverton put up a modest hand.

"I believe there is nothing you could feel." Mr. Waverton recoiled and stared his bewilderment. "You carry a sword, Geoffrey. Oh, that I were a man!"

"To use it upon him! Bah, such rogues are not worth the honour of steel."

"Oh! Honour! Honour!" she cried and flung out her arms, trembling. "The honour of you and me!"

What was Mr. Waverton to make of that? "I believe I have excited you," says he.

"By God, it is the first time," Alison cried and turned on him so fiercely that he started back.

There was a servant at the door saying something which went unheard. Then Susan Burford came into the room, an odd contrast in her placid simplicity to the amazed magnificence of Mr. Waverton or Alison's tremulous, furious beauty. Alison was turned away from her and too much engaged to hear or be aware of her.

"Here is Miss Burford," said Waverton in a hurry.

Alison whirled upon her. "You! You have nothing to do here."

"My dear Alison!" Waverton protested. "Miss Burford, your very obedient."

Susan made him a small leisurely curtsy and sat down. "Oh, please give me a dish of tea," she said.

"We have not seen you at Tetherdown in this long while," Mr. Waverton complained genially.

"I believe not," says Susan.

Alison stared at her. "Why do you come here? You know you despise me."

"I do not come to people I despise," says Susan placidly.

"Well. I am private with dear Geoffrey, if you please."

"My dear Alison! I must be riding. We have finished our business, I think. I'll not fail to be with you again soon. I hope to have news for you. Miss Burford, your most obedient." Susan bent her head. "Alison—" he held out his hand and smiled at her protective affection.

"Geoffrey," said Alison, and looked in his eyes. She did not take the hand. She was very pale.

Mr. Waverton's smile was withered. He took himself out with a jauntiness that sat upon him awkwardly.

Then Alison turned again upon Susan. "You want to know what I have to do with him?" she said fiercely.

"No," says Susan.

Alison stared at the fair, placid face and cried out: "You are a fool."

"Oh, my dear," says Susan.

"I hate that cold, flabby way of yours. You think it is all good and wise and kind. It's like a silly mother with a spoilt child. You've not spirit enough to scold, and all the while you are thinking me vile and base and mean."

"But that is ridiculous. Nobody could think you mean," Susan said.

"There it is again. You believe it is kind to talk so, and it drives me mad. I am shameful—do you hear? I am shameful and perhaps I want to be, and I loathe myself. Now, go. I shall not stay with you. Go."

Susan stood up. "Alison, oh, Alison," she said. Alison flung out of the room.

XXIII

The House in Kensington

L ate in that evening one of Alison's servants rode up to the "Hand of Pork" and inquired for Mr. Boyce. After some parley, he was told that Mr. Boyce had not been in the tavern that day. So he left a letter in the tap and rode back to Highgate.

That letter, which was not heard of till long afterwards, ran thus:

> Mr. Boyce,
>   I desire that you would come to me at Highgate. I have to-day heard from Geoffrey Waverton what you must instantly know. And the truth is, I cannot be content till I speak with you. But I would not have you come for this my asking. Pray believe it is urgent for us both that we meet, and I do require it of you, not desiring of you what you may have no mind to, but to be honest with you, and lest that should befall which I hope you would not have me bear.
>
>   A.

An ungainly, confused composition, as you see, but it set forth very clearly the state of Alison's unhappy mind. She was revolted, of course, by Geoffrey's scheme of spying and trapping, loathed him for propounding it to her, and was eager to warn Harry against it and clear herself of any part in the vile business. But she would not have Harry suppose that she was praying him to come back to her. This time, at least, there should be no wooing on her side. If she wanted him hungrily, shamefully, he should not know till he chose to take her. But he must come to her and be told all the tale, and hold her free of any part in Geoffrey's baseness.

So she fought with herself and wrote of her strife, and, as things went, it mattered nothing to Harry, for he never knew of it till much else had happened.

When he woke on the morning after his affairs with Captain McBean and the Mohocks and his father—woke with a sore head and a very stiff shoulder, he was a prey to puzzled excitement. There is no doubt that McBean had engaged his affections. He was not, indeed, very grateful for the fantastic duel. Of all men, Harry Boyce was the least likely to be pleased by oddity or an extravagance of chivalry. He always thought, I believe, that Captain McBean was a little mad, and liked him none the better for it. But he confessed that with the madness there was allied a most persuasive mind, a very reasonable reason. The combination may not be so surprising to you as to Harry Boyce. He thought that McBean's exposition of the affair of his father, and his consequent duty, was exactly and delicately true—which means, of course, that it agreed with his own temper. He had no more doubt than McBean that his father had planned, was planning, treachery which, win or lose, would disgrace him. He admitted that it was his own wretched duty to do what he might to make an end of these plans.

You smile, perhaps, at Harry Boyce claiming for himself the commands of duty. He was eminently not a saint. He was not delicate. And yet, thrust upon an awkward choice, it is certain that he chose what must be difficult, hazardous, and distressing, rather than stand aloof and let his father's villainy go its way.

I make no pretence of exalting him into a tragic fellow. He had no affection for his father, no respect. Merely to work against his father's will, to smash his father's schemes, would certainly not have cost him one twinge. He had no hate for his father either, not the least ambition to ruin him or make him suffer. But he would heartily have liked to bring these murderous plots to nothing and yet save his father from vengeance. Harry had his share of the common human instinct to keep one's family out of mischief—or at least out of the newspapers.

And it is not to be denied that there was also active in him a simple human animosity. He bore his father a grudge for being publicly a knave: a man who had received nothing from his parents but the gift of birth might fairly demand that they should not bother him with their rogueries. He did not extenuate his father's share in the catastrophe of the marriage. Perhaps it was in itself fated to miscarry, but if Colonel Boyce had not mixed up his affairs with it, the end need not have been ignominious. Harry vigorously condemned the old gentleman's meddling. It was an impertinence at the best to manipulate other folks, and a father who did it so stupidly as Colonel Boyce was a pestilent nuisance. But all this, I believe, rankled less than the behaviour of Colonel Boyce on the night before. If the old gentleman had acknowledged his offences, if he had even been content to talk of them frankly, man to man, he might have been forgiven. But his affectation of profound wisdom, his patronage, and above all, his parade of mystery infuriated Harry's lucid mind.

It sought further causes of offence and had no difficulty in finding them. Everything about that conversation was suspicious. For how did it begin? With a broken head, with every button of his clothes torn open as though he had just been searched to the skin, he woke up in his father's presence. The father might pose as a good Samaritan who had come upon a sufferer by the wayside, but he should not have shown so nervous an anxiety to know what the sufferer had been about. The father talked of Mohocks; but what Mohocks were these who knocked a man down before making sport of him and, not content with taking his money, went through all his clothes? Why was a Mohock's club lying there beneath the father's swords? Harry made a ready guess at the riddle. His father must have fellows watching McBean's house. They had knocked him down to search him for papers. Then the father must have known that he had been with McBean, and those anxious questions were to discover how much he was McBean's friend. Colonel Boyce must have a lively interest in the affairs of McBean—and yet he professed that he had now nothing in hand. What if he knew of the secret of the Pretender's coming to London? What if he was still seeking a chance to accomplish his plot of murder?

Well, Captain McBean expected no less of him. Captain McBean was in the right of it. It became a good son's duty to confound his father's politics. There's no denying that Harry went into the business with zest.

While he ate his breakfast in the taproom, he caught sight of a fellow lurking about outside. Whose spy this was is, in fact, not certain. Afterwards Colonel Boyce vehemently denied that he had commissioned any man against Harry. Though you may not believe him, it is possible that the fellow was one of those in Waverton's pay. Harry made no doubt that his father was the offender.

He went upstairs again and put a book in his pocket. (He had been commissioned for a translation of Ovid, which, let us be thankful, never came into print.) Thus characteristically provided, he went out to baffle the spy and the father. In the courts between Drury Lane and Bow Street he did some ingenious marching and counter-marching whereby—he was always confident and we cannot be quite sure—the spy was shaken off. He then came into St. Martin's Lane by the north end, and dodging in and out of it more than once, made for a tavern close to his father's lodging. He planted himself inside by a window, called for a tankard and a pipe, and divided his attention between the Tristia and his father's door across the lane.

It soon appeared that Colonel Boyce was to have a busy morning. By ones and twos a dozen men went into his house. They were not, even to Harry's hostile eye, brazenly ruffians. Something of the bully they might have about them, for they ran to brawn and swagger, but they were trim enough and brisk, and had no smack of debauch—a company of old soldiers, by the look of them, and still not past their prime. They were with Colonel Boyce a long time, and Harry grew very sick of the Tristia, and had to drink more beer over it than was his habit of a morning.

They came out at last singly, and yet with very short intervals between them. They all turned the same way—across Leicester Fields. There seemed to Harry something so uncommon in this that he was moved to follow. He made his way out by the back door and the tavern yard. As he came into Leicester Fields, he saw that the units had already amalgamated into three companies. They were all steadily marching westward. Keeping behind a cart he followed them, and after a while bought for twopence a lift in an empty hay wagon. I record all this because he seems to have been very proud of it, which is characteristic of his simple nature. The hay wagon rumbled him past two companies of them halted and coalescing at an inn. The first still headed him at a good round pace all the way to Kensington.

The wagon was going through Kensington village when he saw that this vanguard too had found an inn. A little farther on he abandoned his wagon and, buying bread and cheese at a farm, made his dinner under the hedge. It was a long while before he saw anything more of the gentlemen of the inn, and lying among primroses and cowslips he nearly forgot all about them and his excitement and his wonderful tactics. He was, in fact, becoming sentimental, and had made three neat hendecasyllabics to the cowslips when the gentlemen came out again. They split into pairs and marched on briskly. Harry went through the hedge, and from behind it he watched them pass. Then, as now, the road ran straight, and it was not safe to come out and follow them till they were far ahead. While he waited he heard more tramping, and in a little while the rest of the company went by. He peeped out after them and saw an odd thing: though the road ran straight for a mile or more, the first party had vanished already.

Harry climbed a tree. It was some little time before he discovered the lost party. They had scattered, they had taken to the fields and, under hedges, they were making southward. The rest of the company did likewise. Soon he saw what they were after. There was a lane running from the high road towards Fulham. A little way back from it, in a good garden, stood a house of modest comfort, doubtless the place to which some gentleman about town came for his pleasures or a breath of fresh air. About its grounds the company went into hiding.

Harry came down from his tree in a hurry and, like an honest man, took to the high road. It was, you know, his one uncommon capacity to go easily at a round pace. He did his best along the road and down the lane and, though he caught a glimpse of a coat here and there, unchallenged he came up the drive and across the garden to the door of the house. He had hardly knocked before he was being inspected through a peep-hole. The door was opened and instantly shut behind him. He was in darkness dimly lit by one candle. The windows had their shutters closed and barred.

"What's your will, sir?" says the man who let him in.

"The master of the house, if you please," Two other men lounged into the hall.

"And your name, sir?"

"You may say that I came from Captain McBean."

The man appeared to think it over. "That's true enough, faith," says another, advancing out of the shadow. Harry recognised one of the solemn seconds of the duel, Patrick O'Connor. "Will I serve your turn, sir?"

"If you're master here."

"I am not. Come on now." He led the way to a room where a cadaverous man, richly dressed, sat huddled over a fire. "'Tis a gentleman from the captain, my lord. Mr. Boyce, my Lord Sale."

Harry bowed. My lord yawned. "You've a devil of a name, Mr. Boyce," says he.

"I deplore it, and hope to disgrace it."

"Is it possible?" said my lord, and yawned again.

"I had the honour to tell you, my lord, that I answer for the gentleman," says Mr. O'Connor.

"You may endorse the devil, if you please," my lord sneered.

Harry struck in, "I came to tell you, my lord, that your house is watched, and by now surrounded."

"Damn them, they have found it out, have they?" says my lord, and spread out his lean hands to the fire.

"How many, if you please?" says O'Connor.

"A dozen or so. They marched out this morning, scattered, and met again in the village and came here across country. They are well-armed, I believe, and look men who would fight."

"Ods fish, that nets this hole," says my lord. "Pray, Mr. Boyce, when will they put the ferret in?" Harry shrugged. "Oh, there's a limit to your kindness, is there? Do you choose to tell us who sent them?"

Harry was silent a moment and then blurted out: "They came from Colonel Boyce's lodging."

My lord laughed.

"Sure, 'tis an honour to know you, sir," says O'Connor, and bowed to Harry.

"Damned filial, indeed," my lord chuckled.

O'Connor turned upon him. "They have you beat easily, my lord," he said fiercely. "Damned courageous indeed." But my lord only nodded at him. "What, we be six—to count Mr. Boyce. Sure, we could hold the house against the devil's christening."

There came in briskly a tall fellow crying: "Come, Sale, it's full time, I believe."

My Lord Sale got on his feet, "Stap me, sir, I believe not," he drawled. "We must stay at home. They have smoked us. Here's a gracious youth come to tell us that his Whiggish friends beset the house."

The Pretender frowned and seemed slow to understand. Harry looked him over. He was certainly a fine figure of a man, and bore himself gallantly enough. His face was darkly handsome in a melancholy fashion, not unlike the youth of his uncle, Charles II. He turned upon Harry. "What is all this, sir?"

"Oh, sir, it's that old rogue Noll Boyce," my lord put in. "And here's his son betraying the father."

"Faith, my lord, I'll remind you of that," O'Connor said. "Sir, the gentleman is an honest gentleman."

"Colonel Boyce—he is your father, sir?" the Pretender bent his black brows over Harry.

"He begot me, he says." Harry shrugged. "I desire to defend you from him. He has surrounded your house here with a dozen sturdy knaves who intend you, I believe, the worst."

"I am obliged by your service, sir," says the Pretender coldly. "Pray, my lord, is the coach ready?"

My lord shook his head. "I don't advise it, sir. The good Mr. Boyce cannot be lying. Or allow the knaves mean but to frighten you. I dare not risk your person."

"Dare? You dare too much, my lord, who command neither my person nor my honour. I do not thank you for your advice. You will have the coach brought instantly."

"I ask your pardon, sir, and beg you to consider. What will the world say of me if I let you run into a gang of murderers? We can maintain the house against them till our friends come seeking us. In the open we are outnumbered desperately. Nay, sir, be advised; what is to lose by waiting? If you go, you grasp at a shadow and may throw away your life for it."

"I say, my lord, I do not thank you for your care of me, which is careless of my honour and your own. I am promised to our friends. Do you desire me to go afoot, my lord?"

"I have done, sir." My lord bowed and went out.

"Sir, I believe they will not spare you," says Harry.

"I have heard you," the Pretender said haughtily, and waved him away.

"I'll not be put off so." The Pretender turned upon him. "Sir, I have done what I could to save your life from a base plot. If it succeeds, the shame of it must fall upon me and my name, for it's my cursed father that planned it. And you choose to run upon the danger. I entreat you, do me right. Your blood should not be upon my head."

"You have done your duty, Mr. Boyce," the Pretender bowed. "I thank you. But I must do mine."

"Why, faith, sir, 'tis the right principle of war to wait the rogues here," says O'Connor. "You will not?"

"Go to, man, I say it again and again."

For the first time in their acquaintance, Harry saw Mr. O'Connor smile. "I have the honour to take your orders, sir. But sure, we are not at the end of our tactics. I'll presume to advise you. Let the coach come to the door, and me and the other gentlemen will make some display of mounting her and guarding her; she moves off slowly; it's any odds the rogues will believe we have you with us and deliver their main attack, while you'll be mounting quietly in the yard with my lord and ride off with him to Kensington."

"The plan is well enough. Have it so," said the Pretender carelessly.

O'Connor went out in a hurry and Harry followed him. "I'll join you, if you please, Mr. O'Connor."

O'Connor laughed. "Oh, your servant, your servant. No offence, Mr. Boyce. I profess I have an admiration for you. But, faith, you are not a man of war. Do you go round to the stable-yard, now, and watch there to see they prepare nothing against us from the back." He bustled off, calling up his fellows.

So Harry, with a long face, I suppose, drifted away to the back of the house. The coach was already moving out of the yard, and he saw no sign of his father's legion. In a moment the groom, with one of O'Connor's men to help him, was busy again in the stable. Still the legion did not reveal themselves. O'Connor's man ran back into the house, leaving two horses saddled in the stable. Then the Pretender and my lord hurried out, and the horses were brought to meet them. As they mounted, Harry heard the clatter of the coach and then pistols and shouts, and the clash of fighting.

The Pretender spurred off, my lord taking the lead of him through the gate. As they passed, a shot was fired out of the hedge. My lord swayed, fumbling at his holsters, and crying out: "Ride on, sir, ride," fell from the saddle. His foot was caught in the stirrup, and the frightened horse dragged him along the ground.

Harry ran up and snatched the bridle. "How is it with you, my lord?"

"I have enough, I believe," my lord gasped. "Damme, sir, don't fumble at me. Mount and after him."

So Harry went bumping in the saddle after the Pretender.

XXIV

Queen Anne is Dead

The Pretender looked over his shoulder as Harry came up. "Where is he hit?"

"He has it in the body and he suffers."

The Pretender muttered something. "I bring ill-luck to my friends, you see. Best ride off, Mr. Boyce."

"You can do me no harm, sir. God knows if I can do you any good."

The Pretender looked at him curiously. "I think you are something of my own temper. In effect, there is little to hope with me."

"Who knows?" Harry shrugged. "*Par exemple,* sir, do you know where we are going now?"

"This is a parable, *mordieu*! I leave my friends to be shot for me and die, perhaps, while I ride off and know not the least of my way."

"Egad, sir, you were in enough of a hurry to go somewhere." Harry reined up. "Am I to be trusted in the affair?"

The Pretender amazed Harry by laughing—a laugh so hearty and boyish that he seemed another man from the creature of stiff, pedantic melancholy.

"Oh Lud, Mr. Boyce, don't scold. You might be a politician. Tell me, where is this damned palace?"

"Kensington, sir? Bear to the left, if you please."

So they swung round, and soon hitting upon a lane saw the village and the trees about the palace. In a little while, "Mr. Boyce: how much do you know?" the Pretender said; and still he was more the boy than the disinherited king.

"Egad, sir, no more than I told you: that my father had bullies watching for you."

"And I believe I have not thanked you."

It was Harry's turn to laugh. "Faith, sir, you ought to be grateful to the family of Boyce."

"I shall not forget."

"He takes care that you shall remember him, my honourable father."

"I do not desire repartees, Mr. Boyce. Come, sir, you carry yourself too proudly. You are not to disdain what you have done, or yourself."

Harry bowed,—permitted himself, I suppose, some inward ironic smile,—he was not born with reverence, and the royal airs of this haughty, gloomy lad had no authority over him. Then and always the pretensions of the Pretender appeared to him pathetically ridiculous. But for the man he would sometimes profess a greater liking than he had learnt to feel for any other in the world.

Harry was careful to avoid most of the village. As they came into it on the eastward side a horseman galloped up to them. "From my Lord Masham, sir. Pray you follow me at speed." He led them on to the palace, but not by the straight approach, and brought them to a little door in the garden wall upon the London side.

There a handsome fellow stood waiting for them, and bowed them in with a "Sir, sir, we have been much anxious for you. I trust to God nothing has fallen out amiss?"

"There was a watch set for me, my lord, and I fear some of our friends are down. But for this gentleman I had hardly been here."

Masham swore and cried out, "They have news of the design! I profess I feared it. Pray, sir, come on quickly. The Queen is weaker, and my lady much troubled for her. By God, we have left it late. And the ministers must still be wrangling, and my Lord Bolingbroke like a man mazed. We must be swift and downright with the Council."

Then at last Harry understood. The Pretender was to be brought face to face with his sister, the weakening weak Queen, and a Privy Council was to be in waiting. Suppose she declared him her heir; suppose she presented him to a Council all high Tories and good Jacobites! A good plot, a very excellent plot, if there were a man with the courage and the will to make it work.

Within the palace it was now twilight. They were hurried up privy stairways and along corridors, and Harry fancied behind the gloom a hundred watching eyes, and could not be sure they were only fancy. As they crossed the head of the grand staircase Masham made an exclamation and checked and peered down. The Pretender turned and Harry, but Masham plunged after them and wildly waved them on.

"What is it, my lord? Have you seen a ghost?" The Pretender smiled.

"Oh God, sir, go on!" Masham gasped. "We can but challenge the hazard now," and he muttered to himself.

"You are inconvenient, my lord," says the Pretender with a shrug. "Go before. Conduct me, if you please," Masham brushed by him and hurried on.

Harry understood my lord's alarm. He, too, had seen a little company below by the grand entry, and among them one of singular grace, a rare nobility of form and feature, a strange placidity. There was no forgetting, no mistaking him. It was the gentleman of the bogged coach, the Old Corporal, the Duke of Marlborough.. Marlborough, who was in disgrace, who should be in exile, back at the palace when the Tories were staking their all on a desperate, splendid throw: Marlborough, who had betrayed and ruined James II, come back to baffle his son! No wonder Lord Masham was uneasy for his head.

They were brought to a small room, blatantly an antechamber, and Masham, brusquely bidding them wait, broke through the inner door. He was back in a moment as pale as he had been red. "Come in, sir," he muttered. "I believe we had best be short." And through the open door Harry heard another voice. It was thin and strained, and seemed to make no words, like a baby's cry or an animal's.

Across another antechamber, they came into a big room of some prim splendour, and as they passed the door Harry made out what that feeble voice was saying: "The Council, Abbie: we must go to the Council: we keep the Council waiting, Abbie:" that came over and over again, and he knew why he had not understood. The words were run together and slurred as if they were shaped by a mind drowsy or fuddled.

A great fire was burning though the day was warm enough, and by the fire sat a mound of a woman. She could be of no great height, perhaps she was not very stout, but she sat heaped together and shapeless, a flaccid mass. She had a table by her, and on it some warm drink that steamed. Through the drifting vapour Harry saw her face, and seemed to see it change and vanish like the vapour. For it was all bloated and loose, and it trembled, and it had no colour in it but a pallid grey. And as he looked there came to him a sense of death.

Yet she was pompously dressed, in a dress cut very low, a dress of rich stuff and colour, and there was an array of jewels sparkling about her neck and at her bosom, and her hands lay heavy with rings.

There hung about her a woman buxom and pleasant enough, yet with something sly in her plump face. "Fie, ma'am, fie," she was saying, "the Council is here but for your pleasure:" she looked up and nodded imperiously at Masham.

"The Prince James, ma'am," Masham cried.

The Queen, who had seemed to see nothing of their coming, started and shook and blinked towards him. "He is loud, Abbie. Tell him not to be loud," she complained.

"Look, ma'am, look," Lady Masham patted at her. "It is your brother, it is Prince James."

The Pretender came forward, holding out his hand. "Am I welcome, Anne?" he said heavily.

The Queen stared at him with dull eyes. "It is King Charles," she said, and stirred in her chair and gave a foolish laugh. "No, but he is like King Charles. But King Charles had so many sons. Who is he, Abbie? Why does he come? The Council is waiting."

"I am your brother, Anne," the Pretender said.

"What does he say, Abbie?" the Queen turned to Lady Masham and took her hand and fondled it feebly. "I am alone. There is none left to me. My boy is dead. My babies—I am alone. I am alone."

"I am your brother and your King," the Pretender cried.

She fell back in her chair staring at him. Her mouth opened and a mumble came from it. Then there was silence a moment, and then she began to shake, and one hand beat upon the table with its rings. So they waited a while, watching the tremulous, shapeless mass of her, and the tap, tap, tap of her hand beat through the room.

Lady Masham took command. "Nay, sir, leave her. You can do no more now. Let her be. I will handle her if I can." She rustled across the room and struck a bell. "Masham, bring Dr. Arbuthnot. He irks her less than the rest."

Harry followed the Pretender into the outer room, shambling awkwardly. The progress from failure to failure dazed him. He recalled afterwards, as many petty matters of this time stayed vivid in his memory, a preposterous blunder into a chair. The Pretender sat down and stretched at his ease. "We are too late, I think," he said coldly. "It is the genius of my family." He took snuff. "You may go, if you will, Mr. Boyce."

Harry looked up and struggled to collect himself. "Not till you are in safety," he said, and was dully aware of some discomfort. The dying woman, the sheer ugliness of death, the sordid emotions about her numbed the life in him. He felt himself in a world inhuman. Yet, even afterwards, he seems not to have discovered anything ignoble in his admired Pretender. The blame was fate's that mocked coldly at the hopes and affections of men.

"I am obliged, sir," said the Pretender, and so they waited together. . .

After a little while of gloomy silence in that bare room, Masham broke in, beckoning and muttering: "Sir, sir, the Queen is dead."

The Pretender stood up. "*Enfin*" said he, with a shrug.

XXV

Sauve Qui Peut

S ir, you must be gone instantly," says Masham.
"You are officious, my lord." The Pretender stared at him. "I have nothing to fear."

"I warrant you have," Masham cried. "And so have others."

"I believe that, *pardieu*. Come, my lord, command yourself. Where is this Council? I may still show myself to the lords and challenge them."

"Damme, you cannot be so mad! 'Tis packed with Whigs. They must have wind of you, curse them. Marlborough is there, and Argyll and Sunderland, burn his foxy face. It might have gone amiss though the Queen armed you to her chair. Now she is dead, there is no hope for you. Go to the Council! Go to the Tower—go to the block."

The Pretender turned to Harry with a smile and a shrug. "He trims his sails quickly."

"That's unworthy, by God," Masham cried.

"My lord is in the right, sir," Harry said. "It's true enough, Marlborough is here and he makes sure. You'll but extinguish yourself to try more now. The need is to bring you safe to your friends."

"You also!" The Pretender shrugged again. "Faith, Mr. Boyce, you show yourself vastly anxious for my life. You are not much concerned for my honour."

"Egad, sir, I should have thought your honour was to maintain your cause. You'll not do that from a prison or coffin."

"Who knows?" the Pretender said. "My grandfather—"

Masham was stamping with impatience. "Oh Lud, sir, must we gossip about your grandfather? Stay here, you cannot. It is not decent. The Queen's a corpse behind that door. Why, and if they take you in the palace, it's ruin for you and for us all. Oh, we shall not be spared if you are caught."

"Yes. I am a curse to my friends." The Pretender laughed drearily. "Well, my lord, you shall be delivered at least. Lead the way." Masham hurried out on the word. As they followed the Pretender took Harry's arm. "I wish you may be right, Mr. Boyce," he said. "But my heart bids me stay."

"Oh, sir, a king has no right to a heart," says Harry.

They were suddenly thrown upon Masham as he checked and drew back without warning. He had come upon a woman who was leaving the Queen's apartments, a woman who had once been handsome, and was still proud of it. She stared haughtily at Masham and his companions, and swept on before them. He was much agitated.

"What alarms you, my lord?" The Pretender sneered.

"Carrots from Somerset, egad," Masham muttered, gazing after the disdainful lady's red head. "It's the Duchess of Somerset, sir, the damnedest Whig, and she came from the Queen. Now they will all know the Queen is gone. Come on, sir, come on for God's sake."

They hurried after him through the palace. All was quiet enough. Afterwards, indeed, Harry could hardly believe that fancy had not played tricks with his memory; for the emptiness, the silence of the corridors must needs have been a dramatic invention of his own mind and no reality. But it is true that as they hurried their retreat he was haunted by the quiet of the place—the quiet of death, a quiet ominous of storm.

They were down at the door by which they had entered, and Masham's servant-in-waiting there was dispatched for the horses. Masham fumed at the minutes of delay, ran out and in again, and then with some awkwardness apologized for himself. "Egad, sir, I warrant you we have done what we could. It is for you I fear, by God. I promise you, I doubt damnably how things may go. Pray, sir, put yourself in safety."

"I am grateful for your emotions, my lord."

Masham stared at him and then cried out, "Ods life, what now?" The horses were coming, but before the horses came two of the Guards at the double. They halted at the door, panting, and grounded their muskets. "What the devil's this, my lad?" says Masham.

"None is to leave the palace, my lord."

"Damme, sirrah, you know me?"

"It won't do, my lord. That's the order. You must go speak with the captain at the main gate."

"Come, sir, I have no time. Forget that you were here soon enough to stop me. You shall not lose by it."

"It won't do, my lord. Nay, nay, don't force me to it." The corporal crossed muskets with his fellow as Masham was thrusting by. "Order is to spare none."

"Damme, sir, what do your mean?"

"Sure, my lord, you know better than that." The corporal grinned. "Ask the captain, if you please."

Masham recoiled and drew the others back into the palace. They heard the corporal shout: "Put the nags up, my bully. My lord won't ride to-day."

"They know you are here, sir," Masham said, with a very white face. "Damn the Somerset! She lost no time. What is to do now?"

"It seems my own plan was the best, gentlemen. If I had gone into the Council we should at the worst have been in no worse case."

"Oh Lud, sir, must we wrangle that out again?"

"You are impudent, my lord. I will do without your company."

"Good God, sir, it's no time for forms. What would you be at?"

"I shall go to the main gate of your palace and see who will stand in my way."

"That's ruin for certain," Masham groaned.

"Be easy, my lord. I shall not boast myself your guest."

"Oh, you are mad."

"By your leave, sir," says Harry. "We need not so soon despair, I think, nor you run upon your death. There is something more to be tried. These sentries, they'll be on the watch for a gentleman of your distinction and in my lord's company or of some noble attendance. But a common fellow may pass them. If you would lend me your fine clothes and that great wig, and condescend to my subfuse and bob, there's no one would take so shabby a fellow for yourself. Maybe I might make a show to break out one way, while you slipped past by another."

"And left you to bear the brunt for me? I complain of you again, Mr. Boyce—you do not much value my honour."

"And I say again, sir, your honour is to maintain your cause. Nay, but what can they do to me? Faith, it's no sin to wear fine clothes. And I—well, I think the Whigs will never bring me into court. I know too much of my father."

"Oh, you are specious, Mr. Boyce," the Pretender smiled at him. "Nay, if all my friends were such as you, I should not be in this queer plight." He put his hand on Harry's shoulder. "How am I to thank you, sirrah?"

"Pray, sir, do as I advise."

The hand pressed harder. "Be it so then."

"Egad, I like it very well," says Masham heartily. The two exchanged a shrug and a sneer at him. "If Mr. Boyce will risk it, he may make a show of marching out by the garden entrance while you slip away by the servants' wicket beyond."

"I believe I can trust you to get rid of me, my lord," the Pretender shrugged. "Pray, where may we exchange our characters—and our breeches?"

"Oh, sir, follow me; we must be private about that."

Harry burst out laughing. "Aye, faith, he is a gentleman of delicacy, our Masham," the Pretender said.

But my lord had no ears or no understanding for irony. He brought them to his own quarters and, fervidly entreating them to lose no time, shut them in and mounted guard outside the door.

They cut queer figures to their own eyes when they came out, and Masham was distressed by their laughter. "What ails you?" he protested nervously. "It does well enough, I swear."

"I am flattered by your admiration, *pardieu*," says the Pretender, with a rueful grin down at the shabby clothes which were so tight upon him, and a clutch at the bob-wig's jauntiness.

"Some are born great," says Harry, "and some have greatness thrust upon 'em. I believe I can keep inside your periwig, sir, but damme if I am sure about your breeches. They disdain me, egad."

"God's life, sir, if you make a jest of it you'll ruin us all," Masham cried. "I vow it's not seemly, neither. The Queen's dead but this half-hour, and—and, by God, our own heads are loose on our shoulders."

"My lord's in the right, sir. It's no laughing matter," says Harry.

"Aye, he's all noble feeling," the Pretender shrugged.

"Come on, sir, in God's name," Masham groaned.

"Look you, thus it goes. I'll bring you within sight of the garden entry. Then you make to go out, Mr. Boyce, with what parade you can. And you, sir, I'll take you to the head of the back stairs. You have but to go straight down and out, and I wish you God speed with all my heart. Come, come!"

They marched along the corridor and must needs pass the end of that which led to the Queen's apartments. Masham was a little ahead of the others. He passed the corner. Then he checked and he turned sharp about and charged back on them, crowding them against the wall, trying to stand in front of both of them and hide them.

It was Marlborough who alarmed my lord, Marlborough who came, alone, pacing slowly from the room where the Queen lay dead. No dismay, no emotion troubled his supreme grace. He disdained his splendours and his beauty with the wonted calm.

He saw them, could not but see them, huddled together as they were and striving not to be seen. His face betrayed nothing. He paced slowly up to them. It seemed to Harry that from the first his placid eyes looked at none of them but the Pretender. "We have met before, sir, I think," he said gently.

"On the field of battle," says the Pretender in French.

Marlborough bowed. "Give me your company."

"Oh, your family has always been too kind to mine."

Marlborough pointed the way.

The Pretender shrugged, and "*Enfin*," says he with a bitter laugh, and marched on with an air.

Masham, leaning against the wall and very white, muttered to himself, "My God, my God!"

Harry ran forward to look after them. He saw Marlborough glance over the Pretender's shabby clothes and then, making some ostentation of it, put on his hat. The Pretender with a stare of disdain put on his—or Harry's. They came to the head of the grand staircase and went down. The servants in the hall sprang up and ran to open the doors for His Grace. Harry heard a din and a clang and saw a flash of steel as the guard outside presented arms. The two passed out and out of sight. For a little while the servants stood staring after them, and then came back to their chairs whispering.

Harry turned round to Masham. "What now?"

"Now?" Masham stared. "Now we may go hang ourselves."

"Like Judas? Damme, I don't feel the obligation. Do you, my lord?"

Masham swore at him and began to walk off.

"Can you lend me a humbler coat, my lord?" Harry cried. "I am no more use in this."

"I'll do no more in it," Masham growled. "Look to yourself."

"*Enfin*, as His Majesty says," quoth Harry with a laugh, and went on to look for the garden entry or any other humble door. He found it soon enough and was going through it—to be instantly beset by a sergeant's party and a joyful shout, "Odso, 'tis himself, 'tis the Chevalier."

"You flatter me," says Harry, and they marched him off.

XXVI

REVELATIONS

Harry was kept a long time in a guard room. Once or twice an officer came in and looked him over, but he was asked no questions, and he asked none. He was ill at ease. Not, I believe, from any fear for himself. He knew, indeed, that he might hang for his pains. What he had done for the Pretender was surely treason, or would be adjudged treason, with the Whigs in power and the Hanoverian King. But death seemed no great matter. He was not a romantic hero, he had no faith, no cause to die for, and he saw the last scene as a mere horror of pain and shame. Only it must be some relief to come to the end. For he was beset by a hopeless, reckless distrust of himself. Everything that he did must needs go awry. He was born for failure and ignominy. Memories of his wild delight in Alison came stabbing at his heart, and he fought against them, and again they opened the wounds. Yes, for a little while he had been given the full zest of life, all the wonder and the glory—that he might know what it was to live maimed and starving. It was his own fault, faith. He should never have dared venture for her, he, a dull, blundering, graceless fool. How should he content her? Oh, forget her, forget all that and have done. She would be free of him soon, and so best. Best for himself, too; it was a dreary affair, this struggling from failure to failure. Whatever he put his hand to must needs go awry. Save the Pretender from the chance of a fight and deliver him into the hands of Marlborough! Marlborough, who would send him to the scaffold with the noblest air in the world! Why, but for that silly meddling at Kensington, the lad might have won free. Now he and his cause must die together before a jeering mob. So much for the endeavours of Mr. Harry Boyce to be a man of honour! Mr. Harry Boyce should have stayed in his garret with his small beer and his rind of cheese. He was fit for nothing better, born to be a servitor, an usher. And he must needs claim Alison Lambourne for his desires and rifle her beauty! Oh, it was good to make an end of life if only he could forget her, forget her as she lay in his arms.

The door opened. The guard was beckoning to him. He was marched to a room in which one man sat at a table, a small man of a lean, sharp face. Unbidden, Harry flung himself into a chair. He must have been a ridiculous figure, overwhelmed by the black wig and the rich clothes too big for him. The sharp face opposite stared at him in contemptuous disgust.

"Your name?"

"La, you now!" Harry laughed. "I don't know you neither. And, egad, I can do without."

"I am the Earl of Sunderland."

"Then, damme, I am sorry for you."

"Your name, I say?"

"Why, didn't your fellows tell you? They told me."

"Impudence will not serve you. I warn you, the one chance to save yourself is to be honest with me."

Harry began to hum a song, and, between the bars, he said, "You may go to the devil. I care not a curse for anything you can do. So think of your dignity, my lord. And hold your silly tongue."

Sunderland considered him keenly. A secretary came in and whispered. "I will see him," Sunderland said, and lay back in his chair.

It was Colonel Boyce who broke in, Colonel Boyce something flushed and out of breath. "Egad, my lord," he began. Sunderland held up his hand. Colonel Boyce checked and stood staring at his son.

Harry began to laugh. "Oh, sir, you're infinitely welcome. It only needed you to complete my happiness."

"Od's life, sirrah." Colonel Boyce advanced upon him. "Are you crazy? What damned folly is this?"

"You know him then?" says Sunderland.

"Oh, my lord, it's a wise father knows his own son. And he is not wise, you know. Are you, most reverend? No, faith, or you would never have begot me. No, faith, nor enlist me to do murder neither. For I do but bungle it, you see. And make a fool of my Lord Sunderland, God bless him."

"Is he mad?" says Sunderland.

"I profess I begin to think so." Colonel Boyce frowned. "Lud, Harry, stop your ranting. What brought you here?"

"You, sir, you. Your faithful striving to do my Lord Sunderland's murders for him. *Imprimis*, that work of grace. But, finally, some good soldiers who assured me I was the man my lord wanted to murder."

"You came here with the Pretender?"

Harry laughed and began to sing a catch:

"'Tis nothing to you if I should do so,
And if nothing in it you find,
Then thank me for nothing and that will be moe
Than ever I designed."

"What a pox are you doing in his clothes, sirrah?" Colonel Boyce cried.

"Faith, I try to keep them on me. Which is more difficult than you suppose. If I were to stand up in a hurry, my lord, we should all be shamed."

"The lad is an idiot," said Sunderland, with a shrug.

"Come, Harry, you have fooled it long enough. I had a guess of this mad fancy of yours. But the game is up now, lad. King George is king to-day, and his friends have all power in their grip. There's no more hope for your Jacobites. Tell me now—the Pretender is in your clothes, I see—where did you part from him?"

"Why, don't you know?" Harry stared at him. "Oh, faith, that's bitter for you. You who always know everything! And your friends 'with all power in their grip.' Oh, my dear lord, I wonder if there's those who don't trust you?"

Some voices made themselves heard from outside. Sunderland and Colonel Boyce looked at each other, and my lord bit his fingers. The Colonel muttered something in Sunderland's ear.

Harry laughed. "Do you bite your thumb at me, my lord? No, sir, says he, but I bite my thumb. Odso, I bite my thumb."

"Be silent, sirrah," Sunderland cried.

The door opened. "Announce me," says a placid voice, and the secretary cried out in a hurry: "His Grace the Duke of Marlborough."

Harry went on laughing. The contrast of Marlborough's assured calm and the agitation of the others was too impressive. "Oh, three merry men, three merry men, three merry men are ye," he chanted. "No, damme, it's more Shakespeare. The three witches, egad. And I suppose Duncan is murdered in the next act. When shall you three meet again? In—"

"Oh, damn your tongue, Harry," his father exploded.

Marlborough was not disturbed. His eye had picked out Sunderland. "Is this the whole conspiracy, my lord?" said he.

"I beg your Grace's pardon," Sunderland started up. "You see, I am not private," and he called out: "Guard, guard."

"No," Marlborough said, and, as the soldiers came in, dismissed them with "You are not needed."

Sunderland fell back in his chair. "Oh, if you please," he cried peevishly. "At your Grace's command."

"You have no secrets from Mr. Boyce, my lord." He turned to Harry. "Sir, we have met before," and he bowed.

"Yes. The first time your wife was stuck in the mud. Now it's you."

"Sir, you have obliged me on both occasions," Marlborough said. "Well, my lord? You had Mr. Boyce under examination. Pray go on."

"I don't understand your Grace," Sunderland said sulkily. "I have done with the gentleman."

Colonel Boyce thrust forward. "By your Grace's leave, I'll take the lad away. Time presses and—"

"You may be silent," said Marlborough. For the first time in their acquaintance Harry saw his father look at a loss. It was an ugly, ignominious spectacle. Marlborough turned to Harry, smiling, and his voice lost its chill: "Well, Mr. Boyce, how far had it gone? Were they asking you what you had done with Prince James?"

Harry stared at the bland, handsome condescension and hated it. "Oh, you have always had the devil's own luck," he cried. "Devil give you joy of it, now."

"You mistake me, I believe. I can forgive you more easily than some others." He turned upon Sunderland. "I will tell you where Prince James is, my lord. Safe out of your reach. On his way to France."

Sunderland made a petulant exclamation and spread out his hands. "Your Grace goes beyond me, I profess. Do you choose to be frank with me?"

"Frank?" Marlborough laughed. "You know the word, then? By all means let us be frank. I found Prince James in the palace. He accepted my company. We had some conversation, my lord. I present to you the results. You have used my name to warrant a silly, knavish plot for murdering Prince James in France. You entered upon a silly, knavish plot to murder him on this mad visit to London, and while engaging me to aid your motions against the Jacobites you gave me no advice of this damning folly. To complete your blunders—but for the chance that I came upon him and took him through your guards you would have been silly enough to plant him on our hands in prison. I do not talk to you about honour, my lord, or your obligations. I advise you, I resent my name being confused with these imbecilities."

Sunderland, who had been wriggling and become flushed, cried out: "I'll not submit to this. I don't choose to answer your Grace. You shall hear from me when you are cooler."

"My compliments," Marlborough laughed. "I do not stand by my friends? I lose my temper? You will easily convince the world of that, my lord. Colonel Boyce!" Before Harry's wondering eyes his father came to attention and, with an expression much like a guilty dog's, waited his reward. "You have had some of my confidence and I think you have not lost by it. You have repaid me with an impudent treachery. I shall arrange that you have no more opportunity at home or abroad."

"Pray leave to ask your Grace's pardon," Colonel Boyce muttered. "I swear—"

"You may be silent," Marlborough said, and turned away from them. "Pray, Mr. Boyce, will you walk?" Something bewildered by this time, Harry stood up and they went out together. "I require a carriage for this gentleman," said Marlborough to the sergeant of the guard, and with a smile to Harry, "That will be convenient, I think?"

"Egad, sir, you might say, decent," says Harry with a wary hand on his breeches.

"Spare me a moment while you wait," Marlborough turned into a recess of the corridor. "Prince James expressed himself much in your debt, Mr. Boyce. Consider me not less obliged. Thanks to you, I have freed myself of suspicions which I profess it had irked me to bear."

"Your Grace owes me nothing. I never thought of you. Or if I did you were the villain of the piece."

Marlborough laughed. "And now you are sorry to find I am not so distinguished. Why is it a pleasure to despise me, Mr. Boyce?"

Harry had to laugh too. "It's a hit, sir. I suppose your Grace is so great a man that we all envy you and are eager for a chance to defame you and bring you down to our own level."

"You're above that, Mr. Boyce," Marlborough said. "I make you my compliments on your conduct in the affair. And pray remember that I am in your debt. I don't know your situation. If I can serve you, do me the pleasure of commanding me."

"Oh, your Grace does everything magnificently," says Harry, with a wry smile, and liked him none the better.

XXVII

Virtue is its Own Reward

There is reason to believe that the Earl of Sunderland and Colonel Boyce fell out. Sunderland, never an easy man, suspected that he had been ridiculous and was nervously eager to make some one smart for it. Colonel Boyce was in a despondent rage that any one should have heard Marlborough rate him so. They seem to have had some cat and dog business before they parted: each, I infer, blaming the other for their ignominy.

But they took it in very different fashions. Colonel Boyce suffered in the more respectable part of his soul. Sunderland merely fumed and felt venomous. For it is certain (if absurd) that Colonel Boyce had a sincere reverence for Marlborough. He much desired (one of his few simple human emotions) that Marlborough should think well of him. If he had tacked Marlborough's name to a dirty business about which Marlborough knew nothing, he had honestly believed that His Grace would be very well content to know nothing of the means, and profit by the end. That his hero should retort upon him disgust and contempt wounded him painfully. Final proof of his devotion—he never thought of questioning Marlborough's judgment. He had no doubt that he had managed the affair with miserable stupidity, and bowed a humiliated head.

Unfortunately, he was not ready to bow it before Sunderland. If there was to be scolding between him and Sunderland, he had a mind to give as much as he took. My lord had been art and part in the whole affair, and could have his share, too, in the disaster. But Sunderland had no notion of accepting Marlborough's opinion of him. Sunderland had no reverence for any of God's creatures, and with Marlborough safe out of the room, snarled something about an old fellow in his dotage. This much enlivened the quarrel, and they parted in some exhaustion, but still raging.

The night brought counsel. Sunderland might tell himself and believe that Marlborough had become only the shadow of a great name. But the great name, he knew very well, was valuable to himself and his party, and he had no notion of throwing it away for the sake of his injured dignity. In his way, Colonel Boyce was quite as necessary to my lord. The fellow knew too much to be discarded. Moreover, he would still be valuable. His talents for intrigue and even that weakness of his, his fertility in multiplying intrigue, much appealed to Sunderland. So before noon on the next day, Colonel Boyce was reading a civil letter from my lord. He sneered over it, but it was welcome enough. He did not want to be idle, and could rely on Sunderland to find him agreeable occupation. He walked out to wait on my lord, and they made it up, which was perhaps unfortunate for Mr. Waverton.

Later in the day my lord heard that a gentleman was asking to speak with him, a gentleman who professed to have information about the Pretender which he could give only to my lord's private ear. Thereupon my lord received a large and imposing young gentleman, who said: "My Lord Sunderland? My lord, I am Geoffrey Waverton of Tetherdown, a gentleman of family (as you may know) and sufficient estate. This is to advise you that I am in need of no private advantage and desire none, but only to do my duty against traitors."

"You are benevolent, sir, but I am busy."

"I believe you will be glad to postpone your business to mine, my lord," says Mr. Waverton haughtily. "Let me tell you at this moment of anxious doubt," Mr. Waverton hesitated like one who forgets a bit of his prepared eloquence,—"let me tell you the Pretender has come to these shores. He has come to England, to London. He was in Kensington yesterday."

"You amaze me, Mr. Waverton."

"My lord, I can take you to the house."

"You are very obliging. Is he there now?"

"I believe not, my lord."

"And I believe not too. Mr. Waverton, the world is full of gentlemen who know where the Pretender was the other day. You are tedious. Where is he now?"

"My lord, I shall put in your power one who is in all his cunning secrets: one who is the treasonous mainspring of the plot."

Sunderland, who was something of a purist, made a grimace: "A treasonous mainspring! You may keep it, sir."

"You are pleased to be facetious, my lord. I warn you we have here no matter for levity. I shall deliver to your hands one who is deep in the most dangerous secrets of the Jacobites, art and part of the design which at this moment of peril and dismay brings the Pretender down upon our peace."

"Mr. Waverton, you are as dull as a play. Who is he, this bogey of yours?"

"He calls himself Boyce," said Mr. Waverton, with an intense sneer. "Harry Boyce, a shabby, scrubby trickster to the eye. You would take him for a starveling usher, a decayed footman. It's a lurker in holes and corners, indeed, a cringing, grovelling fellow. But with a heart full of treason and all the cunning of a base, low hypocrisy. Still a youth, but sodden in lying craft."

Sunderland picked up a pen and played with it, and through the flutter of the feather he began to look keenly at Mr. Waverton. "Pray spare me the rhetoric," says he. "What has he done, your friend, Harry Boyce?"

"He has this long time past been hand and glove with the Jacobites of Sam's. I have evidence of it. Now mark you what follows. Yesterday betimes he slunk out to Kensington, using much cunning secrecy. And there he made his way to a certain house—I wonder if you know it, my lord? It was close watched yesterday, and a coach that came from it was beset. I wonder if you have been asking yourself how the Pretender evaded that watch. I can dispel the mystery. This fellow Harry Boyce went in with news of the guard about the house. It was in his company that the Pretender rode away."

"Why do you stop?" said Sunderland.

"Where they went then I cannot tell you. You will please to observe, my lord, that I am precisely honest with you and even to this knave Boyce just. But it is certain that in the evening when Harry Boyce came back to the low tavern where he lodges—and he came, if you please, in a handsome coach—he was wearing the very clothes of the Pretender—aye, even to the hat and wig. I believe I have said enough, my lord. It will be plain to you that the fellow is very dangerous to the peace of the realm and our good and lawful king. If you lay hands on him, which I advise you to do swiftly, you will quench a treason which has us all in peril, and well deserve the favour of King George. For my own part I seek neither favour nor reward, desiring only to do my duty as a gentleman." Mr. Waverton concluded with a large bow in the flamboyant style.

"Your name is Waverton?" Sunderland said coldly. Mr. Waverton was stupefied. That such eloquence should not raise a man's temperature! That he should not have made his name remembered! He remained dumb. "Pray when did you turn your coat?"

"Turn my coat?" Mr. Waverton gasped.

"You once professed yourself Jacobite. You went to France with a certain Colonel Boyce. You quarrelled with him because he was not Jacobite. Now you desire to get his son into trouble. You do not gain upon me, Mr. Waverton."

"I can explain, my lord—"

"Pray, spare me," says Sunderland. "You are not obscure. I see that you have a private grudge against the family of Boyce. Settle it in private, Mr. Waverton. It is more courageous."

Mr. Waverton stared at him and began several repartees which were only begun.

"I find you tiresome," Sunderland said. "I advise you, do not make me think of you again," and he struck his bell. But when Mr. Waverton was gone: "I fear he has not the spirit of a louse," my lord remarked to himself with a shrug.

Thus Mr. Waverton's virtue was left to seek its own reward.

XXVIII

In the Tap

When Harry came back to his tavern, he was, you'll believe, not anxious to be seen. He made one step from the coach to the door, scurried through the tap and upstairs. But the coming of a coach, and a coach of some splendour, to the humble "Hand of Pork" had brought folks to the windows, and at the staircase window Harry bumped into his landlady, who gasped at him and began a "Save your lordship—" which ended in "God help us, it's Mr. Boyce."

"Cook me a steak, Meg," Harry said, and went up the stairs three at a time.

She screamed after him "Ha' you seen your letter? There's a letter for you in the tap."

When Harry came down in his natural clothes, his best and one remaining suit, and shouted for his supper she was quarrelling with the potman and searching the shelves: "Meg, you villain—Meg, where's my steak?"

"Lord love you, it's to the fire. I be looking for your letter. Ain't you had it now? Days it's been here, I swear, and I saw it again only this morning. By the black jar of usquebaugh it was, George, Od rot you."

"Burn the letter," says Harry. "Go, bring me that steak, you slut."

"Oh, God save you," Mrs. Meg cried in a pet, and so for Alison's letter there was no more search. But indeed they would not have found it.

Harry, if he ever thought about it, supposed it one of the grumbling screeds of the bookseller for whom he scribbled and was glad to be rid of it so easily. But he was in no case to think usefully of anything. The amazement of his deliverance left him in a queer state of excited lassitude. His nerves were all tremulous, he must needs do everything vehemently, and felt the while as if he were being whirled along, passive, in the grip of some force outside himself One moment he was dreaming himself capable of miracles, the next he was limp with weariness and utterly impotent. And naturally, as soon as he had food inside him, weariness won and he was overwhelmed with great waves of languor. He hardly dragged himself up to his attic before he was asleep.

When he woke, the world was grey. He could survey himself cynically and wonder why he had been such a fool as to be in a fluster overnight. Faith, it was a grand exploit to dabble in conspiracies and come out with your head still (for a while) on your shoulders. And that only by a turn of the luck, not any wit of his. Well! Neither winners nor losers would want more of the blundering offices of Mr. Harry Boyce. He was back again after his conversation with royalty—and royal breeches—a hack writer in his garret. And Alison as far away as ever. The wonderful Alison! The beauty of her flashed into his squalor. He felt her passionate life. Be hanged to Alison! Let the hack writer get to his writing.

All that day he strove with the fluency of Ovid, and to this hour his labours, much flaccid verse, survive in a decent obscurity. It was late in the afternoon before he yielded to his growing disgust with the whinings of the Tristia and sought relief in the open air.

There was not much movement in the air of Long Acre. The day had been warm and languorous, with heavy showers steaming up again in the sun. Clouds were darkening across the twilight for more rain. Harry turned off to stretch his legs and find some freer air across the fields by the Oxford road. But he was soon tired of them. The moist heat oppressed him still and lowering darkness across the sky threatened a storm. He had no desire for a wetting and an evening spent in the Pretender's clothes. He made for his tavern again by St. Martin's Lane and there came full upon his father.

Colonel Boyce touched his hat. Harry touched his, gave him the wall and was going by. Then the Colonel laughed and caught his son's arm. "Well met, Harry. I was coming to seek you." (It's not known whether that was true.)

"And I, sir—I had no notion of seeking you."

"Fie, don't be haughty. I bear no malice."

"Egad, sir, that's kind in you," Harry sneered and pushed on.

Colonel Boyce linked arms with him. "Why, what's the matter? You went off with the honours. Od's heart, you left us like a pair of whipped dogs."

"You've to thank yourself for that, sir. Not me."

"No, zounds, you did very well. I profess I was proud of you, Harry."

"Then I have to envy you."

Colonel Boyce laughed. "You play that game well, you know. But sure, you need not play it all the time. No, but I never knew you could put on such an air, Harry. You carried it off *à merveille*. My lord was a whipper-snapper to you. I allow you were a thought too free of your wit. It's a young man's fault. But in the main you were admirable."

"You make me uneasy," Harry said. "I hoped that I had quarrelled with you."

"Oh Lud, Harry, why be so bitter? You have won, and sure you can afford to be civil. You have beat me and broken as pretty a plot as ever I knew. Why the devil should you snarl at me?"

They were now turning into Long Acre and the coming storm had already brought darkness. Harry stopped and freed himself from his father's arm. "If you please, we'll have no more of this. I've no will to make an enemy of you. But if you seek to be friends, enemies we must be."

"Why then? Harry, you are not so mad as to declare Jacobite now? It's a lost cause, boy. There's not a thing in it but noble hole-and-corner work and not a guinea for your pains. You—"

"Aye, now we have it!" Harry laughed. "You want to be in my secrets. Sir, I'm obliged to you, and by your leave I'll discontinue your company."

"I swear I wish you nothing but well," his father cried.

"Dear sir, it's your good wishes that I dread. Pray cut me off without a blessing." He waved his hand to his father and strode off.

For a moment Colonel Boyce looked after him—shrugged—went his way.

So Harry walked alone upon his danger. He was near the tavern, he was passing the end of a court. From the blackness there men rushed upon him. They managed it well. He was almost borne down by the first onset, but hearing something in time, seeing a glimmer of steel, he swung aside and staggered back into the kennel slashing at them with his stick. They were borne past him by their vehemence, but he carried no sword and their swords were all about him. There was no hope. Two blades seared through his body and he fell.

Colonel Boyce heard the clatter of ash and steel and turned at his leisure to look. It was a moment before he made out Harry in the midst of the mêlée. Then he shouted of help and threats and ran on with ready sword.

He came too late. Harry was down and the dripping blades again at his body. Colonel Boyce had one fellow pinked before they were aware. The others bore upon him furiously and he was hard beset. He made a good fight—it's the best thing in his life—he understood the sword, and they were but hackers and hewers, they were in a mad hurry to finish him and he had a perfect calm. But he was hampered and overborne. He would not give ground for fear of more thrusts into the body at his feet, and they closed upon him and he could not break them.

But now doors were opening and heads out of windows. From Harry's tavern a man came at a run. As Colonel Boyce reeled back with a point caught in his shoulder, gripping at the blade and thrusting at empty air, another sword shot into the fight. One man went down upon Harry's body. The other three broke off and bolted down the court by which they had come.

"*Canaille*," says the deliverer mildly, and plucked at the cloak of the man he had overthrown to wipe his sword. "Is that a friend of yours underneath, sir?"

"Egad, they have tickled me," quoth Colonel Boyce, feeling at his shoulder. "Pray, lend me your hand, sir."

The deliverer looked him over without much sympathy: "And, egad, it's the ancient Boyce," he said. "Oh, you'll survive, *mon vieux*. Who is this in the mud?" He rolled his own victim, who groaned effusively, off Harry's body. "It's the boy, *mordieu*!" he cried.

"In effect, Captain McBean, it's the boy," says Colonel Boyce, who was trying to fix a pad of handkerchief on his own wound.

McBean was down on his knees beside Harry, handling him gently. "Twice through the body, by God," says he. "What does this mean, Boyce? Damme, did you set your fellows on him?"

"I am not an imbecile," Colonel Boyce said fiercely, stared at McBean and laughed his contempt. Then with another manner, he turned to the little crowd which was mustered: "Bring me a shutter, good lads. We've a gentleman here much hurt. And some of you call the watch."

McBean rose with bloody hands. "He has it I believe," he muttered. "Hark in your ear, Boyce. If this is your work, I'll see you dead, by God, I will."

"Oh, damn your folly," says Colonel Boyce. "I struck in to help him. I know nothing who the knaves were. Your own tail, maybe."

"Aye, aye," McBean looked at him queerly. "You would say that. Well, maybe this rogue can speak. He groans loud enough." Down he dropped again by his victim to cry out "Ben! You filthy rogue! Ben! Who a plague set you to this business?"

"Oh, you've found a friend, then?" Colonel Boyce sneered.

The man who groaned was Harry's old friend, Ben the fat highwayman of the North Road. He rolled his eyes and made hoarse, grievous noises. "Captain! Lord love you, captain, I didn't know you was in it. Oh, gad, and you ha' been the death o' me,'

"I shall be if you lie," quoth McBean. "You rogue, who set you on Mr. Boyce?"

"How would I know he was a friend of yours? 'Twas a squire out of Hornsey. Squire Waverton of Tetherdown. Paying handsome to have him downed. Oh, gad, captain, don't be hard. I ha' had no luck since you turned me off."

Now the constables came running up and Colonel Boyce turned to them: "Secure that fellow. He and some others which have escaped stabbed my son who lies there. I am Colonel Boyce at the Blue House in St. Martin's Lane."

The wretched Ben was haled off, groaning.

Harry, lifeless still and bleeding, for all McBean's work, they lifted and carried away to his father's lodging.

"What's your Waverton in this, sir?" says McBean.

"The silly gentleman wanted Harry's wife. Egad, I never thought he had so much gall in him."

"I believe I'll be letting some of it out," says McBean.

"You'll be pleased to leave that to me," quoth Colonel Boyce.

McBean looked up at him oddly. "*Ventrebleu*, I wonder if I'll make you my apologies. Have you bowels after all, sir?"

"You're impertinent."

"If you like." McBean cocked a wicked eye at him.

"You concern yourself with the affairs of my family. I resent it, Captain McBean."

"I believe you, *mon vieux*."

"You have done me a notable service to-night and I am ready to forget the older injuries, your ill offices with my son. Let us call quits and part, sir."

"It won't do," said McBean with a grin.

"What now, sir?"

"I must know how Harry does and make sure that he has the best there is for him. Surgery and friends—he will need both, sound and sure."

"Be satisfied. I shall well provide him."

Captain McBean shook his head.

"Damn your infernal impudence." Colonel Boyce's temper gave way. "Od's life, sir, this is infamous. You put upon me that I would mishandle my own son as he lies wounded and near death! I shall murder him, I suppose. You had that against me before. Shall I rob him too, or torture him maybe? This is raving. Carry it where you will, I'll none of it. You may go."

"Fie, what a heat!" says McBean placidly.

They were now come to Colonel Boyce's lodging and he bade the bearers take Harry up to his own room.

"I sent a brisk lad for Rolfe," says McBean. "I could but stop the blood. He'll be here soon enough. It's but a step to Chancery Lane. He knows more of wounds than any man in the town."

Colonel Boyce was for a moment speechless. "I shall send for Dr. Radcliffe and Sir Samuel Garth," says he majestically. "I wish you good night, sir."

"I believe they have sense enough to do no harm," said McBean. "And now, Boyce, a word with you. Not in the street."

"I don't desire it, sir," which McBean answered by passing in front of him into the house. Colonel Boyce came after, fuming. "Egad, sir, you presume upon my wound," he cried. "You—"

"Not I. Patch yourself up and I'll meet you at your convenience. There's more urgent matter. When the boy comes to himself—if ever he comes to himself—I must have speech of him."

Colonel Boyce, who now completely commanded himself, had grown very pale. "You have gone too far, Captain McBean. I desired to forget that I have you in my power. You force me to use it. If you thrust yourself upon me I shall have you arrested as a traitor."

McBean flushed. "Odso, then there is some villainy of yours in the affair! Devil take you, I have a mind to finish you now, a wounded man as you are." He had his hand on his sword.

"Will you go, sir?"

"Not I. If you ha' murdered him, you"—he slapped his sword home again—"no, *mordieu*, I can't touch you so. And you may meddle with me if you dare."

"Oh, you have a great devotion to the boy," Colonel Boyce sneered with pallid lips. "You would have him deeper dipped in your mad treasons? I think you have done him harm enough." He struck his bell.

"Harm?" McBean cried. "Is it harm? You that begat him for the heir to your damned infamy? You that soured him with your husk of a soul and your cold cunning? You that made a dirt-heap of his life to suit your muddling need? You—"

But Colonel Boyce swayed in his seat and fell sideways fainting.

A moment McBean surveyed him as if he thought this too a trick. Then, *"Ventrebleu"* says he, "here's Providence takes a hand," and he whistled, and it is not to be denied that he looked covetously at the cabinet which held Colonel Boyce's papers. "The poor old devil," he said with a shrug. "He grows old, in fact. I suppose there's more blood in his shirt now than his damned body," and he knelt down and began to feel about the wound.

He was at that when a woman announced the surgeon. "Mr. Rolfe? Never more welcome. Here's old Colonel Boyce with a hole in his shoulder, and young Mr. Boyce with two holes through and through. A street brawl. Pray go up, sir, the lad's in bad case."

"Faith, it's Captain McBean," says Rolfe, a brisk, big man, as they shook hands. "What have you to do with Noll Boyce?"

"A friend of the family," says McBean. "Away with you to the lad;" and he knelt again and ministered to the unconscious Colonel. "A friend of the family, old gentleman," says he with a grin.

XXIX

ALISON KNEELS

So all this while Alison lacked an answer to her letter. She fretted at the delay, she grew angry soon, but it does not appear that she allowed herself any new pique against Harry. She was angry with circumstance, with herself, and something much more than angry with Mr. Waverton. It was detestable of Geoffrey to dare spy and plot against Harry, intolerable in him to suppose that she would favour the villainy. But she had been a fool and worse to give him any chance of insulting her so. And yet she might have hoped that her letter—sure, she had been humble enough in it—that her letter would bring Harry back in a hurry. It was maddening that some trick of circumstance should have kept it from him or him from her. For she had no notion that he would read the letter and toss it aside or delay to come. There was nothing petty about Mr. Harry, no spite. Nothing of the woman in him, thank God.

What had happened that he gave her no answer? For certain the letter had gone safely to the tavern. She could be sure of her servant. Harry was living at the tavern. The people there gave assurance of that. It was strange that he made no sign. The servant, indeed, had waited for an answer late into the night and seen nothing of him. Perhaps he had discovered Geoffrey's spies and gone into hiding. It would be like Geoffrey to devise some mighty cunning villainy and so manage it that it was futile. Perhaps Harry really was at some secret politics, captured again by his father and sent off to France, or too deep in some matter of danger to show himself. Perhaps—perhaps a thousand things, so that she made no doubt of Harry. He would not deny her when she came seeking him.

She had no fear either. Her nature could not imagine perils or disasters. There was too proud a force in her life for her to admit a dread of being defeated. Her man must live and be safe, because she needed him. Harry could not fail her. But she was desperately impatient. She wanted him every instant, and even more she wanted to stand before him and accuse herself, confess herself. For the truth is that Geoffrey Waverton had profoundly affected her. When she found Geoffrey daubing her with patronizing congratulations, when he dared to claim her as ally in mean tricks against her husband, she discovered that she must be miserably in the wrong. Approved by Geoffrey, annexed, used by Geoffrey—faith, she must have sunk very low before he could dare venture so with her. She received illumination. She saw herself in the wrong first and last, the sole sufficient cause of their catastrophe, a petty mean creature, snarling and spiteful and passionate for trivialities—just like Geoffrey, just such a creature as she hated most. Pride and honour instantly demanded that she must seek Harry, indict herself and read her recantation. She needed that, longed for it, and to satisfy herself, not him. It is possible that she then began to love.

So monsieur must be found instantly, instantly. When she thought of all her tale of sins, she must needs think also of Mrs. Weston. Poor Weston had enough against her too—Weston—his mother. It still seemed almost incredible that poor, grey, puritan Weston should be mother to Harry. But if she was indeed, she might know something of him. At least, it would be good to make peace with her again; it was necessary. And so on the day that Harry fell, Mrs. Alison marched off to the little cottage behind the High Street.

It was a room that opened straight from the path, and it seemed very full. Susan was sitting there, who was now Susan Hadley. Her fair placidity admitted no surprise. She smiled and said, "Alison!"

Mrs. Weston stood up in a queer frozen fluster. "What do you need, ma'am?" says she.

"Oh, Weston, dear, don't take me so," Alison cried, and she edged her way between the little table and the stiff chairs, holding out her hands.

Mrs. Weston flushed. "Your servant, ma'am," says she with a curtsy, but she ignored the hands.

Then Susan stood up. "I must go, I believe," she smiled, and bent to offer one fair cheek to Mrs. Weston. The other was then given to Alison. She smiled upon them both benignly and made for the door.

"Susan! You'll dine with me to-morrow," Alison put in.

"Oh. Mr. Hadley will be at home."

"But of course you bring him."

"Thank you then." The door shut behind her, and the room was larger.

"I can't tell why you have come," says Mrs. Weston tremulously.

"To say I was wrong and I'm sorry. Oh, Weston, dear, to say I have been a peevish wicked fool."

Mrs. Weston sat down again. "Where is Harry?" she said.

"I have writ to him to beg him come back to me."

"I am asking you to come back to us."

"You—"

"Where is he?"

"Ah, you don't know then?"

"I have not seen him since he left your house."

"He has been living at a tavern in the Long Acre. I have made sure of that, and I wrote to him there. But he has not answered me. He does not answer me. I can't tell if he has gone away."

"Where is his father?" Mrs. Weston asked quickly.

"His father? Colonel Boyce? Oh, Weston! Colonel Boyce is his father, then?"

"Did you come to pry?" Mrs. Weston flushed.

"I do not deserve that," Alison said, and then very gently, "Oh, my dear, but I have been cruel enough to you."

"It's very well," Mrs. Weston said faintly. "Where is Colonel Boyce?"

"I know nothing. Does it matter, Weston, dear? He cannot help us to Harry."

"I am afraid of him. Oh, it's all wrong maybe. I am so weak and stupid. But I am afraid what he may do with Harry."

"Indeed, I think Mr. Harry can keep his head even against Colonel Boyce," Alison smiled.

"His head?" Mrs. Weston looked puzzled. "I don't mean that, I believe. I am afraid he may win Harry to be like himself. He is so clever and dazzling, and he is full of wickedness. He cares for nothing but his own will and to have power. When I saw him so friendly with Harry I thought I should have died."

"My poor Weston," Alison said gently. "But I am not afraid of that. Mr. Harry won't be dazzled."

"You dazzled him."

"Oh, and am I full of wickedness too?" Alison laughed. "Dear, forgive me."

"No, but you are strong and hard as his father was."

Alison drew in her breath. "I shall teach you not to call me that, Weston," she said. "And Harry—well, Harry shall find me for him."

There was silence for a while, and Alison watched with new emotions the tired, wistful face. "Weston, dear, I want you to come back to me. I want Mr. Harry to find you with me when he comes home."

Mrs. Weston cried out, "He does not know who I am!" in anxious fear, and clutched at Alison's hand.

"No, indeed. But he loves you already, I think."

"But I do not want him to know," Mrs. Weston cried. "I—I was not married to Colonel Boyce."

"Weston, dear," Alison pressed the hand.

"I lived at Kingston. My father reared us strictly. He was harsh. I think that was because my mother died so young. Mr. Boyce—he was a gentleman in the Blues then, and very fine, much gayer than Harry and more handsome. He used to ride out to Hampton Court to an old cousin of his, who had a charge at the Palace. He met me one day by the river. I don't know why he set himself upon me. I was never much to his taste, I think. But I thought him the most wonderful man in the world. I let him do what he would with me. I don't blame him for that. He never promised me anything. In a while he grew tired. Then Harry came. My father could not forgive me. Afterwards they said that I had killed him. Harry was born. I lay very ill and they believed that I should die. I never knew whether it was my father or my brother sent for Mr. Boyce. My brother boasted afterwards that it was he made him relieve them of the baby. And I—I did not die, you know. When I began to be well again my baby was gone. My father lay dying then. He would not see me. My brother was the head of the family, and he—I could not stay there. I tried to find Mr. Boyce, but he had left the regiment. He had gone to Holland, they said, after the Duke of Monmouth. I could do nothing. And my brother had told me that Mr. Boyce would soon find a way to be rid of my baby. I—I believed that he had. I never saw Harry again till—you know. I never saw his father till that day at Lady Waverton's. He told me afterwards that they had said to him I was dying, and he supposed me dead. I believe that is true. He would not have troubled himself with the child else."

"Oh, Weston, dear," Alison murmured, and caressed her.

Mrs. Weston pushed back the hair from her wrinkled brow. "Mr. Boyce promised me that Harry need know nothing of me now. I do not know if he has kept his word about that."

"There's nothing about Harry that is not safe with me," Alison said. "Oh, my dear, now I know where Harry has his strength from and his gentleness."

Mrs. Weston looked at her in a puzzled fashion. "I wonder what he is doing now?" she said wearily. "I think I have told you everything,

Alison. Oh! Your father. Your father was very kind to me. When I did not know what to do—I had no money left—they gave me five pounds—I went to him. He used to come to my father's house, you know, when he had business in Kingston. He used to go all over the country about his trading. My father said he was a godless man, but he was always kind to me. I told him everything. He took me into his house, and indeed I did not know where to go for food. I was your mother's servant while she lived, but I think she doubted me. Your father never told her anything, and she—but she let me be."

"Oh, Weston, Weston," Alison said. "And you have spent all your life caring for me."

"There was nothing else to do. But I was glad to do that." She looked at the girl with strange, puzzled, wistful eyes and saw Alison's eyes full of tears. She put out her hand shyly, awkwardly, and touched Alison's cheek.

Alison smiled, laughed with a sob in her voice. "It is a long while since I cried," she said, and put her arms round Mrs. Weston and laid her head on Mrs. Weston's bosom and cried indeed.

Mrs. Weston held her close. "Alison! But this isn't like you."

"Indeed it is," Alison sobbed.

XXX

Emotions by Mr. Waverton

You behold Mr. Waverton exhibiting a high impatience. He was alone in the best room of the "Peacock" at Islington, a well-looking place after its severe old oak fashion. Disordered food upon the table showed that Mr. Waverton had been trying to eat with little success. Mr. Waverton's hat upon one chair, his whip upon another, and his cloak tumbled inelegantly over a third proved that he was not himself. For he was born to treat his clothes with respect. Mr. Waverton would be jumping up to look out of the window, flounce down again in his chair to drink wine and stare with profound meaning at the table, start up and stride to the hearth and glower down at its emptiness—and repeat the motions in a different order. He must be theatrical even without an audience.

But he had some excuse for his uneasiness. It was the evening of his conversation with my Lord Sunderland, and that fiasco had stimulated him, you know, to a grand exploit. He was waiting for news of it.

The twilight darkened early. Mr. Waverton pushed the window open wider, and leaned out only to come in again in a hurry as if he were afraid of being seen. The room was close, and he wiped his large brow and flung himself down and drank. There was a dull sound of thunder rolling far away. In a little while came the beat of rain—slow, big drops. That was soon over. Then lightning stabbed into the room, and the storm broke.

Candles were brought to Mr. Waverton's petulant appeal, and an excited maid-servant bustled and blundered over clearing his table with pious invocations at each thunder-clap. She fretted Mr. Waverton, who admonished her and made her worse.

Upon him and her there came a man cloaked from heel to eye, streaming rain from every angle. He shook a shower from his hat. "Hell! What a night," says he, breathless. "Save you, squire!"

"Begone, girl! Begone, I say. Od's life, leave us, do you hear?" says Mr. Waverton, in much agitation.

"Bring us a noggin of rum, Sukey, darling," says the wet gentleman, dragging himself out of his sodden cloak. He flung it upon Mr. Waverton's.

"Run, girl!" says Mr. Waverton, in a terrible voice. "Go, you fool." He advanced upon her, and she stopped gaping, and got herself out with a great clatter of crockery.

"Od burn and blast it! I want it," says the wet gentleman, and collapsed into a chair. "I believe you, squire. I want it."

"What is the news with you?" Mr. Waverton said.

"Od's bones, ha' you got the megs? The megs, I say. Oh, rot you, the ready, the hundred guineas?"

"Is it done then?" Mr. Waverton's voice dropped.

"Out with the cole, burn you."

Mr. Waverton put a bag of money down on the table. The man snatched at it, tore it open, and began to count. "Is it done, Ned, I say?" Mr. Waverton cried.

Ned showed some broken teeth. "I believe you, by God. He has it. He's dead meat. Two irons through and through his guts."

Mr. Waverton flung back in his chair. "How then?" he said, in a low voice. "Ned—was it in fight? You brought him into a fight?" Ned went on counting the guineas, and sometimes tried one in his yellow teeth. "Oh, have done with that!" Mr. Waverton cried. "They come straight from my goldsmith, man. Tell me—you said you would force a fight on him. Did he—"

"Lay your life!" Ned grinned. "There was a fight, sure. Old Ben knows that, by God. Aye, aye, you're fond of fighting ain't you, squire?"

"I fight with gentlemen, sirrah," says Mr. Waverton. "For such base rogues as this fellow, I must provide otherwise."

"Provide my breeches!" says Ned coarsely, and swept up his money. "Where's that damned rum?"

"You may take it in the tap." Mr. Waverton rose. "Nay, she'll bring it. Nay, but, Ned—how did he take it?"

"Rot you, how would you take an iron in your gizzard?"

"He said nothing?"

"Now, stap me, do you think we waited for him to say his prayers?"

"Prayers!" says Mr. Waverton grandly, "They would little avail him."

"Well now, burn me, you're a saint yourself, ain't you?"

The rum arrived, and the servant, with frightened eyes upon the bedraggled Ned, went stumbling out of the room again. "You are impertinent, sirrah," says Mr. Waverton. "The fellow well deserved his end. I may tell you that I was advised to deal with him thus privately by a noble lord in high place."

"Then it's worth more than a hundred megs."

"You have your pay, I believe. I am satisfied with you."

"Damn your airs," says Ned, but something awed by this parade. "Well, I must quit."

"It is better," Mr. Waverton agreed.

"Oh! There was a letter for my gentleman at his tavern. We pouched that while we were waiting for him. D'ye care for it? It's a pretty, tender thing. I reckon it's cheap for another five pieces."

"You are a scoundrel," said Mr. Waverton, and tossed another guinea on the table.

"Pot to you," says Ned, but slapped down the letter. "Well, I'll march. Maybe you'll have some more in my way. I won't forget you, squire," and out he went.

Mr. Waverton, left alone, fingered the letter contemptuously. His great mind was indeed possessed by thoughts of victory. He had hated Harry rarely with the chief count in his enmity that Harry was a low fellow, hireling, menial. He could have borne defeat with some grace, he might even have sought no revenge for being made ridiculous, if the offender had been of a higher station than his own. But such insolence from a pauper! The fellow must needs be crushed like an insect. Only such ignominious extinction could satisfy Mr. Waverton's dignity. He inclined to despise himself for a shadow of human concern about the manner of Harry's death. Faith, it was an extravagance of chivalry to desire that the rogue should have had a chance to fight—that generous chivalry which had ever been his bane. He felt nothing but exultation at the issue. The wretched creature had been properly punished—stamped out by knaves of his own class in a vulgar street brawl—a dirty hole-and-corner end. Egad, my lord was very right. These petty, shabby knaves should be dealt with privately. Mr. Waverton found revenge very sweet.

So Mr. Harry Boyce had gone to his account, and Alison was happily delivered. Dear child! Mr. Waverton felt a pleasant warmth of heroism steal over him, felt himself a knight-errant rescuing his lady from the powers of darkness. Dear Alison! She was free now. To be sure, she need not be told the manner of the deliverance. That would be an outrage on her delicacy. Enough for her that the cunning wretch who had cozened her was dead, and she a happy widow. She had but to show a pretty penitence, and Mr. Waverton proposed to be magnanimous. The prospect much pleased him. He saw himself grandly accepting her; permitting her to be very tender; wittily, but with a touch of magnificence, restraining her from too much humility. . .

He came out of this golden dream in the end, and was conscious again of the letter, and sneered at it. A nasty, infected thing, to be sure, damp and filthy from Ned's handling. What was it the fellow said? A tender composition? Pah, some blowsy paramour of the knave Boyce. But, perhaps it would be well that Alison should know the fellow had paramours in his own class. She ought to be made to feel how low she had sunk by yielding to him.

Mr. Waverton opened the letter and saw Alison's writing:

MR. BOYCE,

I desire that you would come to me at Highgate. I have to-day heard from Geoffrey Waverton what you must instantly know. And the truth is, I cannot be content till I speak with you. But I would not have you come for this my asking. Pray, believe it is urgent for us both that we meet, and I do require it of you, not desiring of you what you may have no mind to, but to be honest with you, and lest that should befall which I hope you would not have me bear.

A.

Mr. Waverton read with swelling eyes.

It was a little while before the meaning came home to him. He was never quick. Then (a sin to which he was not prone) he used oaths. The treacherous, besotted woman! She was still craving for her shabby lover, then. She offered a fair face to her too generous, too faithful Mr. Waverton, only to obtain his confidence and betray him again. Egad, she was too base. Rotten at the very heart of her. Why, some women must lust after a low, common fellow, as dogs after dirt. So she would have saved her Boyce from his master's punishment? Mr. Waverton laughed. She would have had him back in her arms again? Mr. Waverton continued to laugh.

But faith, she went too far when she tried to trick Mr. Waverton a second time. Much she had gained by her treachery. Her fine husband was out of her reach now. It would be a pleasure to advise her of his death. Nay, faith, a duty. The miserable creature had been saved from herself. She must be shown that—oh delicately, with something of a cold grandeur, a touch of irony maybe, but always in a lofty manner as became one who moved upon heights far above her grovelling soul. Mr. Waverton, for all his high irony, rode back home through the dregs of the storm very furiously.

XXXI

Captain McBean Takes Horse

C aptain McBean, healthily red and brown, showed no sign of having been out of bed all night. From cold water and a razor in his own lodgings he came back at a round pace to St. Martin's Lane. He found his aide, Mr. Mackenzie, taking the air on the doorstep of the Blue House, and rebuked him. "I bade ye bide with the lad, Donald."

"The surgeon has him in hand, sir."

"*Tiens*. He's a brisk fellow, that Rolfe."

"I'm thinking Mr. Boyce will need him."

"Eh, is there anything new?"

"I would not say so. But he's sore hurt. And I'm thinking he takes it hard."

"Aye, you're the devil of a thinker, Donald." Captain McBean grinned. "And the Colonel, has he made a noise?"

"He's in the way of calling for liquors, but he's peaceable, the women say."

"You'll go get your breakfast and be back again. And bring O'Connor with you. I'll hope to need the two of you." Captain McBean relieved guard on the doorstep till the surgeon came down. "I'm obliged to you, Mr. Rolfe. What do you make of him?"

"Egad, Captain, you're devoted. Why, the old gentleman has put in for some fever, but I doubt he will do well enough."

"Be sure of it. What of the young one?"

Mr. Rolfe pursed his lip. "Faith, there's no more amiss. But—but— why, he was hard hit, I grant you—but you might take the young one for the old one. D'ye follow me? The lad hath no vigour in him."

McBean nodded. "I'll be talking to him, by your leave."

"Od's life, I would not talk long. I don't like it, Captain, and there's the truth. Go easy with him. I will be here again to-day."

Captain McBean went up to the room where Harry lay as white as his pillows. A woman was feeding him out of a cup. "You made it damned salt, your broth," says Harry, in a feeble disgust.

"'Tis what you lack, look you." Captain McBean sat himself on the bed and took the cup and waved the woman off. "'Tis the natural, hale salinity and the sanguineous part which you lose by a wound, and for lack of it you are thus faint. Therefore we do ever administer great possets of salt to the wounded, and—"

"And pickle me before I be dead," says Harry. "Be hanged to your jargon."

"You'll take another sup, my lad, if I hold your long nose to it. And you may suck your orange after."

Harry made a wry face, swallowed a mouthful and lay back out of breath. After a while, "You were here all night, weren't you?" he said.

"I am body physician to the family of Boyce, *mon brave*."

"My father?"

"Has a hole in his shoulder, praise God, and a damned paternal temper. He will do well enough."

"How do you come into it?" McBean grinned. "Who were they?"

"I am here to talk to you, *mon cher*. You will not talk to me, for it is disintegrating to your tissues. *Allons*, compose yourself and attend. Now I come into it, if you please, out of gratitude. Mr. Boyce—I have it in command from His Majesty to present you with his thanks for very gallant and faithful service."

"Oh, the boy got off then?"

"King James is returned to France, sir," says McBean with dignity. "Look 'e, tie up your tongue. His Majesty charged me to put this in your hands and to advise you that he would ever have in memory your resource and spirit and your loyalty. Which I do with a great satisfaction, Mr. Boyce."

Harry fingered a pretty toy of a watch circled with diamonds, and wrought with a monogram in diamonds and sapphires. "Poor lad," says he.

"It's his own piece and was his father's, I believe. *Pardieu*, sir, there's many will envy you."

Harry's head went back on its pillows. "It's a queer taste."

"Mr. Boyce, you may count upon it that when His Majesty is established in power, he—"

"He will have as bad a memory as the rest of his family. Bah, what does it matter? You are talking of the millennium."

"You will talk, will you?" says McBean. "I'll gag you, *mordieu*, if you answer me back again. Come, sirrah, you know the King better. It's a noble, generous lad. So leave the Whiggish sneers to your father. So much for that. Now, *mon ami*, you have put me under a great obligation.

It was a rare piece of work, and to be frank, I did not think you had it in you. But I did count upon you as a gentleman of high honour, and, *pardieu*, I count myself very fortunate I applied to you. I speak for my party, Mr. Boyce, when I thank you and promise you any service of mine."

Harry mumbled something like, "Damn your eloquence."

But McBean was not to be put off. "You will like to know that the King when he was quit of Marlborough—egad, the old villain hath been a gentleman in this business—made straight for me and was instant that I should concern myself for you. I held it my first duty to get His Majesty out of the country. Between ourselves, I was never in love with this plan of palace trickery and Madame Anne. But the thing was offered us, and we could not show the white feather. *Bien*, His Majesty took assurance from Marlborough of your safety, so I had no great alarm for you. I could not be aware of your private feuds. But now, *mordieu*, I make them my own. I promise you, it touches me nearly that you should be hacked down, and egad, before my eyes."

Harry tried to raise himself and said eagerly, "Who was in it? Who were they?"

Captain McBean responded with some more of the salt broth. "Now I'll confess that I had some doubts of your father. As soon as I was back in London I made haste to find you. I was waiting at that tavern of yours when I heard the scuffle. You were down before I could reach you, and there was your father fighting across you most heroical. Faith, I did not know the old gentleman had it in him. He had pinked one, I believe, but he is slow, and they were too many for him. He took it badly in the shoulder as I came. But they were not workmen. I put one out at the first thrust, and the rogues would not stand. I tickled one in the ham as he ran, but missed the sinew in his fat. So it ended. Now I'll confess I did the old gentleman a wrong. I guessed the business might be one of his damned superfine plots. It would be like him to have you finished while he made a brag of fighting for you. But I was wrong. *Mordieu*, I believe he has a kindness for you, Harry."

"What?" says Harry, startled by the name.

"Oh, *mon ami*, you must let me be kindly too. Egad, you command my emotions, sir. No, the old gentleman hath his humanity. He would have died for you, Harry, and faith he is so rheumatic he nearly did. No, it was not he played this damned game. Who d'ye think it was that I put on his back? That rascal Ben—you remember Ben of the North Road?

I put the villain to the question who set him on you. *Bien* he was hired to it by that fine fellow Waverton."

"Geoffrey!" Harry gasped.

"Even so. Now, Harry, what has Master Geoffrey Waverton against you? If he wanted to murder your father I could understand it. That affair at Pontoise is matter enough for a life or two. Though he should take it gentlemanly. But why must he murder you?"

"I am not dead yet," said Harry, and his mouth set.

Captain McBean laughed. "Not by fifty year:" and he contemplated Harry's pale drawn face with benign approval. "But why does Mr. Waverton want you dead now?"

"That's my affair," said Harry.

"*Enfin.*" Captain McBean shrugged, with a twist of the lip and a cock of the eye.

"Is there more of that broth?" says Harry.

Captain McBean administered it. "I go get another cup, Harry." He nodded and went out.

His two aides, Mackenzie and O'Connor, were waiting below. "Donald, go up. The same orders. None but Rolfe is to come to him without you stand by. And shorten your damned long face, if you can. Patrick, we take horse."

XXXII

PERPLEXITIES OF CAPTAIN McBEAN

C aptain McBean and Mr. O'Connor halted steaming horses before the door of Tetherdown. The butler announced that Mr. Waverton had gone out, and then impressed by the evidence of haste and the martial elegance of McBean, suggested that my lady might receive the gentleman.

"How? The animal has a mother?" says McBean in French, and shrugged and beckoned the butler closer. "Now, my friend, could you make a guess where I should look for Mr. Waverton?" and money passed.

"Sir, Mr. Waverton rides over sometimes to the Hall at Highgate. Miss Lam—Mrs. Boyce's house;" the butler looked knowing.

"Mrs. Boyce? Eh, is that Colonel Boyce's lady?"

The butler smiled discreetly. "No, sir, to be sure. Young Boyce—young Mr. Boyce, sir."

Captain McBean wheeled round in such a hurry that the butler was almost overthrown. They clattered off.

It was not till they were riding through the wood that McBean spoke: "Patrick, my man, would you say that Harry Boyce is the man to marry wisely and well?"

"Faith, I believe he would not be doing anything wisely. That same is his charm."

"*Tiens*, it begins now to be ugly. Why must the boy be married at all, *mordieu*?"

"It will be in his nature," says O'Connor. "And likely to a shrew."

"If that were all! Ah, bah, they shall have no satisfaction in it. But no more will I. . ."

There were at the Hall two women who had almost become calm by mingling their distress and their tears. It's believed that they slept in each other's arms, and slept well enough. In the morning another messenger was sent off to the Long Acre tavern. If he came back with no news it was agreed they should move into town. They said no more of their fears. Each had some fancy that she was putting on a brave face for the other's sake. There is no doubt that they found the stress easier to bear for consciousness of each other's endurance.

So Mr. Hadley and his Susan were received by an atmosphere of gentle peace. Much to Mr. Hadley's surprise, who would complain that venture into Alison's house was much like a post over against the Irish Brigade; for a man never knew how she would break out upon him, but could count upon it that she would be harassing.

"We are so glad," says Susan.

"She loves to march her prisoner through the town. It's a simple, brutish taste."

"Oh. I am so, I believe," says Susan, and contemplated Mr. Hadley with placid satisfaction.

"She is too honest for you, Mr. Hadley," Alison said.

"Oh Lud, yes, ma'am. The mass of her overwhelms me, and it's all plain virtue—a heavy, solemn thing. Look you, Susan, you embarrass madame with your revelations."

"It is curious. He is always ill at ease when I am with him."

"Because you make me tedious, child."

"That's your vanity, Mr. Hadley." Alison tried to keep in tune with them.

"Look you, Susan, I am cashiered by marriage. Once I was Charles. Now I am without honour."

"Mr. Geoffrey Waverton," quoth the butler.

Alison's hand went to her breast and she was white.

"Dear Geoffrey!" Mr. Hadley murmured. "I do not know when last I saw dear Geoffrey," and he turned a sardonic face to the door.

Susan leaned forward. "Alison, dear—if you choose—" she began in a whisper.

"Sit still," Alison muttered. "Stay, stay."

Mr. Waverton came in with measured pomp, stopped short and surveyed the company and at last made his bow. "Madame, your most obedient. I fear that I come untimely."

Alison could not find her voice, so it was Mr. Hadley who answered, "Lud, Geoffrey dear, you're never out of season: like mutton."

"I give Mrs. Hadley joy," says Geoffrey. "Such wit must be rare company."

Alison was staring at him. "You have something to say to me? You may speak out. There are no secrets here."

"Is it so, faith? Egad, what friendship! But you have always been fortunate. And in fact I bring you news of more fortune. You are free of your Mr. Boyce, ma'am. You are done with him. He has been picked up dead." He smiled at Alison, Alison white and still and dumb. Mrs. Weston gave a cry and fell back in her chair and her fingers plucked at her dress.

Mr. Hadley strode across and stood very close to Geoffrey. "Take care," says he in a low voice.

"Well. Tell all your story," Alison said.

"They found him lying in the kennel in Long Acre," Geoffrey smiled. "Oh, there was some brawl, it seems. He was set upon by his tavern cronies in a quarrel about a wench he had. A very proper end."

"Geoffrey, you are a cur," says Mr. Hadley in his ear.

"You are lying," Alison cried.

Mr. Waverton laughed and waved his hand. "Oh, ma'am, you are a chameleon. The other day you desired nothing better than monsieur's demise. Now at the news of it you grow venomous. I vow I cannot keep pace with your changes. I must withdraw from your intimacy. 'Tis too exacting for my poor vigour. Madame, your most humble."

"Not yet," Alison cried.

"Let him go, ma'am," Mr. Hadley broke in sharply. "Go home, sirrah. You'll not wait long before you hear from me."

"From which hand?" Geoffrey flicked at the empty sleeve. "Nay, faith, it suits madame well, the left-handed champion."

Mr. Hadley turned on his heel. "Pray, ma'am, leave us. This is become my affair."

"I have not done with him yet," Alison said.

But the door was opened for the servant to say: "Captain Hector McBean, Mr. Patrick O'Connor," and with a clank of spurs and something of a military swagger the little man and the long man marched in.

Captain McBean swept a glance round the room.

"So," says he with satisfaction and made a right guess at Alison. "Mrs. Boyce, I am necessitated to present myself. Captain McBean."

"What, more champions!" Geoffrey laughed. "Oh, ma'am, you have too general a charity. My sympathy is in your way," and he made his bow and was going off.

"*Mordieu*, you relieve me marvellously," says McBean, and O'Connor put his back against the door.

Mr. Waverton waved O'Connor aside.

"You'll be Mr. Waverton?" said O'Connor.

"Od's life, sir, stand out of my way." But O'Connor laughed and McBean tapped the magnificent shoulder. Mr. Waverton swung round.

"Hark in your ear," says McBean. "You're a lewd, cowardly scoundrel, Mr. Waverton."

Mr. Waverton glared at him, stepped back and turned on Alison. "Pray, ma'am, control your bullies. I desire to leave your house!"

"Let him be, sir," Alison stood up. "Leave us, if you please, I have to speak with him."

"You have not," McBean frowned. "The affair is out of your hands. Come, sir, march. There's a pretty piece of turf beyond the gates. Your friend there may serve you."

"Not I, sir," Mr. Hadley put in. "I have myself a meeting to require of Mr. Waverton."

"So? I like the air here better and better, *pardieu*. Well, Mr. Waverton, we'll e'en walk out alone."

"Your bluster won't serve you, sirrah. If you be a gentleman, which you make incredible, you may proceed in order and I'll consider if I may do you the honour to meet you."

"Gentleman? Bah, I am Hector McBean, Captain in Bouffiers' regiment. Come, sir, now are you warmer?" He struck Mr. Waverton across the eyes.

Mr. Waverton, drawing back, turned again upon Alison: "My God, did you bring your bullies here to murder me?"

"I did not bid you here," Alison said.

"*Lâche*," says Mr. O'Connor with a shrug.

"*En effet*," says McBean and sat down. "Observe, Waverton: I have given you the chance to take a clean death. You have not the courage for it. *Tant mieux*. You may now hang."

Mr. Waverton again made a move for the door, but Mr. O'Connor stood solidly in the way. "Attention, Waverton. You have bungled your business, as usual. Your fellow Ned Boon hath been taken and lies in Newgate. He has confessed that he and his gang were hired for this murder by a certain Geoffrey Waverton."

"It is a lie!"

"Waverton—I have a whip as well as a sword."

"I do not concern myself with you, sir," says Mr. Waverton with dignity. "You are repeating a lesson, I see. But I advise you, I shall not permit myself to be slandered. This fellow Ned Bone—Boon—what is his vulgar name? I know nothing of him. If he pretends to any knowledge of me, he lies."

"You told me that you had hired men to spy upon Mr. Boyce," Alison said.

Mr. Waverton laughed. "Oh, ma'am, I thank you for a flash of honesty. Here's the truth then. In madame's interest, I had arranged with her that a party of fellows should watch her scurvy husband. She suspected him of various villainies, infidelity, what you will. And, egad, I dare to say she was right. But I have no more concern in it. So you may his back to your employers, Captain Mac what's your name, and advise them that I am not to be bullied. I shall know how to defend myself."

Alison came nearer Captain McBean. "Sir, this is a confection of lies. It is true the man told me he was planning a watch on Mr. Boyce. But not of my will. And when I knew I did instantly give Mr. Boyce warning."

"I shall deal with you in good time," McBean frowned. *"Dieu de dieu!* I do not excuse you. Attention, Waverton! You lie stupidly. Your bullies, *mordieu*, blunder in your own style. It would not content them to murder Mr. Boyce. They must have his father too. They could not do their business quietly nor finish it. The rogue Ben was caught and the Colonel has only a hole in his shoulder. You may know that he is not the man to forgive you for it. So, Waverton. You have suborned murder and furnished evidence to hang you for it. You must meddle with Colonel Boyce to make sure that his Whiggish party who hold the government shall not spare you. You set every Jacobite against you when you struck at Harry. However things go now there'll be those in power urgent to hang you. Go home and wait till the runners take you off to Newgate. March!"

Mr. O'Connor opened the door with alacrity.

"I am not afraid of you," Waverton cried. "And you, madame, you, the widow—be sure if I am attacked, your loose treachery shall not win you off. What I have done—you know well it was done for you and in commerce with you." Mr. O'Connor took him by the arm. "Don't presume to touch me!" he called out, trembling with rage. Mr. O'Connor propelled him out.

"I believe Patrick will cut the coat off his back," said McBean pensively and then laughed a little. He brushed his hand over his face and stood up and marched on Alison. "Now for you," he said. "I beg leave of the company." He made them a bow and waved them out of the room.

"Sir, Mr. Boyce?" Mrs. Weston said faintly.

"Madame, Mr. Boyce is not dead. He lies wounded. I make no apology, *pardieu*! It is imperative to frighten the Waverton out of the country—since he would not stand up to be killed. You, madame," he turned frowning upon Alison, "you must have him no more in your neighbourhood."

Alison bent her head. Mr. Hadley came forward. "Captain McBean, you take too much upon yourself."

"I'll answer for it at my leisure, sir."

"Pray go, Charles," Alison said gently. So they went out, Mrs. Weston upon Susan's arm, and Captain McBean and Alison were left alone, the fierce little lean man stretching every inch of him against her rich beauty.

"You do me some wrong, sir," Alison said.

"Is it possible?" McBean's chest swelled to the sneer.

"Pray, sir, don't scold. It passes me by. Nay, I cannot answer you. I have no defence, I believe. Be sure that you can say nothing to make my hurt worse."

"How long shall we go on talking about you, madame?"

Alison flushed dark, and turned away and muttered something.

"What now?" McBean said. In another moment he saw that she was crying. Some satisfaction perhaps, no pity, softened his stare. . .

She turned, making no pretence to hide her tears. "I beg of you—take me to Mr. Boyce."

"I said, madame, Mr. Boyce is not yet dead." The sharp, precise voice spared her nothing. "I do not know whether he will live." Alison gave a choking cry. "I do not now know whether he would desire to live."

"What do you mean?" A madness of fear, of love perhaps, distorted her face.

"You well know. When I rode out this morning, I had it in mind to kill the Waverton and conduct you to Mr. Boyce. But I did not guess that Waverton would refuse to be killed like a gentleman or that I should find you engaged in the rogue's infamy."

"But that is his lie! Ah, you must know that it is a lie. You heard how he turned on me, and his vileness."

"*Bien*, you have played fast and loose with him. I allow that. It does not commend you to me, madame."

"I'll not bear it," Alison cried wildly. "Oh, sir, you have no right. Mr. Boyce would never endure you should treat me so."

"*Dieu de dieu*! Would you trade upon Harry's gentleness now? Aye, madame, he would not treat you so, *mordieu*. He would see nothing, know nothing, believe nothing. And let you make a mock of him again. But if you please, I stand between him and you."

"You have no right," Alison muttered.

"It is you who have put me there. You, madame, when you played him false with this Waverton."

"That is a lie—a lie," she cried.

"Oh, content you. You are all chastity. I do not doubt it. But you drove Harry away from you. You admitted your Waverton to intimacy— you let him hope—believe—bah, what does it matter? You were in his secrets. You knew he put bullies upon Harry. Now he has failed and you are in a fright and want your Harry again. Permit me, madame, not to admire you."

"What do you want of me?" Alison said miserably.

"I cannot tell. I want to know what I am to do with Harry. And you—you are another wound."

Alison shuddered. "For God's sake take me to him. I will content him."

"Yes. For how long?"

"Oh, I deserve it all. I cannot answer you. And yet you are wrong. I am not such as you think me. I have never had anything but contempt for Mr. Waverton. If he were not what he is, he must have known that. He came to me after I left Harry. He told me that he was having Harry spied upon. The moment he was gone I wrote to Harry and gave him warning and begged him come back to me. He has never answered me. And I—oh—am I to speak of Harry and me?"

"If you could I should not much believe you. From the first, madame, I have believed you."

"It was I who drove him away from me. I have been miserable for it ever since. I humbled myself."

Captain McBean held up his hand. "I still believe you. Pray, order your coach."

"Where is he?"

"He lies at his father's lodging. Observe, madame: I have said—he is not yet dead. Whether he lives rests, I believe to God, upon what you may be to him."

"Then he will be well enough," she sobbed as she laughed.

"Oh! I believe in your power," says McBean with a twist of a smile.

She stayed a moment by the door and flung her arms wide. "What I am—it is all for him."

Captain McBean left alone, took snuff. "A splendid wild cat—and that mouse of a Harry," says he.

XXXIII

Remorse of Colonel Boyce

C aptain McBean was strutting to and fro for the benefit of his impatience when Mr. O'Connor returned to him. "Patrick, you look morose. Had he the legs of you?"

"He had not," says O'Connor, nursing his hand. "But he had a beautiful nose. Sure, it was harder than you would think. And I have sprained my thumb."

"What, did he fight?"

"He did not—saving the tongue of him. But I had broke my whip upon him, so I broke his nose to be even. Egad, he was beautiful before and behind. He cannot show this long while. Neither behind nor before, faith. What will he do, d'ye think?"

"Oh Lud, he'll not face it out. He would dream of hangmen. He'll take the waters. He'll go the grand tour. D'ye know, Patrick, there's a masterly touch in old Boyce. To choose that oaf for his decoy at Pontoise! Who could guess at danger in him? No wonder Charles Middleton saw no guile! Yet, you observe, the creature's full of venom."

"He bleeds like a pig," says Mr. O'Connor. "What will we be waiting for, sir?"

"The lady."

"She goes to Harry? Oh, he's the lucky one. What a Venus it is!"

"Aye, aye. She should have married you, Patrick. You would have ridden her."

"Ah now, don't destroy me with envy and desires," says Mr. O'Connor. "But, sure, there was another, a noble fat girl. Will she be bespoke?"

"She belongs to the one-armed hero."

"Maybe she could do with another. There's enough of her for two. Oh, come away, sir, before I danger my soul."

They heard the wheels of the coach and marched out. Alison was coming downstairs with Mrs. Weston. "What now?" says McBean glowering. "Do you need a duenna to watch you with your husband?"

"Madame is Harry's mother, sir," Alison said.

For once Captain McBean was disconcerted. "A thousand pardons," says he, and with much ceremony put Mrs. Weston into the coach.

As they rode after it, "You fight too fast, sir," says O'Connor with a grin. "I have remarked it before."

Captain McBean 'was still something out of countenance. "Who would have thought he had a mother here?" he growled.

"Oh, faith, you did not suppose the old Colonel brought him forth—like Jove plucking Minerva out of his swollen head."

"I did not, Patrick, you loon. But I did not guess his mother would be here with this gorgeous madame wife."

"Fie now, is it the Lord God don't advise you of everything? 'Tis an indignity, faith."

Captain McBean swore at him in a friendly way, and they jogged on through the Islington lanes. . .

So after a while it happened that Colonel Boyce, raising a hot and angry head at the creature who dared open his bedroom door, found himself looking at Mrs. Weston. "Ods my life! Kate! What a pox do you want here?" says he.

"You are hurt. I thought you would want nursing."

"I do not want nursing, damme. How did you hear of the business?"

"That Scotch captain rode out to tell us."

"Od burn the fellow! Humph. No. Maybe he is no fool, neither. Us? Who is us, Kate? Mrs. Alison?"

"She is gone up to Harry now."

Colonel Boyce whistled. "Come up and we will show you a thing, eh? That is Scripture, Kate. You used to have your mouth full of Scripture."

"You put me out of favour with that."

"Let it be, can't you? What, they will make it up, then?"

"Does that hurt you? Indeed, they would never have quarrelled but for you."

"Oh, aye, blame it on me. I am the devil, faith. Come, ma'am, what have I done to the pretty dears? She's a warm piece and Harry's a milksop, and that's the whole of it."

"With your tricks you made her think Harry was such as you are. And that wife you married came to Alison and told her that Harry was base-born."

"Rot the shrew! She must meddle must she? Egad, she was always a blunder, Madame Rachel." He swore at her fully. "Bah, what though? Why should jolly Alison heed her?"

"Alison knows everything now. I told her."

"Egad, you go beyond me, Kate. You that made me swear none should ever know the boy was yours. You go and blab it out! Damn you for a woman."

The woman looked at him strangely. "You have done that indeed," she said.

"No, that's too bad. I vow it is." For once Colonel Boyce was stung. He fell silent and fidgeted, and made a long arm for the herb water by his bed. Mrs. Weston gave it him. "Let be, can't you?" he cried, and drank all the same. "Eh, Kate that came over my guard. . . She has made you suffer, the shrew. Egad, I could whip her through the town for it."

"Yes. Whip her."

"Oh, what would you have?" Colonel Boyce shifted under a rueful air, strange in him. "I am what I am. I have had no luck in women. She was a blunder. And you—you have paid to say of me what you will. Egad, you have the chance now."

"Are you in pain?"

"Be hanged to pain! Don't gloat, Kate. That's not like you, at least."

"Oh, I am sorry. I am sorry."

"No, nor that neither. Damme, what should I be with you pitying me? Let it be. Come, you want something of me, I suppose. Something for your Harry, eh? What is it?"

"I want nothing but that he should live. He has no need of you or me."

"Oh Lud, he will live. But you were always full of fears."

"Yes. You used to say that long ago."

Colonel Boyce winced again. "Eh, you get in your thrusts, Kate, I swear I did what I could to save him."

"I could not have borne to come to you else."

"Humph. I see no good in your coming. There's little comfort for you or me in seeing each other. I suppose it's your damned duty."

"I don't know."

"Oh Lud, then begone and let's have done with it all."

"I want to stay till you are well."

"Aye, faith, it's comfortable to see me on my back and helpless."

Mrs. Weston did not answer for a moment. She was busy with setting his table in order. "I want to have some right somewhere. She is with Harry."

"By God, Kate, you're a good soul," Colonel Boyce cried.

"I am not. I am jealous of her," Mrs. Weston said with a sob.

"Does Harry know of you?"

"What does it matter? He'll not care now."

"Kate—come here, child."

"No. No. I am not crying," Mrs. Weston said.

XXXIV

HARRY WAKES UP

Harry lay asleep when Alison came into his room.

She made sure of that and sat herself beside him to wait. It was not, you know, a thing which she did well. She looked down at him gravely. Afterwards Harry would accuse her that what first she felt was how little and miserable a man she had taken to herself.

He lay there very still and his breath hardly stirred him. Indeed, the surgery of Mr. Rolfe had bound him up so tightly that he was in armour from waist to neck. After a moment, she started and trembled and bent over him and put her cheek close to his lips. She felt his breath and rose again slowly almost as pale as he. That cheating fear had stabbed cruelly, and still it would not let her be. His face was so thin, so white and utterly tired. The life was drained out of him. . .

She sat beside him, still but for the beat of her bosom, and it seemed that the consciousness in her was falling from a height or galloping against the wind. She seemed to try to stop and could not.

She tried to change the fashion of her thought and had no power in that either. It was a strange, half-angry, half-contemptuous pity that moved in her, and a fever of impatience. He was wicked to be struck down so, rent, impotent. Why must the wretch go plunging out into the world and measure himself against these swashbuckling conspirators? He had no equipment for it. He was fated to end it with disaster. Faith, it was a cruel folly to throw himself away and drag up her life by the roots as he fell. She needed him—needed him quick and eager, and there he lay, a shrunken thing that could use only gentleness, help, a tedious, trivial service like a child.

He was humiliated, a condition not to be borne in her man. As she watched him, she saw Geoffrey Waverton rise between them, blusterous and menacing, and his lustiness mocked at the still, helpless body. But on that all other feeling was lost in a fever of hate of Mr. Waverton. He was branded with every contemptible sin that she knew, she ached to have him suffer, and (unaware of the contusions and extravasations administered by Mr. O'Connor) tried to console herself by recalling the ignominious condition of Geoffrey in the hands of the truculent gentlemen at Highgate. Bah, the coward was dishonoured for ever, at least. He would never dare show his face in town or country. How could he? Mr. Hadley would spit him like a joint. The good Charles! She found some consolation in the memory of Mr. Hadley's sardonic contempt. Nay, but the others, that fire-eating little Scotsman and his lank friend, they were of the same scornful mind about Mr. Waverton. His blusterous bullying went for nothing with them but to call for more disdain. They had no doubt that he cut a miserable figure, that it was he who was humiliated in the affair. And so all men would think, indeed. It was only a fool of a woman who could be imposed upon by his brag, only a mean, detestable woman who could suppose Harry defeated.

Why, Harry must needs have done nobly to enlist these men on his side. He was nothing to Captain McBean, nothing but what he had done, and yet McBean took up his cause with a perfect devotion, cared for nothing but to punish his enemies, and to assure his safety. Faith, the little man would be as glad to thrash her as to overthrow Master Geoffrey. He had come near it, indeed. She smiled a little. The absurd imagination was not unpleasant. Monsieur was welcome to beat her if it would bring Harry any comfort. Aye, it would be very good for her. She would be glad to show Harry the stripes. Nay, but it was Harry who should beat her—only he never would. And these fantastics were swept away in a wave of tenderness.

Mr. Harry was not good at making others suffer. He left it to his wife, poor lad, and she—she had done it greedily. Well. There was to be an end of that. Pray God he might ever be strong enough to hurt her. She bent over him in this queer mood, and her eyes were dim, and she kissed him, and whispered to herself—to him. Yes. She must make him hurt her. She must have pain of him to bear. . .

Harry slept on. She began to caress his pillow, and crooned over him like a mother with her child, and found herself blushing and was still and silent again. Indeed, she was detestable. To make a show of fondling after having driven him to the edge of death! To chatter and flutter about him when he had no more than strength enough for sleep! Why, this was the very way for a light o' love. And, indeed, she was no better, wanting him only for her pleasure, for what he would give, watching greedily till he should be fit to serve her turn again. Yes, that was the only way of love Mrs. Alison understood.

It was some satisfaction to scold herself, to make herself believe that she was vile. For she wanted to suffer, she wanted to be humbled. Not so much for the comfort of penance, not even for the luxury of sensation which makes self-torture pleasure, but that she might be sure of realizing her sins against the love which was now in command of all her being, and go on to serve it with a clean devotion. One thing only was worth doing, in one thing only could there be honour and joy, to make him welcome her and have delight in her. . . And so she fell among dreams. . .

She saw something glitter on the table by the bed, and idly put out her hand for it. She found herself looking at the diamonds of the Pretender's watch. How did Harry come to such a gorgeous toy? J.R., the diamonds wrote. Who was J.R.?

"Alison," Harry said.

She started, stared at him, and stood up. His eyes were open, and he frowned a little.

"Alison? It is you?" he said, and rubbed at his eyes.

"Yes."

"Why have you come?"

She fell on her knees by the bed. "Oh, Harry, Harry," she murmured, and hid her face.

"Is it true?"

"I will be true," she sobbed.

"I want to see you."

She showed him her face pale and wet with tears. . .

After a while, "Why have you come?" he said again.

"Harry, I knew about Geoffrey. He told me."

"You—knew?"

I wrote you warning. I begged you come back to me. Oh, Harry, Harry, you are proud."

"I had no warning. Proud? Oh, yes, I am proud. What were you with Geoffrey?"

"Harry! Oh, Harry! No, it's fair. Well. I tried to trick him for your sake to save you."

"I am obliged for your care of me."

She cried out "Ah, God," and hid her face again. Harry lay still and white as death. . . "Oh, Harry, you torture me," she murmured. "You have the right. No man but you has ever had a thought of me. Harry—I want to pray you—oh, I want to lie at your feet. Only believe in me— use me—take me again."

"I am a fool," Harry said, and she looked up and saw that he, too, was crying. "Oh, curse the wound," he said hoarsely. "Egad, I am damned feeble, child."

"I love you, I love you," she sobbed, and pressed her face to his. . . "Oh, Harry, I am wicked."

She raised herself. "You are hurt, and I wear you out."

"That's a brag." Harry smiled faintly, "It takes more than you can give to kill me, ma'am."

"Ah, don't."

"Stand up and let me look at you." Which she did, and made parade of her beauty, smiling through tears. "Aye, you're a splendid woman," and his eyes brightened.

She made him a curtsy. "It's at your will, sir." "Yes, and why? Why? What made you come back?"

"My dear!" She held out her arms to him. "I have wanted you ever since I lost you. And now—now I am nothing unless you want me."

"Oh, be easy. There is plenty of you, and I want it all."

"Can you say so? Ah, Harry, you have known enough bad that's me, cruel and greedy and hard and cheating. I have always taken, and given nothing back."

"Damn your humilities," Harry said.

"Oh, sir, but I want them, my new humilities. I have nothing else to cover my nakedness."

"You look better without them, ma'am."

"Fie, I will stop your mouth." But it was a cup of herb water that she offered him instead of a kiss.

"You are a cheat," Harry spluttered. "You presume on my infirmities."

"No. No. I have made you talk too much. You must be still and rest again."

"Burn your maternal care! I have hardly seen you yet a minute."

"A minute! Oh!" She looked at the jewelled watch. "Aye, sir, an hour. And what's this pretty toy?"

Harry laughed. "Why, now I have you. Sure, ma'am, it's a love token."

"I shall go away, sir."

"Not till you come by the secret. I know you."

His ear was pinched. "J.R. Who is J.R., sir?"

"Jemima Regina. A queen of beauty, ma'am. She fell in love with my nose. And offered me a thousand pound for it."

"Harry! I am going to say good night."

"Hear the truth, Alison. Do you remember—you told me I was born to be a highwayman—my stand-and-deliver stare—my—"

"Oh! Don't play so. I was a fiend when I taunted you so."

"Why, child, it's nothing. Come then—J.R., it's Jacobus Rex, the poor lad, Prince James, who will never be a king, God help him. He gave me that for the memory of some little service I did him. McBean brought the toy to-day."

Alison nodded. "I will have that story from Captain McBean, sir. You tell stories mighty ill, do you know—highwayman. Yes, Harry, you are that. You pillage us all. Love, honour, you win it from all. And I—I am the last to know you."

"Bah, you will never be a wife," Harry said. "You have too much imagination. But you make a mighty fine lover, my dear."

A Note About the Author

H.C. Bailey (1878–1961), also known as Henry Christopher Bailey, was a British author born in London. He studied at Oxford University where he published his first book, *My Lady of Orange* in 1901. He also worked as a journalist, contributing war coverage as well as reviews and editorials. Although Bailey penned historic and romance novels, he is best known for his detective stories including *Call Mr. Fortune* (1920), *Mr. Fortune's Practice* (1923) and *Mr. Fortune's Trials* (1925).

A Note from the Publisher

Spanning many genres, from non-fiction essays to literature classics to children's books and lyric poetry, Mint Edition books showcase the master works of our time in a modern new package. The text is freshly typeset, is clean and easy to read, and features a new note about the author in each volume. Many books also include exclusive new introductory material. Every book boasts a striking new cover, which makes it as appropriate for collecting as it is for gift giving. Mint Edition books are only printed when a reader orders them, so natural resources are not wasted. We're proud that our books are never manufactured in excess and exist only in the exact quantity they need to be read and enjoyed.

Discover more of your favorite classics with Bookfinity™.

- Track your reading with custom book lists.
- Get great book recommendations for your personalized Reader Type.
- Add reviews for your favorite books.
- AND MUCH MORE!

Visit **bookfinity.com** and take the fun Reader Type quiz to get started.

Enjoy our classic and modern companion pairings!